SOMETHING
TO
HIDE

SOMETHING TO HIDE

PETER LEVINE

ST. MARTIN'S PRESS ● ⚏ NEW YORK

Design by Julie Duquet

Library of Congress Cataloging-in-Publication Data

Levine, Peter.
    Something to hide : a novel / by Peter Levine.
        p.   cm.
    ISBN 0-312-14047-9
    I. Title.
PS3562.E8998S66   1996   95-39982
813'.54—dc20   CIP

First Edition: March 1996
10 9 8 7 6 5 4 3 2 1

But, after all, why must we say loudly and with so much enthusiasm what we are, what we want, and what we do not want? Let us consider it in a colder, higher, shrewder way; let us say it as if among ourselves, so privately that all the world fails to hear it, and fails to hear *us!*

—Friedrich Nietzsche, *The Dawn*

CHAPTER 1

1 • The heart of campus was a long mall surrounded by stately buildings, each graced with the name of a generous benefactor: in short, the traditional arrangement. But the university's architects had been aesthetic revolutionaries, far too emancipated and visionary to sanction the porticoes and shady avenues, brick and ivy of a conventional American campus. Instead, they had raised the main quadrangle several stories above ground level, paved it with concrete, and lined it with intimidating structures of steel and reflecting glass. This arid plateau lay shimmering under the August sun, deserted except for one rather slight man who trudged wearily toward its rim.

He was twenty-seven, with short curly black hair. He had slung a heavy corduroy jacket over his right shoulder, and in his left hand he grasped by its neck a plastic bag full of books and papers. Whenever his eyes began to sting from sweat, he raised his left hand, bag and all, and wiped his eyebrows with his thumb. Now and then, his jacket slid off his shoulder and he had to stop to readjust it. He plodded from one leafless sapling to another down the side of the mall, hopelessly seeking shade; and as he walked he muttered mild curses under his breath.

Zach Blumberg was a graduate student, just a few months away from a PhD. To support himself over the summer, he was teaching a course on existentialism at a branch of the state university. His goal: to instill angst and foreboding in his eight credulous pupils, much as Nietzsche had announced to Europe the death of God. Unfortunately, Zach lacked Nietzsche's eloquence; and even the Antichrist couldn't have persuaded the students in the back row to do their reading. Zach's own teachers at Yale had captivated huge audiences with their thoughts on modernity, nihilism, and art, enlivening their lectures with dry quips in foreign languages and personal recollections of Sartre and Edmund Wilson. This was a far cry from Zach's performance as a summer-school instructor. His students, he knew, would leave his class with their lives totally and blissfully unchanged.

As he reached the edge of the raised campus, he was still considering his lackluster performance in class. He flinched when he recalled a particularly awkward, rambling answer that he had given to a student's question. He descended to ground level by means of a long flight of cement steps and then walked along the side of a highway. The intermittent shade from the trees that lined the road partly compensated for the traffic noise. At last he reached the plastic bubble of a bus stop and sat down alone on the bench.

Zach was living that summer in New York City, fifty miles to the south. Not having a car, he had to commute to his teaching job twice a week by a combination of bus, train, and subway. Now, as he began the first leg of the journey home, his thoughts shifted from his class to his dissertation: like a cranky toddler, it always seemed to want his attention. If anything, his thesis was a more depressing subject than his class, for it was still rife with obscurity and vagueness, contradictions and omissions, even though it was now several months overdue. He recalled the chapter that he had been rewriting over the summer; he tried to remember its overall structure and began moving imaginary blocks of text around in his head.

Like most graduate students, Zach felt toward his dissertation a blend of jealous, protective love and bitter resentment. In his own case, the proportion of resentment was perhaps higher than usual, because of the peculiar way in which he had selected his topic. In fact, he had not really chosen the subject at all; instead, it had been forced upon him. After passing his orals at Yale five years earlier, he had stalled, unwilling to embark on a huge project for which he was afraid that he lacked the necessary stamina and ability. After several months of procrastination, and to his utter amazement, he had been summoned to an "interview" with the august chairman of the department, Professor H.P.T. Davies. Even now, as Zach boarded the local bus, he recalled that appointment with a shiver of recollected terror.

Hannibal Davies (pronounced "Davis" by anyone who hoped to avoid the chairman's ire) was the fourth member of his family to teach at Yale and the twelfth to attend the university. A respected logician, he was the author of several classic essays and a widely used textbook. On campus, he was a formidable political presence, feared alike by deans and presidents. Clad permanently in tweed, sporting a Victorian white mustache, with his trouser legs clipped for bicycle-riding, he could have been his own great-grandfather, Diomedes P. Davies (the twenty-third president of the university), returned from the dead to revive academic standards. During the sixties, he had publicly thrashed a campus protester with an umbrella when the young man had tried to prevent him from entering Davies Hall to lecture on introductory logic. This episode had been very much on Zach's mind as he had prepared feverishly for his interview with the chairman, for he had expected it to turn into an impromptu logic exam that would terminate his career.

On the day of the appointment, he had been admitted by Davies's personal secretary into the chairman's office, a dark, paneled room the size of a lecture hall, complete with oil portraits, a panoramic view of Gothic spires, but not a book or typewriter (let alone a computer) in sight. The chairman had sat behind a vast desk, his chin resting lightly on the tips of his fingers. Zach had approached the desk and stood before Davies, who occupied the only chair in the room.

"Ah, Mr. Blumberg," said the chairman. Like Bertrand Russell, he was said to have no visual memory at all; he had no capacity to form or retain mental images, for he thought only in clear and distinct propositions. Whether or not this was true, he had certainly never addressed Zach by name before.

"Sir?"

"Yes. Your supervisor informs me that you are dillydallying on the choice of a dissertation. True?"

"Well, I—"

"You have no topic? True or false?"

"True, sir."

"And you are an expert, or so I am reliably informed, on the history of political philosophy?"

"I would hardly say—"

"Fine. I know what you are going to say; you are just beginning your studies, etcetera, etcetera. But Mr. Bamburg, philosophy has only gained its rigorous scientific basis in the last hundred years; and political theory, which deals with the welfare of boobs, has no potential whatever for rigor. Therefore, I count you as an expert on the subject, insofar as expertise is available at all regarding such hokum."

"Thank you, sir."

"Brumberg, I have a topic I would like you to work on. Your supervisor approves of it."

"You do?" Zach was thoroughly intimidated by the chairman, but even in Davies's inner sanctum he retained enough dignity to find this suggestion rather offensive. His dissertation topic was supposed to be his own choice, after all.

"Yes, I do, and you will complete it with the maximum dispatch. As a scholar in the field of political philosophy"—he sneered at the very phrase—"you will be familiar with the writings of Joseph Marie, comte de Maistre?"

Zach was not, although he recognized the name and could at least identify Maistre as some kind of early-nineteenth-century reactionary. "Minimally, sir," he said.

"Well, I think it's time that someone completed a study of his work. For reasons that I will not go into, I wanted recently to consult a précis of Maistre's ideas. There appeared to be nothing competent in the library. You will remedy this lack."

"But—"

Davies smiled ingratiatingly. "True, the chairman of the philosophy department does not normally involve himself in academic counseling. In general, his contact with students is limited to decisions about whether to provide them with adequate *funding.*" Here Davies's voice adopted a menacing tone, but immediately a smile returned to his face. "In your case, however, having taken a personal liking to you, I have decided to help you make one of the most difficult choices that a young man can make, the choice of his dissertation topic. No need to thank me, Mr. Cohen; our interview is closed."

But for the story of the thrashing, Zach might have tried to make an issue out of Davies's tyrannical abrogation of a graduate student's most fundamental right. But instead of provoking a confrontation that could only end in the loss of his stipend, or perhaps even in physical injury, Zach had decided to take a preliminary look at Maistre's works. Perhaps Davies's advice would actually turn out to be helpful. Zach's high-school French was rusty and Maistre's largely untranslated *Complete Works* was forbiddingly large. However, he gradually began to form an idea of Maistre's basic themes. And while these were in many ways offensive, Zach at least admired Maistre's eccentricity and found him a stimulating adversary for imaginary debates. For five years he had struggled with Maistre, interrogated him, defended him, denounced him—in short, he had developed a relationship with the dead Frenchman that was probably the most intense and enduring of his life so far.

According to Maistre, civilization could survive only if it was based on total, unquestioned faith and obedience. Attempts to reform societies on a rational basis were doomed to failure, because rationality was incapable of justifying or proving anything. In the end, rational thought would reveal that all ideas and institutions were merely arbitrary, the product of local cultural values and accidents of history. Even the belief in rationality was culturally relative, a product of Europe in the Age of Enlightenment. But reason was different from other arbitrary values: it led toward the discovery that there was no objective difference between good and evil, truth and falsehood. Once such a discovery was widely recognized, man would return to the beasts. Nothing would be true and everything would be permitted. The only alternative, then, was repression, faith, and ignorance.

2 • *Z*ach arrived in New York at about five that afternoon. On his way home, he stopped at a cash machine and with-

drew twenty dollars, dismayed to see that there was only about $120 left in his account. His next stipend check would arrive in four weeks, assuming that he could convince his department that his dissertation would be done by the end of the fall semester. Otherwise, it was conceivable that they would cut him off; he had already persuaded them to extend his financial aid by more than six months, and sooner or later they would run out of patience with him.

His apartment on upper Broadway was a tiny place in an ex-welfare hotel, facing an air shaft, which he shared with a computer programmer named Judah. There was no door between the common space and the bedroom, but they had hung a curtain across the opening to give Judah some privacy, and Zach had created a kind of bedroom for himself behind a row of bookcases. The remaining, rather narrow common space in the apartment contained a filthy kitchenette with appliances from the fifties, a black-and-white television sitting on the floor, Judah's desk and computer, a Formica-topped kitchen table, and a shabby purple couch.

Judah was Orthodox, a pious, gentle soul (those were the very words that always ran through Zach's mind when he thought of him); but he and Zach had argued once about Israel and after that their relationship had been a bit cool. Nevertheless, their books managed to cohabitate peacefully enough on the living-room bookcases. In one section were Judah's computer books: manuals and textbooks with titles like *Mastering Macros*. The titles on the next bookcase were unintelligible to Zach because they were printed in Hebrew: Judah owned a large collection of religious texts. And the remaining shelves contained Zach's collection of nineteenth- and twentieth-century philosophy. Sitting on the couch, Zach wondered, What would Nietzsche have thought of macros? or Rabbi Hillel of Nietzsche? or the author of *Debugging*

Made Simple of Moses Maimonides? or Moses of Jean-Paul
Sartre? Like the philosophy student he was, Zach stopped
to consider whether there could possibly be any understanding across such gaps of culture and ideology. If each
discipline and each era had its own grounds for deciding
what was true and good, then the person who beheld this ca-
cophony of values from afar could have no faith in any truths.
Maistre was right: nothing was true and all was permitted.

Zach stuck an old slice of pizza in the oven and ate it while
it was still half cold. When he was done, he sat immobile on
the couch, trying to persuade himself to work. The horror of
being a graduate student was that you could always work, but
nobody made you do anything at any particular time. You
could ruin endless years by procrastinating, as Zach had discovered. His whole youth had been a casualty of academic
work postponed.

At last, sadly and wearily, he switched on the computer
and typed, "Retrieve Document: thesis/58." He stared at the
monitor, waiting for a fragment of his prose to appear. Instead, the computer replied: "File not found. Abort Y/N?"
"Y," typed Zach, and at the prompt he requested a directory. Suppressing a surge of panic, he scanned the list of files,
which conspicuously lacked all sixty-two parts of his precious dissertation. He changed the directory, searched the
hard drive, and consulted the manual. No dissertation.

No need to worry, Zach thought: I keep a back-up copy
in my desk. You can never be too careful with computers.
He inserted a key, opened the drawer, and saw that the neat
little stack of disks was missing. Back to the computer, more
hurriedly typed commands, but the dissertation was clearly
gone. Stunned, Zach let his face sink into his hands. After
a few moments of blind desperation, he realized that his fac-

ulty advisor would at least have a hard copy of his dissertation. It would mean a lot of retyping, but it was better than losing the whole thing. His fingers shaking as he dialed, he called his advisor in New Haven.

"Vat can I do for you, Zachary?" said Professor Mollendorff.

"I was wondering if you had gotten a chance to look at the copy of my dissertation I sent you."

"Vat copy?"

"The copy I left in your pigeonhole when I was up there two weeks ago," Zach said, his voice faltering.

"No. I check it every day. No dissertation. I vas vaiting. You know, Zachary, you must submit it soon or you'll be in very big trouble."

There was a long pause. Zach said: "Would you mind looking around the office for it, when you get a chance?"

"Ja, sure."

Zach said good-bye and hung up.

He could not believe the series of calamities that had befallen him. He looked down at his clothes and considered that when he had put them on that morning, he had been a man with a dissertation—not a great piece of work, not as close to finished as it should have been, but nevertheless hundreds of pages' worth of scholarship and detailed argument. Now it was gone, and so was almost any hope of retaining his stipend or continuing his career as an academic. With $120 to his name and no marketable skills, he could be in real trouble: not the kind of trouble that you ran into when your term paper was late, but the kind that involved being evicted from your apartment, kicked out of your graduate school, and left (at best) to find refuge in your parents' house in Massapequa. Zach spent a sleepless night pondering his future and trying to comprehend what had happened to him.

3 • Judah was due home the next morning, and Zach stayed in the apartment to wait for him. He couldn't concentrate on work—for all he knew, his entire project was lost anyway—and he found it equally impossible to focus on a current book of philosophy that he was trying to read for his general edification. He decided to pass the time by watching daytime television, his last refuge whenever he couldn't face work. He grasped the remnants of the TV's channel-control knob with a pair of pliers that he and Judah kept on top of the set for that purpose, and used it to flip past several indistinct stations, but every one seemed to be running a commercial—it was just before ten, and the networks were between programs. However, a public-affairs station was carrying congressional hearings of some kind. Zach watched idly for a minute.

From a high perch in an ornate committee chamber, a distinguished-looking senator with pomaded white hair was saying:

"Neither this committee nor the Senate of the United States ever faces any more momentous duty than the confirmation of a nominee for the Supreme Court of the United States." The senator was reading from a prepared text and playing to the cameras.

"I might say," he continued, clearing his throat, "that ours is no mere rubber-stamp function. The Founding Fathers obliged us to give our advice and consent to all judicial nominations, making us, in effect, coequal partners with the president. The practice of soliciting our advice has, alas, long since been abandoned, but our consent is still required. In good conscience and in accordance with our constitutional oath of office, we shall not give our consent without due deliberation.

"Judge Wendell Frye, we welcome you to these proceedings. We intend to treat you with the respect and consideration that you deserve as a member of the federal bench and as the president's nominee for the Supreme Court. Furthermore, you are an alumnus of a certain law school in Connecticut, one which conjures up fond memories for many of us on this panel."

He smiled broadly. But the camera shifted to another senator several seats away, who said, "Mr. Chairman, if I may interject a comment. In some cases our fondest memories of Yale involve passing by it on the train and thanking our lucky stars that we attended an institution farther to the north."

There was laughter from off-camera. Zach reflected on the obnoxious reputation that his university had acquired—and often deserved. The chairman replied, "Judge Frye, please forgive the senator for his rude interruption; he has a second-class education and this sometimes shows." More snickering could be heard in the background. Addressing the nominee, the chairman began to speak again from notes. "Sir," he said, "both your character and your judicial philosophy are appropriate topics for our consideration. We shall exert ourselves to the limits of our capacity to ascertain your fitness for this exalted position. The klieg lights that now shine upon you can be intimidating at first, but think of them as the benign yet penetrating eyes of the American people, and you will have nothing to fear."

Zach rolled his eyes and thought about switching channels; but before he could get to work with the pliers, Judah burst into the apartment, looking pleased with himself. Zach had developed a theory and prepared a speech. Judah walked into his room without saying a word of greeting, but Zach shouted, "It really isn't very funny. I laughed, I admit, but the joke's over. Please give it right back."

"What's your problem?" said Judah, strolling back into the living room and grinning slightly.

Zach switched off the TV. He said: "Look, I know you're a computer genius. For you to hide my files is easy; it's not even a good trick. Please give them back."

"You erased your files, stupid?"

"No, you did," said Zach, sounding childish and shrill.

"Hey, back off. Why would I do a stupid thing like that? I have better things to do than play with your dumb little twenty-megabyte computer. Don't be stupid."

The truth was, Zach couldn't picture Judah stealing his dissertation, nor could he imagine a motive. He sat down wearily on their threadbare couch.

"Look, dummy," said Judah, "when did you last open your files?"

"Wednesday morning," said Zach.

"What time?"

"About ten."

"And they were okay?"

"Yes."

"Well, I was already in Williamsburg. I was there straight through till this morning. You want to ask my father?"

"You got someone else to do it. One of your friends came in here and stole my dissertation."

"Yeah, that's it. I made a copy of my key, gave it to a friend, he picked the lock of your desk drawer, stole three copies of your extremely valuable thesis that I didn't even know existed—sure. You know what, my friend? I think maybe you're going a little nutso. Huh?" Judah made a circling motion with one finger near his forehead.

Zach felt sorry for his insinuations, and Judah could see

that. "Look," he said, "I can get your stuff back."

"How?"

"If it was deleted from the hard drive, it's really still there. The computer just basically puts a mark on it saying it can be written over. Until you type new stuff in, it can be retrieved."

"Unbelievable." Zach beamed. Judah went to his desk and pulled some disks out of a software box. "I am so grateful," said Zach.

"Don't mention it." Judah began typing abstruse commands and conjuring up screens filled with little funny-faces and strings of periods.

"Weird," said Judah.

"What?" said Zach, with a tremor in his voice.

"I told you, if you delete a file, it's still there. Right?"

"Right."

"But you can also write over a file. That wipes it out for real. Except that's not too easy, because basically you don't have any way of knowing where the computer's going to put your new files. In other words, let's say somebody deleted your dissertation, then started a bunch of new files. That would wipe out some of your stuff, but it wouldn't take it all out unless the files they downloaded were huge."

"You're saying that my stuff *has* been wiped out completely?"

"Right. That means either someone downloaded huge files onto your hard drive, files of random ASCII codes, and then deleted them, wiping out all your stuff—"

"Or?"

"Or they went into your hard drive with a program like this one and basically entered random stuff directly onto the memory. You could write software to do that real fast if you wanted to."

"But it would have to be deliberate?"

"Unless it's a virus. Do you ever use your disks in other computers?"

"Never."

"Sure?"

"Sure. I don't even know how."

"Weird," said Judah. "I guess you're screwed, then."

4 • The next few days passed slowly and miserably. Zach tried to distract himself with work, television, long walks— but a sense of helpless distress kept reasserting itself, along with a deep feeling of nostalgia for the days when he had still had a dissertation to work on. He didn't completely trust his roommate, whom he watched suspiciously out of the corner of his eye. Professor Mollendorff couldn't find any copy of his thesis in the department office, and neither could Zach, on a trip back to the university. He thought maybe he *was* going crazy. Perhaps in a moment of self-loathing he had destroyed the whole thing, and then developed a case of amnesia to cover it up. Meanwhile, the beginning of the semester was rapidly approaching, and with it the need to show his department an almost-finished dissertation. Finally, on his way up to the state college on Tuesday, Zach suddenly remembered with joy that the chair of the department there would have a copy: he had submitted it in support of his job application months before.

Timidly he knocked on the chairman's door. Professor Demetrios Papadakis was a tough New York intellectual of the old school, a Marxist, an ex-journalist, a heavy smoker, and a hard drinker. Today he wore shorts, sandals with black socks, and a Giants T-shirt over his beer belly. He taught Marx, critical theory, and (at a prison nearby) self-defense. He had known Che Guevara.

"Zach! My man! Come on in. Too goddamn hot out. You wanna drink?"

"No, thanks, I'm about to teach a class."

"Then you need a stiff one." He poured Zach a straight glass of rye and threw the empty bottle into a garbage can twenty feet away. There was a miniature basketball net attached to the rim. "Three-pointer," he growled. "Swish."

"Professor Papadakis, do you think you still have a copy of my dissertation in your files?"

"Yeah, sure. I didn't read it, so it's still there. Whatssa matta, you want it back?"

"I'd like to make a copy if I could. I'm having a problem with my computer."

"I told you, only wimps use computers. You think Lukács knew goddamn WordPerfect? Serves you right. Here, I'll give you your thesis back. You think we were gonna read it anyway?"

He opened his filing cabinet with a key. "Let's see, Blumberg, Z. Yup, here's your file, and your dissertation is—no dissertation. Sorry, Zach, the file's empty, as the Feds always say when you slap a Freedom of Information suit on them."

"It can't be."

"Don't tell me what I can see with my own eyes, hombre. No dissertation; nada. *Il n'y a pas de texte.* It's deconstructed itself. That's the fact, Zach."

Class participation was at an all-time low that afternoon, and Zach, unable to concentrate, dismissed the students fifteen minutes early. They showed no signs of disappointment at missing his analysis of Heidegger's concept of death. He shouted a reminder about the final paper and then watched them hasten past his desk to freedom.

Among the first to exit were a trio of gum-chewing young

women who sat silently at the back of the class and showed great skill and experience at the art of avoiding eye contact with their teacher. Also quick on his feet was Jim, a wild-eyed senior citizen who sat in the front row and, at random intervals, blurted out questions about artificial intelligence, Lenin, Helen Keller, and quantum mechanics. Fred, a fat Ayn Rand enthusiast whose comments were always zealous, if never strictly relevant, had been seated near the door, so he was able to make a relatively quick exit despite his lethargic pace. And bringing up the rear was Zach's favorite student, the earnest Dorothy, who wrote solid papers and smiled encouragingly at him in class, although she seemed afraid to speak.

Once they were all gone, Zach collected his books in a plastic bag and walked back toward the bus stop. As usual, the sun beat down relentlessly on the vast, inhumane, high-modernist plaza. There were no human beings in sight. Zach sweated profusely under the corduroy jacket that he always wore to make himself look like a professor. He wondered what the hell he should do about his dissertation.

It was clear that more than coincidence was at work. Five copies of the thesis had disappeared, two locks had been picked, three cities visited. But why would anyone go to so much trouble to ruin *his* academic prospects? Granted, the job market was tough, but he wasn't exactly serious competition. More than three hundred people had applied for a position at Harvard, many of them hotshots, and nobody could steal that many dissertations.

Zach wondered for the hundredth time if he had destroyed the dissertation himself. Sometimes he had a masochistic urge to pull out the plug on his computer before saving a document that he'd been working on for hours. But he'd really have to be crazy to destroy his thesis five times over, and then suppress the memory. Besides, he wouldn't have known how to break into Professor Papadakis's files. No, someone had stolen his dissertation. Maybe the thief was going to turn it in as his own project. On second thought, that wouldn't work: Professor Mollendorff knew his research, and would be able to unmask the plagiarist sooner or later. Unless, of course, the thief was Professor Mollendorff. The bottom line, Zach reflected sadly, was that his work was widely believed to be mediocre. If someone wanted to plagiarize a dissertation, it would hardly be his.

There was only one thing to do: rewrite all four hundred pages of typescript by September, four weeks away. Many of Zach's notes would still be in his locker in the library basement; and he remembered virtually every word he had written, so often had he gone over the manuscript. Perhaps a new draft would even be an improvement: more terse, pointed, elegant. On the other hand, he wasn't sure that it was humanly possible to write a thesis in four weeks. Joseph de Maistre could have cranked out enough pages in that time, but he hadn't been required to provide footnotes and a bibliography. The thought of rewriting the whole book filled Zach with loathing and weariness. But if he was going to do it, he'd better start right away. He would ride all the way down to Grand Central, he decided, and then head up to New Haven on the first available train. Judah had not been in the apartment much lately, so Zach could get a lot done. If he didn't make much progress, he would at least know that it was all over.

5 • The campus bus came only once an hour; Zach settled down at the bus stop to wait. Cars and trucks roared by, irritating his head, which already ached from the heat. He looked idly at the *New York Times* but found that he couldn't concentrate on political battles in Washington.

After a few minutes, he spotted a lone figure approaching down the side of the highway. His eyes were not good but soon he could make out that the figure was a woman, and this gave him a momentary burst of anticipation. But then he recognized Dorothy from his class. She was at least as shy and socially awkward as he, and now they would have to make conversation until a bus arrived to rescue them.

"Professor Blumberg, may I sit down?" She was a very thin, bony, pale woman with frizzy hair and a heavy backpack.

"I'm not a professor—yet—but sure."

They sat next to each other, staring off into the heat. Zach didn't want to look at the paper for fear of being rude, but his eyes kept turning to it. "Are you going all the way into the city?" he asked.

"No." That was a relief.

"Are you enjoying the class?" asked Zach, partly just to break the silence but also because he felt he ought to solicit his students' opinion of his performance.

She paused, then nodded, but not very forcefully.

"Okay," said Zach, "tell me this, how would you make it better?"

"No, really, I think it's very good. Although." Silence fell.

"Although it's not very interesting? Or is it too hard? What?"

"No. You're a very interesting teacher and the reading is like, really weird"—she laughed—"but it's not too hard. It's just that I can't quite figure out one thing."

"What's that?"

"Why all that stuff is important."

"Ah," said Zach, who had wondered about this himself from time to time. At least it was good to have something to talk about. "Why it's important?" He paused to collect his thoughts, considering how to put the case in simple language, then began: "Do you think it's true that everything we do, we choose to do because of some basic values?"

"I guess so."

"Okay. And let's say that our values are based on some core beliefs, like 'There is such a thing as the truth.' And then someone comes along, like Nietzsche, and says, 'No, there is no truth.' Don't you think that matters?"

"I guess so. Except." Silence. "Except on second thought, I don't believe that I do everything because of basic values."

"Oh, you're not a moral person?" Zach was kidding; she was probably all too pure and incorruptible.

"No. It's not that. It's just that I couldn't tell you exactly what my values are. I don't decide what I'm going to do by, like, referring to a list of values in my head. It's more like, I know what I should do because it just *seems* right, and I don't care if you could prove it logically."

"So you don't reflect on your values? That's what philosophy's supposed to teach you to do. The unexamined life is not worth living for man," said Zach, regretting his pomposity immediately. "Or woman," he added hastily.

"No, I think about moral questions a lot. I just don't think about them, I guess, in a philosophical way."

"Okay. So how *would* you decide what the right thing to do was if you faced some kind of moral dilemma? Would you get the answer from the Bible?" Zach guessed that she might be a pious woman, perhaps a Catholic or a devout Jew.

"Not really. I'm an English major. My favorite books are novels, Jane Austen best of all. Sometimes, that's how I decide what I should do: I imagine that Jane Austen was writing a novel about me. She would make fun of me if I was self-centered."

"But Jane Austen has values too, even if she doesn't say them right up front. You have to learn to identify the values and criticize them, make sure they're right."

"Okay. Thanks, that helps. Although."

"Although what?"

"Although it would spoil Jane Austen if there was, like, too much philosophy in her books. You know what my English teacher used to say in high school? Show it, don't say it. Plus, I wouldn't enjoy reading her as much if I had to think about her the way—the way you think about books. But maybe that's just me."

She got up to leave.

"Aren't you going to take the bus?"

"No. I just wanted to ask you a couple of questions. Thank you very much."

Surprised, Zach watched her as she walked off into the distance toward the towers of the state college.

6 • The journey to Yale took almost five hours and required one bus journey, one subway ride, two train trips, and a walk through ominously empty New Haven streets to campus. It was early in the evening by the time Zach arrived in the university library, which was practically deserted. He fumbled with the combination to his locker, then winced as the door finally swung open, half expecting to find nothing inside. With relief, he recognized the cardboard box full of manila files that contained his laboriously collected notes on the *Oeuvres complètes* of Joseph de Maistre. The box was satisfyingly heavy. He carried it through the stacks to his carrel, switched on the bare light bulb, and opened the box. It was full of old copies of *Vogue*.

On the late train back to New York, Zach contemplated suicide. He imagined various methods, and decided that he lacked the courage to go through with any of them. He could vividly picture the moment at which he pressed the icy blade of Judah's kosher Swiss Army knife against his wrist. He would falter at that moment, he knew. No amount of Camus and Heidegger could prepare him to terminate his own existence, miserable as it might be. He stared through the dirty glass of the train window at the tenement rooftops, water tanks, and telephone lines of the Bronx.

"Zachary! Don't look so glum."

A tall, erect, white-haired woman was steadying herself against the back of Zach's seat, a cardboard tray from the buffet car balanced in her hand. She had a chalky complexion and a deep, refined, stentorian voice, a voice redolent of New Hampshire before the First World War, of Vassar, Harvard, and *The New Yorker.* It was a voice that might have summoned the steward on a Cunard liner, or informed T. S. Eliot that he knew very little about the Jacobean stage. She wore a tartan jacket and a white shirt. She was professor emerita of Renaissance literature at Yale, and her name was Alice Webster.

"Professor Webster. Do you want to sit down?"

Zach craved human company, and Alice Webster had always been friendly to him.

"I will. I was just on my way back from the buffet car with this dreadful whiskey. Do you want some?"

"No, thank you."

"What are you doing on a train so late on a Friday night?"

"I live in New York now."

"I see. Have you finished your dissertation?"

"No, I haven't, but I have a job upstate."

"Excellent. You're lucky, in this market. You are planning to submit soon, though?"

"I had hoped to."

"You *had* hoped to. What happened? You do look rather distraught, Zachary."

"It's a long story, Professor Webster."

"Alice, please. I like stories. Start telling me now, and if you're still in the middle of it when we arrive at Grand Central, you can accompany me off the train and find me a taxi."

"It's not only a long story, it's also rather hard to believe."

"Even better."

Zach described the events of the last week. "If I were you," he added, "I wouldn't believe a word of this."

"Nonsense. Frankly, Zachary, I think it's just a little bit thrilling. What's your next move?"

"I don't think I have a next move."

"Of course you do. It seems to me you have to start doing two things at once, and right away. First, start rewriting that thesis. And second, find out who stole the last version."

"I'm not sure I *can* rewrite the dissertation." Zach felt deeply sorry for himself.

The train was creeping through the long tunnels that approach Grand Central Station. Zach accompanied Alice back to her seat to pick up her book bag and umbrella. A copy of *The Faerie Queene* lay open on her bag, along with a stack of examination books. Alice Webster still taught one class each semester, and hundreds of senior citizens from all over the state came to hear her. The undergraduates loved her, too; it was a rare sophomore whose eyes were still dry at the end of her annual lecture on "Petrarch and Love Deferred."

"Of course you can rewrite your thesis in a month," she said. "And you know something, Zachary? I think it's just the kind of challenge you need. It's time you aimed a little higher, thought a little for yourself. You know everything there is to know about your subject. Now—*just write it down.* Trust yourself. And meanwhile, we'll get you your thesis back."

As Zach and Alice waited on Park Avenue for a cab, Alice said: "I have two ideas. Not for nothing have I read Dorothy Sayers novels all my life. What would Lord Peter

Wimsey do, if he were in our situation? First, he would go over the substance of your dissertation, trying to detect some detail, some fact or interpretation that would cause inconvenience to someone if you ever published the manuscript. On Friday, you must come to my apartment for breakfast, at eight, and you must be prepared to give me a thorough synopsis. At the same time, Wimsey would be playing another card. If I were you, Zachary, I'd let the word get out that you still have a copy of your dissertation. But say that you're ready to talk to whoever stole the other copies. That'll smoke the criminals out."

"How would you go about sending that message?" said Zach, as he opened a taxi door for Alice.

"West Eleventh Street," she told the driver. As the cab pulled away, she leaned out through the window and said in a stage whisper: "I'd put a personal message in the *New York Review of Books.* Don't worry about it; I'll call and have a free one set up for you immediately. They can stop the presses if they have to."

CHAPTER 2

1 • Since the 1930s, Alice had lived in a studio just off Fifth Avenue. Her apartment was lined with great mahogany bookcases. A Persian cat dozed on an overstuffed settee and rubber plants filled the large windows that looked out on leafy Eleventh Street. An old black manual typewriter sat on a messy rolltop desk. Framed photos depicted Alice with Wallace Stevens on a sailboat; Alice with an ancient James Thurber at the Algonquin; Alice giving a commencement address at Bryn Mawr; Alice receiving the National Book Award for *Shakespeare's Moral Vision.*

Zach arrived at five to eight on Friday morning, having paced up and down on Eleventh Street since seven. He had spent his time outside Alice's apartment preparing to explain the basic points of his dissertation to her. He felt nervous, mainly because he was about to describe his academic work to a distinguished scholar.

"Good morning, Zachary," said Alice, as she opened the door. "Bagels and coffee?"

"Great," said Zach. "Thank you."

Alice served breakfast, fed the cat, and opened a stack of accumulated mail as Zach watched and ate. The Pen and

Brush Club and Americans for Social Justice had sent
newsletters. The *Nation* wanted a piece from her on
prospects for women in academia: looking ahead to the year
2000. A gentleman from Los Angeles with poor spelling
pointed out that Petrarch and Chaucer were communists
and should not, under any circumstances, be allowed to
enter the U.S. A librarian from Pittsburgh wanted to thank
Alice very, very much for all she had learned listening to the
Shakespeare program on National Public Radio. An Action
Alert asked for Ms. Alice Webster's immediate financial assistance to Help Defeat Judge Frye.

"Now, Zachary, your dissertation. What is the subject
again?"

"Joseph de Maistre." Zach still hated saying this name,
which came out of his mouth as "Metra," "Mayter," or "Met,"
the last with a throat-clearing rattle that didn't sound authentically French and hurt slightly. This time he did his best
to provide the Gallic suppressed "r," but the results still displeased him. He sounded like an American tourist in a
restaurant, calling for the "mayter dee."

Alice said: "I have not read Maistre, unfortunately." Her
pronunciation was flawless, practically Parisian. "He was the
ultramontane Jesuit theologian and political reactionary,
right?"

"Right. Or so people believe."

"Until they read your thesis."

"If anyone ever does. Anyway, Maistre claims to be exactly what you said: an extremely orthodox theologian and a
right-wing politician. He begins his most famous book, *Con-
siderations on France,* by announcing that we are all bound
to the throne of a Supreme Being by an adamantine chain of
duty. Those who trifle with God, like the French revolutionaries, will bring down righteous divine wrath on all our heads

for generations to come. The sins of the fathers shall be visited upon the sons, so better not start any revolutions."

"But this is not the whole story."

"Right. You see, Maistre did not believe in God at all."

"No?"

"His argument goes something like this, except he doesn't say it in nearly such an obvious way; you have to tease it out of his books. He says that if you investigate matters rationally, you will see that the gods in which men believe are different in every country. Each nation's divinities are a product of its own local values, an idealized self-portrait. Not only religious ideas fit this description: so do ideas of right and wrong, beauty and ugliness, truth and falsehood."

Alice was staring at him attentively. Zach stopped to let her respond, but she simply nodded, so he continued: "Perhaps there is some universal substratum of human nature, but if so, it is prelinguistic, barbaric, animalistic. Joseph de Maistre was one of the first thinkers to recognize that humans did not exist before language; any thinking creature had to think in the arbitrary medium of words. The words used in other cultures were alien and often incommensurable. So there could be no access to truth. Even if all humans agreed about some very simple, obvious matters, such as the existence of space and time, these were still only truths for humans, and not truths per se. Another species would see things differently."

"A lot of people think that's true."

"Yes, but Maistre's conclusions were unusual. He said: given that all this is true, we must believe in God. Otherwise, everything will collapse. We must take the infallible teachings of pope and church to be true, absolutely, certainly, without question. Otherwise, we shall perish. But do you see what I mean about his not exactly believing in God?"

"Yes. His work seems to be actually inconsistent."

"Or duplicitous. You see, I think he was deliberately writing for two audiences. The simpletons would get the Jesuit message, and keep the faith. There's lots of straightforward polemic against the wanton Protestants and the excesses of the French Revolution. But a second audience, a select and clever audience, would see that strictly speaking, this was all garbage. But necessary garbage. If people recognized that the vast superstructure of culture that they had built lacked foundations, they would no longer give it their allegiance. We would return to the beasts."

"Do you find this plausible, Zachary?" said Alice, after a pause.

"You mean, do I really believe that this is what Maistre thought?"

"No. I mean, do you, Zachary Blumberg, agree with it?"

"Yes," said Zach after a minute. "I think so. Maybe, anyway."

"Philosophy is a funny business, isn't it?" Alice got up to make more coffee. "I got a B in philosophy at Vassar. It never was my strong point. You see, Zachary, I couldn't take it *seriously*. But go on."

"There's not that much more to say. I am interested, though, in Maistre's practical activities, his political career."

"That sounds more promising."

"This was the period of the Terror and the Napoleonic Wars. It was also the age of the secret societies: the illuminati, the Freemasons, the Jacobins. Maistre was up to his neck in all of it: an ex-Mason with ties to the Jesuits, a diplomat in Saint Petersburg during Napoleon's Russian campaign, a royalist agent active in émigré circles. I wanted to know who he was really working for, what he wanted to achieve, and what he left behind."

"And?"

"All I know so far is fragmentary. Also, my detailed notes are lost, but I tried to reconstruct some of it this morning." Zach pulled some ragged pieces of notebook paper out of his jacket pocket and looked at them for a moment.

"For example," he said, "there's evidence to suggest that, despite Maistre's violent attacks on Freemasonry, he remained a Mason all his life, or perhaps a member of some secret inner circle or splinter group."

"What kind of evidence?"

"Well, in print, he called the Masons a 'synagogue of Satan,' and he denied that he had ever had much to do with them. But his early Masonic writings have recently been published, and they show him to have been the 'Grand Orator' of the Lodge of the Three Martyrs in Chambéry. He also had something to do with a secret rite of Freemasonry based on the esoteric works of one Martinez Pasqualis, about whom virtually nothing is known."

"What's that name?"

"Somebody Martinez Pasqualis. I don't remember his first name. Actually, I'm not sure anyone knows it. I do recall, though, that the Martinez Pasqualis sect was some kind of inner-circle Masonic group whose membership was absolutely secret. They tended to preserve this secrecy by vehemently attacking Freemasonry in public, as Maistre did. They were known by the initials "SOT" for Stricte Observance Templière. As well as being Templars, they were also Rosicrucians—whatever that means exactly."

"Good. So he was an anti-Masonic Mason, a hypocrite."

"Here's another tidbit. In Saint Petersburg, Maistre discovered that the Russians were intercepting his mail home, so he started writing letters that were deliberately intended to be read by the czar, Alexander I. These so impressed and flattered Alexander that Maistre was made his confidant, and he helped convert the czar from liberalism to authoritarianism."

"Clever," said Alice. "I should try something like that with the president of Yale—with the opposite goal, of course."

Zach laughed politely, then continued: "Following Maistre's advice, a certain courtier named Count Uvarov was able to have philosophy and political economy banned as subjects of study in Russia until the eighteen sixties. This was just when the czarist state was first becoming absolutist, and introducing a secret police, agents provocateurs, Siberian prison camps for intellectuals. I think that Maistre may have been more or less the brain behind the whole business."

"What a fine man you have chosen to spend your life studying!"

"I know. Last night I jotted down my best recollection of a couple of his most interesting quotes. He told the czar: 'The principle of popular sovereignty is so dangerous that even if it were true, we would have to conceal it.' And he wrote: 'Those who teach or speak in such a way as to rob the people of their inherited dogmas should be hanged like burglars.' That's exactly what happened in Russia for many years. By the way, you may recognize Maistre as the Vicomte de Mortemart from *War and Peace*."

"Not offhand, but I probably should."

"Recently, I've been looking into Maistre's legacy. His works were reprinted hundreds of times in Europe and America in the nineteenth century. The early French communists, surprisingly, described themselves as his followers. Saint-Simon admired him greatly. In eighteen thirty, in Boston, a very shady character called O'Flaherty published a translation of Maistre's book on the Spanish Inquisition. It was advertised as 'A Rare Book, and the Best Which Has

Ever Appeared on the Subject.' O'Flaherty was a leader of the Anti-Masonic Party, which actually fielded presidential candidates at the time. But when it turned out that O'Flaherty was really a Mason himself, he was tarred and feathered and ridden out of Boston on a rail. According to a newspaper report from the time, when they searched O'Flaherty's room in a boarding house, they discovered a letter of commendation from the pope. He turned up some years later in South Carolina as a proslavery pamphleteer."

"Really, Zachary, you are spending your time studying the *most* unpleasant characters. But go on."

"I only have a little bit more stuff." Zach examined his notes again. "The main topic that I still want to mention is this whole issue of suppression, which is sinister enough that it might be relevant to my current problems."

"What?"

"Suppression. In seventeen seventy-three—I remember this precisely; the date is important—Pope Clement the Fourteenth suppressed the Jesuits. He said he had 'secret reasons' for this. The Jesuits, of course, were the order that was most strongly committed to papal supremacy. Yet the pope suppressed them, except in Russia, where they may have continued to receive Vatican money. Maistre was educated by the Jesuits, and he was still going to Jesuit retreats at the time of the French Revolution—in other words, nearly twenty years after the order had been banned."

"Not only a secret Mason, but a closet Jesuit, too. As a young girl, I was told to beware papists. I should have heeded the warning."

"Listen to this, though. When he was in Russia, Maistre opened a Jesuit academy. In this school, the doctrine of papal infallibility was taught—although the existence of the Jesuits was supposedly against the pope's orders."

"And this was before papal infallibility was official church doctrine, right?"

"Right. That was a late-nineteenth-century innovation, I think. But Maistre was ahead of his time. Another thing: in seventeen seventy-three, the same year that Pope Clement banned the Jesuits, Maistre joined the Masons. The Masons too had been banned by the pope, twice in fact. The local king where Maistre was then living, Victor Amadeus the Third of Piedmont, was a good Catholic, yet he secretly belonged to Maistre's lodge. So Maistre was a member of two secret organizations that had been banned by the Vatican, but he used both to strengthen the pope's worldly power. Then, at a date that I can't remember (but I'm sure it was when Maistre had Czar Alexander under his thumb), the Masons and the Jesuits were both banned in Russia. Nevertheless, both organizations continued to flourish there and Maistre remained involved."

Alice got up and walked to her kitchenette, saying, "Don't mind me; carry on. I'm just going to boil some more water."

Zach turned around in his seat to face her and said: "If you look at the whole issue of suppressions a little more broadly, you find more interesting things. Take the Knights Templar, for example. This is your period more than mine, but I think I know the basic issues. Way back in the twelfth and thirteenth centuries they were a very powerful crusading order, of course, extremely wealthy, and highly supportive of papal supremacy. The king of France had them suppressed partly for that reason. The last grand master, Jacques de Molay, was burned at the stake. However, the rumor continues up to the present day that they still exist in secret."

Alice, coming back to the table, said, "When Louis the Fourteenth was executed, someone shouted, 'Jacques de

Molay, you are avenged!' After umpteen generations, the House of Bourbon had finally paid the price for executing a Templar."

"That's right. Now, Maistre was technically a Templar himself during the French Revolution, because he was a member of that Masonic inner circle, the Stricte Observance Templière. Whether they had any real connection to the medieval crusading order is another question, of course. But it is certain that Freemason and neo-Templar secret societies had a lot to do with the revolution, in part through Jacobin clubs. That's why it was widely believed that Louis had really been executed to avenge Molay. Okay so far, but Maistre was a royalist spy, remember—not a revolutionary.

"I'm sure ninety percent of this Templar stuff is pure mythology. But take the Action française, the French fascists. They liked Maistre, were banned by the pope, but argued nevertheless for papal supremacy and very strict Catholicism. Do you begin to see a pattern here?"

"Not very precisely, Zachary, to tell you the truth."

"Me, neither. But I think the central point is clear. There are a whole bunch of secret organizations that Maistre either belonged to or influenced. These are constantly being banned by the authorities, despite the fact that the organizations support authority to a fanatical extent. And in the case of the Jesuits in Russia, Maistre was even calling the shots when they were suppressed, yet he remained a secret lay Jesuit.

"The most complicated case is that of the Templars during the French Revolution." Zach counted some key points on his fingers: "First, Maistre seems to have been a member of the Templars. Second, the Templars were widely thought to be behind the revolution. Third, they had been the pope's biggest allies during the Middle Ages, but now they were in-

volved in an anti-Catholic Terror, if they were really linked
to the French Revolution. And fourth, Maistre was acting as
a royalist spy and a Catholic propagandist, and he openly
condemned the Templars and Freemasons. Yet he remained
one in secret."

"Oh, dear," said Alice. "I'm inclined to think that any discussion of this kind of subject will leave one with a
headache, and not much else. However, it could be that you
made someone nervous by discovering that Maistre was a duplicitous author. This someone might be a kook who believes that the Templars commissioned Shakespeare's works
to prove that the Elders of Zion and the pope own the gnomes
of Zurich and are using them to found a separatist UFO
Rosicrucian state in Atlantis, also known as the Bermuda
Triangle. People come up with the most juvenile ideas. Unfortunately, someone is making a nuisance of himself by
stealing your dissertation. So I suppose it wouldn't hurt to
follow up the secret-society angle, just to see if you can find
anything more specific."

"What would you do next?"

"I don't know. Perhaps you could just go to the New York
Public Library and look up books on Freemasonry, Rosi-
crucianism, and paranoid works on the Jesuits. See if you
can find references to Maistre in the indexes. You can go
through a lot of indexes in a short time. Also, look into the
twentieth-century angle. Presumably, whoever stole your
dissertation doesn't care about Maistre per se; he's involved
with some group that still exists. Especially, keep your eyes
peeled for American connections. It occurs to me, after all,
that our own beloved university is famous for its secret societies."

At this, Zach nodded and made a note on one of his scraps
of paper. Alice continued: "You and I think of them as silly

undergraduate fraternities with big budgets. But they're very old, dating back to the great period of Freemasonry and illuminism, the eighteenth century. They're influential not only in the university in general, but in your department particularly. Your department chair is a Crypt man himself, and three or four of the senior faculty are supposed to be alumni of either Crossbones or Bell, Book, and Candle. That's how they got their chairs—it wasn't talent. I've been fighting political battles on campus for so many years, I've learned to recognize Crypt types in a minute. They run the CIA, you know."

Zach was writing all this down.

"Okay," Alice said, "you run along and do some work. I have correspondence to catch up with. Give me a call later if you find anything very exciting. If not, I'll expect you here at eight o'clock on Thursday morning for bagels and coffee. Do you like plain bagels, or should I get another kind?"

"Plain is great, Alice."

"Good. See you then, Zachary." Alice got up and led the way to the door.

2 • *Z*ach left Alice Webster's apartment in a state of high excitement. Not only had she taken an interest in his problems; she was even willing to help. On the way to the Eighth Street subway he bought a copy of the *New York Review of Books.* Down on the subway platform, he opened it up to the advertisements in the back. He couldn't help pausing at the Personals column to see if any of the entries applied to him. Was he, for instance, a handsome, divorced Jewish male, tall, and interested in Proust, Buddhism, and romantic walks? Did he show enough Zest for Life to make him appealing to a pretty Gestalt psychologist, mid-thirties, who

was into European travel and Monet? Did he like Ellington enough to interest a professor of American studies, under fifty, divorced with teenage daughter, who sought male friend with an eye to permanent companionship? The answer, alas, was probably no. As he boarded an uptown train, Zach's eye fell on the Queries column. Here there were only three entries, and one of them was his. "Did you steal my thesis?" it read. "If so, be warned: I still have another copy. Let's talk." His own telephone number was appended.

Zach got off at Forty-second Street and walked across town to the New York Public Library. By now, it was unbearably hot out. In Bryant Park, outside the library, bag ladies and boys on rollerblades mingled with Japanese tourists and yuppies sipping cappuccinos. Zach bought a couple of hot dogs and sat down on a bench. After a minute or two, a large, hairy man holding a cardboard sign sat down next to him. The sign said something about AIDS and Vietnam. The man spoke loudly but unintelligibly in Zach's direction. Zach stuffed the rest of his second hot dog in his mouth and moved quickly away toward the library, while the man with the sign shouted obscenities at him.

He walked up the steps of the library and into its cool, austere, splendid halls. This is what uncouth, cigar-chomping American robber barons and big-time crooks had bought with their millions, he thought: a little bit of the Vatican, a piece of the Louvre for Forty-second Street. Leaving Bryant Park for the main reading room was like crossing the Atlantic. The allegorical ceiling portrayed the wisdom of the centuries: Euclid, Zoroaster, Newton, Washington Irving.

Zach sat down at a computer terminal and punched in some key words. Mason, Freemason, Rosicrucian, Jesuit, Maistre, Conspiracy. The computer contained only recent acquisitions, but still, there were hundreds of titles. Zach jotted down call numbers and turned in request slips. The man at the desk looked strangely at Zach as he handed him the Viscomte Léon de Poncins's *Secret Powers Behind the Revolution: Freemasonry and Judaism.* This was a new paperback book with a Star of David on the cover. It turned out to be a photographic reprint of a work from about 1930, the new edition underwritten by a fundamentalist book club in Orange County. Poncins traced the pernicious influence of Zionist plotters on European history, giving special attention to their decisive role in the French and Russian revolutions. The Jacobin Clubs, Masons, Communist party, and Templars all turned out to be front organizations for the Jewish Sanhedrin, which was plotting world domination. Poncins cited Henry Ford's anti-Semitic tracts with approval, and implied that the great industrialist had been silenced when the Jews of America, working through Hollywood, threatened to crush him. The only solution to the Jewish problem, Poncins said, was extermination. There was no reference to Maistre in the index.

Zach hid the book under some others, and felt suddenly sick. What was he getting himself into? He was just a nice Jewish boy from Long Island. You had to be crazy even to read books like this; it was sick to have anything to do with such maniacs. What would his mother say? But more books kept arriving, and it was hard not to glance at them. It seemed that they fell into several distinct categories. First, there were paranoid, ranting, fascist tracts, like Poncins's. Then there were journalistic exposés, less paranoid but of generally low respectability. These tended to dwell on the Vatican, the CIA, the Red Brigades, Opus Dei, Lee Harvey Oswald, the Mafia, the Masonic connections of contemporary politicians, and the world banking system. They cited a confusing array of sources, from Senate hearings to reports in underground Los Angeles magazines. Then there were more reputable books, popular, but produced by publishers who wouldn't want to be sued for libel. There was one (a spin-off of a British TV documentary) that revealed that the Templars had fled to Scotland after their suppression in 1307, and had existed there clandestinely to the present day. Photographs of a Templar burial site on a remote loch revealed that people were still being flown there from as far away as California to be buried, with Masonic and Rosicrucian symbols on their tombs. An old couple lived in a mobile home nearby and hid their Masonic texts when the TV crew tried to interview them. The bare facts in a book like this were no doubt accurate; but it was impossible to tell whether the incidence of Templar symbolism throughout Scottish history was the result of a real secret brotherhood. Perhaps the Templar story was just a myth that was constantly being resurrected by people who wanted to add a little glamour and mystery to life in their remote, provincial, rainy nation.

Finally, there were serious works of scholarship. After all, the occult and secret societies were important parts of European intellectual and social history, and they had been duly chronicled by competent professionals from around the world. However, Zach discovered that it was somewhat difficult to tell the serious books from the crazy ones. Footnotes and long quotations in Latin or Hebrew were no guarantee; plenty of nuts learned ancient languages. Besides, Zach knew little Latin and no Hebrew, so he couldn't tell if the quotes made any sense. He decided to stick with the university presses and the authors who held professorships at reputable research institutions. Unfortunately, these works tended to cover small areas at great length. Zach wasted forty-five minutes reading about neo-Zoroastrianism at the Medici court, and almost an hour tracing Masonic imagery in Mozart's *Magic Flute*. Maistre showed up in none of the indexes.

3 • By five o'clock, Zach could no longer concentrate. Discouraged and tired, he put down a book on Isaac Newton's occult writings and went outside to get a bite to eat. It was still hot out, but the shadows were getting longer on Forty-second Street. Zach went into a fast-food restaurant and ordered an iced tea and fries. As he paid, he noticed the pyramid of the Illuminati on his dollar bill, with its weird eye and the familiar Latin phrase, "novus ordo seclorum"—a new world order. He had been reading all afternoon about the occult underground of the eighteenth century; now here it was on his money.

He went upstairs to the restaurant's "dining area" and selected a window seat, from which he could watch the shoppers and commuters who jammed the sidewalks of Fifth Avenue. It occurred to him to call home and check if there were any messages on Judah's answering machine. A teenage girl with a jarringly strong New York accent was using the pay phone, and it took her ten minutes to get off. When the phone was finally free, Zach inserted a quarter, and at the sound of Judah's recorded voice, he typed a code number. He listened to three messages from Judah's mother, who sounded as hysterical as ever. There was also a message for Zach from the library at his university, saying that he owed two dollars and ninety-three cents in fines; unless he paid immediately, he would not be allowed to graduate. Not much chance of that anyway, thought Zach. Finally, there was a beep and a long pause, followed by a message in a hesitant, nervous male voice.

"Uh, hello," said the voice. "I, uh, saw your query in the *New York Review of Books*. I did not steal your thesis. But, uh, the same thing happened to me, believe it or not. I have reasons to be kind of paranoid about the whole thing. And frankly, I have no way of knowing this isn't some kind of trap." There was another pause. "Okay. I guess I better take a chance on you. Look, I'll be at the ticket counter at Penn Station at seven o'clock tonight. I'll be coming up from Princeton on the train and I'll be wearing, um, a red T-shirt. Okay? I'm a grad student, twenty-five. Name is Charles. Okay? Bye."

Zach, very excited by this message, decided that he could not stand to return to the library. Instead, he started jogging toward Penn Station, but he slowed down after a few blocks when he realized that it was still before six. To kill time, he went into a discount record store and browsed in the used classical section for a few minutes. He tried to catch the eye of a young woman in a black dress who was looking at compact discs across the aisle, but she studiously ignored him. By peering at the alphabetical dividers in front of her, Zach was able to deduce that she was looking at Schönberg recordings. This meant that she was probably too sophisticated for him anyway.

On Thirty-fourth Street, desperate to kill time, he stopped to watch a mime. He showed up at Penn Station at about a quarter to seven, and began to pace back and forth in front of the ticket kiosks. For a while, he imagined that an old man was watching him, but the man left when the Philadelphia train was announced. Seven o'clock came and went with no sign of a graduate student in a red T-shirt.

At seven-fifteen, Zach called his answering machine again. There was a new message from Judah's mother, but nothing else. He went back to the ticket area and waited until seven-thirty. The crowds of commuters were beginning to thin out, and the bag ladies began to take over the station. Shady characters waited to pick up the public phones as soon as they rang. A couple of cops joked and swung their nightsticks expertly. Trains arrived and left every few minutes, carrying office workers home to New Jersey, and men in Islanders' shirts up to Madison Square Garden for the game. At seven-thirty and eight, Zach tried his machine again. At eight-fifteen, he decided to go home.

4 • Early the next morning, Zach was on his way to Princeton. He had decided that he could lose nothing by trying to find Charles; and anything was better than another day reading paranoid tracts in the New York Public Library. He withdrew another fifty dollars from his bank account and then took the New Jersey Transit train to Princeton Junction, enjoying the ride through the surreal northern New Jersey landscape of wetlands traversed by highways and punctuated by flaming towers. The train was nearly empty, since the morning commuter traffic flowed in the opposite direction. At Princeton Junction he transferred to the "dinky," an ancient two-car electric train that connects the university with the main-line station. This deposited him on the periphery of Princeton's bucolic, leafy, and—in the summer—almost deserted campus. Across the street was a convenience store that (Zach thought as he bought a drink) made all the convenience stores of his prior experience look like hovels beside the Parthenon. It was vast, immaculate, cool, and empty of people. Never had a homeless person held *its* door open for anyone.

Zach found the philosophy department by using a campus map. Once he had identified its front door, he marched rapidly in, trying to look as if he knew exactly what he was doing. To his left was a row of mail slots. Recognizing a name or two, he determined that these pigeonholes belonged to the

department's distinguished faculty. He also noticed that a
middle-aged woman with half-moon glasses was watching
him from behind a three-foot-high partition. On the top of
this partition was another row of pigeonholes; the names underneath were unfamiliar to Zach. He began looking for
someone called Charles.

"Can I help you?" asked the woman.

"No, thanks, I'm just dropping something off," said Zach,
who had nothing in his hand to leave behind. The woman apparently noticed this.

"For whom?" she inquired, her voice rising sharply at the
end of the sentence and emphasizing the *m*, as if to make a
grammatical point. But by then Zach had completed his
search of the boxes and, mercifully, had discovered just one
Charles—a Charles S. Wilson.

"Oh, sorry, this must be the *philosophy* department," he
said with a mock-embarrassed laugh, and left.

After a few minutes of wandering around the building,
Zach found a university directory. This yielded Charles's address. After another glance at the campus map, he set off past
dark stone classroom buildings, two little Greek temples, and
streets of Victorian frame houses toward the graduate school.
This turned out to be a huge Gothic tower, a replica of Mag-
dalen College, Oxford, but built to a scale possible only with
twentieth-century technology and robber-baron wealth. It
was still fairly early in the morning and no one was around.
The front door was locked, but after a few minutes a cleaning woman emerged and allowed Zach to go inside. He found
a cool interior in the American collegiate Gothic style, complete with round-topped doors, spiral staircases, stone floors,
and leaded windows. After wandering around deserted corridors and up several flights, Zach found Charles's door. He

knocked, first timidly, then with more authority. No one answered.

Just then a door to Zach's right opened and a woman emerged, wrapped only in a towel and with wet hair. "Looking for Charles?" she said.

Zach nodded. The woman tried knocking too, and shouted Charles's name. "Strange," she said. "He usually hangs around in the morning. Are you a friend of his from Philosophy?"

"No, not exactly," said Zach. He felt embarrassed to be talking to a woman in a towel; he felt like an intruder, and it would be impossible to explain what he was doing in her hallway. His eyes wandered down from her face toward her neckline and the towel: not because he wanted to see anything, not even out of curiosity, but because he wasn't *supposed* to look and therefore became self-conscious, and then his eyes just wandered down. Before they focused, he realized that she was watching, so he dropped his gaze right down at the floor. Now the problem became: how to look back at her face without retraversing her body. After a gratuitous journey past Charles's door, his eyes returned to meet hers. She had a round, frank face and a direct gaze. "Well, leave him a message," she said and disappeared into her room.

Zach watched her go, then contemplated Charles's notepad. He couldn't decide what to write; he even had a slightly paranoid feeling that he shouldn't write anything. Instead, he sat down on the stairs to wait.

Ten minutes later, the woman emerged, now dressed in shorts and a T-shirt that said "Hamlet." Her brown, shoulder-length hair was still wet and very curly. She was a little bit plump, brown from the sun, pleasant looking. "You don't want to leave a note?" she asked.

"Nah," said Zach, slipping into a mock-casual voice that he used only when insecure. "I'll just wait."

"Good luck," she said, and disappeared downstairs, giving Zach a wide berth as she passed.

Two hours later she returned to find a hungry, discouraged Zach still waiting on the stair. She looked slightly disturbed to see him, and stopped on the landing below as if to leave room for a quick departure.

"Still no Charles?" she asked.

"No Charles."

"You must need to see him right away."

"Sort of."

Zach could see that he was making her nervous. "I'll try back later," he said, and walked past her down the stairs. Just outside the front door, he found a shady bench and sat down. It was hot and a faraway mower emitted a continuous buzzing sound. A half hour passed. A man approached the door and Zach said, "Charles?" but the man just looked back blankly and went inside. After another few minutes, the woman from Charles's floor emerged from the building.

"I can see you from my window," she said.

She sat down next to him and looked off into the haze. "You know," she said after a while, "I'm starting to get a little worried about Charles. He wasn't home last night at eleven, even though there's *nothing* to do in Princeton at night. And he's not here now. Is he late for an appointment with you?"

"It was tentative," said Zach.

"I guess I'm a little jealous," she said. "I wonder where he could have spent the night. Not with me, alas."

"What does he work on?" asked Zach, after a pause.

"Nietzsche," she said. "That's his dissertation topic, I mean."

"Do you know more specifically?"

"I haven't read any of his stuff. We once talked about some allusions to Goethe in Nietzsche, but I don't think that's Charles's main topic. Are you another one of these philosophers?"

"I'm a grad student in philosophy. But not at Princeton; I live in New York."

"Philosophy is not my deal; I'm in art history. But don't panic. I fit neither of the two awful art history stereotypes."

"What are they?" Zach laughed.

"One is the rich woman who's into collecting and connoisseurship; she has great taste and devotion to Beauty, but no interest in ideas. She'll end up working in a museum, dressed fabulously, hobnobbing with donors and collectors. The other type is the po-mo theory-bore, big on deconstruction, SoHo galleries, conceptual art, discourses of liberation, race and gender theory. Actually, they're more like each other than either would admit."

"How about you?"

"I do medieval stuff. But there's another stereotype that I avoid: the whimsical, former Dungeons and Dragons aficionado. Nor am I a nerd who was always great in Latin and decided to do something that allows me to practice my obscure academic skills protected from the real world."

She laughed. "Sorry to be so judgmental; I'm not always like this. I work on medieval narrative art. I'm interested in the way it shows religious and moral ideas without having to spell them out, since the audience was mostly illiterate."

"Medieval art is beautiful," said Zach sincerely.

"Yes. Although the truth is, I have a lousy eye and a terrible visual memory."

"That's great. I'm a philosophy grad student who doesn't know any logic."

"We should start a support group."

A few minutes more passed in silence. Finally, Zach said, "Look, this is silly. Can you do me a favor? I'll give you my number and name. If Charles shows up, can you ask him to call me?"

"Certainly," she said, and watched him from the bench as he walked self-consciously away.

CHAPTER 3

1 • The next morning, the telephone awakened Zach at seven-thirty, at least two hours before he usually got up. He muttered hello.

"Hey, Zach?" It was a woman's voice.

"Yeah, hello."

"Hey, this is Kate from Princeton. I met you yesterday?"

"Right. What's up?" The fog was beginning to lift from Zach's eyes but his mouth still felt like mud. He struggled to sound clear, articulate, vigorous.

"Charles still hasn't shown up."

"Oh, wow."

"I'm really worried."

"Does he go away like that a lot?"

"Never, not without telling me. You know, we're friends. Our relationship is a little bit ambiguous in some ways, but not the friendship part—we're buddies. He would tell me before he went on a trip."

"Have you talked to anyone else about this? Who would know where to locate him?"

"Me, if anyone, I think. Listen, you know more about this than you're letting on. I want you to level with me."

Zach paused for a second, then told the whole story of his

missing dissertation and the phone call from Charles.

After he was finished, Kate said: "Let's get to the bottom of this." She sounded excited.

"I'd certainly like to," said Zach. "My career depends on it."

"Do you want to take a look around Charles's room?"

"Can we?"

"Sure. Come on down as soon as you can."

2 • As arranged, Kate was waiting at the dinky stop when Zach got off. She was wearing dark printed shorts and a white top; she looked good to Zach, who hoped that he was at least presentable. She had been sitting on the bench under the eave of the little station house with a book in her lap. She waved it at Zach; it was a one-volume paperback Nietzsche anthology.

"I figured I'd better get up to speed. But what a wacko! I read *Beyond Good and Evil* one summer in college." She shook her head and raised her eyebrows as if she were describing some crazy relative.

"Yeah, but I like authors who challenge you," said Zach.

"Oh, definitely."

"How are we going to get into Charles's room?" he asked.

"I'll show you."

They walked across some lawns and athletic fields to the graduate school. To fill the conversational void, she played tour guide. "Woodrow Wilson—he was president of the university, you know—wanted the grad school right in the middle of campus," she said. "He wanted to raise the intellectual seriousness of the undergrad scene." She laughed. "Poor deluded fool. Anyway, he was defeated by a faction that wanted an Oxford college replica. It cost him his job, but he went on to even greater defeats as president of the U.S."

She led Zach up to her floor and let him into her room. It was an extraordinary mess, with books strewn across the floor and piled, rather than shelved, on bookcases. The walls were decorated with posters of Italian medieval art; other pictures, slides, and posters lay on the floor as if she had been making a halfhearted effort to categorize them. Her desk was submerged under papers, although the screen of a computer could barely be seen emerging from the chaos. Plants hung from baskets in the window, framed photos cluttered her bedside table, and the bed itself was unmade.

"Sorry," she said, gesturing toward the room in general. She picked her way across the room, trying not to step on anything. "He leaves his window open in the summer."

She opened her own window, a Gothic affair with leaded glass. Zach joined her and looked down the thirty or forty feet to the hard ground below.

"We'll just swing around the sill and into his place," she said. She looked at Zach, who tried to conceal his fright. "Or I can just go and let you in through the door."

She didn't sound condescending, but Zach absolutely did not want to look like a wimp. "No, that's okay. I'm taller; I should go."

"You are?" They sized up each other's heights. He *was* taller, but it was close.

"I'll go," she said. Before he could object, she hitched her leg up over the window ledge, dodged a hanging plant, extended an arm to find the frame of Charles's window, and then scrambled out of sight. Zach swallowed hard and followed her. As he clung to the outside wall, he began to panic. To steady himself, he focused intently on the stones and the exact placement of his feet on the narrow ledge below. He could barely see the ground far beneath him. For a minute he felt as if he were stuck, but it would have been just as hard to go back as forward, so he persevered. He was very pleased with himself when he finally stumbled into Charles's dark room, although his hamstring hurt and his heart was still racing.

"Why did you do that?" she said. "I could have let you in. Men!" But he was still so pleased he couldn't help grinning.

"I guess I'm glad he isn't in here," she said.

"Are you sure he isn't?"

They looked around to make sure that neither Charles nor his body was still in the room. It was neater than Kate's: in fact, it was underfurnished. The bed was neatly made but only with sheets and a wool blanket. There was nothing on the walls except two Monet posters and some gray steel shelves. A desk contained a computer and a stack of books; there were more volumes, mostly Nietzsche's works, in a small bookcase.

Zach looked at the books on the desk. "Is this what he was working on most recently?" he asked.

"I guess so. They're library books. Who's Otto Stern?" Three of the five volumes had Stern's name on their spines.

"Stern is dead now, but he was an interesting figure, actually. A lot of academics think of him as pretty marginal, but he had close intellectual relationships with some of the greatest prewar European philosophers. He founded a school that most people consider eccentric today, but it has a member or two on most of the best faculties in the country."

"And Jules Hausman?" Hausman was the author of the remaining books.

"He's a leading Sternian today. He teaches at Cornell, I think."

"Any connection between these guys and your thesis?"

"There could be, obviously. But nothing specific comes to mind. I haven't really read Stern seriously."

"Interesting." She walked over to Charles's bed and

looked at his answering machine. "What do you think, should we listen to his messages?"

"Do you think so?" said Zach, looking nervously toward the door. "What if he shows up?"

"I'll take responsibility. I'll say I was worried about him, which I am."

"Okay, do it."

She pushed "play." The first voice on the machine was her own. She grimaced as she heard herself inquire nervously about whether Charles was feeling okay. "La dee da," she intoned, drowning out her voice on the tape. "I hate listening to myself."

The second voice was that of a young woman, just calling to say hi. Kate didn't look too happy about that message, either. "Who's she, I wonder," she muttered.

The third voice was instantly recognizable to Zach. "Davies here," it said. "Confound it, where are you? Telephone me immediately, please. Immediately."

Kate could see that Zach recognized the raspy, patrician voice. "Who's Davis?" she asked.

"Hannibal Davies, with an *ie*. He's my chairman."

"Sounds like a great guy."

"Yeah, well, we go way back. It's extremely strange that he should be calling Charles, though."

"I don't know; he's a philosopher, right?"

"Yes, but a totally different kind from Charles and me. He's into pure logic. He thinks Nietzsche was a madman, I would guess."

"Is he a Sternian?"

"Not at all. No, he's what we call a number cruncher. He only does symbolic logic. The Sternians are into cultural decay, nihilism, that kind of thing. You can't diagram cultural decay, so Davies wouldn't be interested."

"Except maybe with a big down arrow?"

"Right."

Zach sat down on the bed. He began to think out loud. "Davies told me what my thesis topic was."

"What do you mean?"

"He picked a topic for me and ordered me to do it."

"How could he do that?"

"He threatened to withhold funding otherwise."

"That's gotta be illegal."

"Davies *is* the law at my university."

"Could this be a deal where he farms out work to grad students, then steals it and publishes it in his own name?"

Zach gave that theory some thought. "How could he have chosen Charles's subject, though?"

"I don't know."

"Wait a second," said Zach. "Did—I mean, *does* Charles have an Austin?"

"The scholarship? Yes, I think so. That's why he doesn't have to teach."

"Guess who's the Eastern Chairman of the Austin Committee?"

"Davies? That's it, then."

"It doesn't make sense, though. Davies wouldn't publish in this field; it's just impossible. Besides, he has a tremendous reputation. He wouldn't want to be associated with work produced by someone like me, even if he were willing to switch fields dramatically. I'm just not a good enough scholar, and he knows it. Plus, Charles and I would surely object when our dissertations appeared under his name. And one more thing: as far as I know, he doesn't have a copy of my work, so he couldn't be stealing it."

"Still, he must be involved somehow with this."

"I guess I should have a talk with him," said Zach. This was like promising to chat with the devil about the problem of evil in the world, but Zach could see no alternative.

"What would you say to him?"

"I don't know. We aren't even sure he's got the dissertations. That might not be it at all."

"Yeah, I think you should know more before you talk to him," said Kate. "I mean, you can't just march in and say, 'Turn over the dissertations, Davies.' Even if he had them, he wouldn't admit it unless you had some kind of evidence."

"True." Zach was grateful for the reprieve.

"We need to figure out why your dissertation and Charles's add up to something that's worth stealing. No offense: I'm sure your work is very valuable on its own—"

"Sure, sure." Zach feigned offense.

"Well, if it was the inherent value of your ideas that they were after, they could have just asked you to *lend* them the manuscript. That's the usual arrangement." She could see that he was just teasing her, so she went on: "Obviously, something a little more sinister is happening here. Do you think you might be able to discover some kind of link to your work by reading these Stern books?"

"Maybe."

"Okay, why don't you skim them this afternoon. If that's okay?"

"Fine. I think it's a good plan."

"Meanwhile, what should I do? I'd like to read this stuff, but it would be kind of a waste of time since I don't know your work."

"I know what you can do," said Zach. "The Sternians have been written up in general-interest magazines from time to time. So has Davies, probably. At least he would show up in *Alumni Magazine* articles and maybe in the *Chronicle*. Do you think you could do some basic research on those two topics?"

"No problem. I may not know much about philosophy, but I'm a professional looker-up of stuff in libraries."

"Should we go there, then?" Zach got up.

"You can't get in, I'm afraid. It would cost us fifty bucks or something to get you a temporary reader's card. Anyway, Charles already has all the relevant books out."

"True. But I don't want to sit in here reading. What if he comes back?"

"Use my room."

They went out of Charles's room but left the door unlocked. "I'll explain what happened if he comes back," said Kate. "I'll take full responsibility."

The door to her room was still open and they walked back in together. She looked for a place where he could sit comfortably, finally opting to push a pile of papers and books off a soft chair onto the floor. "Sit here," she said. "There's diet soda in the fridge if you want. Make yourself at home. I'll report back with what I find, if I find anything. And why don't you answer the phone if it rings? In case it's Charles."

She went out, leaving Zach alone with five weighty volumes of political theory. At least Stern wrote well and with a complete lack of technical jargon or footnotes. Zach settled in to do some hard work. He read quickly, purposefully, with exhausting concentration, skimming some pages, leaving scraps of paper to mark possibly relevant passages, hardly looking up for an hour and forty-five minutes. Vague ideas were beginning to form in his mind. At last he let the book drop, tired but somewhat encouraged by the first stirrings of a theory.

His concentration broken, he looked up at Kate's room and could not resist the temptation to snoop. The pictures on her bedside table showed her, tan and happy, in front of various medieval buildings, unknown to Zach. In one picture she had her arm around the shoulder of a young, Italian-looking man; but she looked a few years younger in the picture. Another showed her with a young woman, perhaps a sister, at a graduation. There was also a photo of a golden retriever with a misshapen rag doll in his mouth. Pinned up above her desk were several postcards, which Zach shamelessly turned over and read. One was from Charles in the Bahamas, who reported that he was having a great time, relaxing, and meeting lots of cool people. Another was from Ridolfo in Firenze; Zach couldn't understand anything except the "carissima Catarina" at the top, the "con amore eternale ed appassianato" at the bottom, and the postmark, which suggested that the card was three years old. So much for Ridolfo, he hoped.

Kate's book collection was difficult to assess when so much of it lay on the floor. Nevertheless, a cursory glance at the scattered titles suggested that many had been bought secondhand, and few concerned art history. Instead, she seemed to own many works on European history; some novels, particularly contemporary ones; some literary theory and women's studies; and a lot of miscellaneous volumes on everything from the birds of New Jersey to Italian opera. At random, Zach flipped open a collection of letters by American slaves and found pencil marks next to particularly poignant passages all the way through the book.

Kate's CD collection was largely classical (but not, in Zach's opinion, very sophisticated); there was also some folk and some prewar jazz. He considered a quick look at her clothes in the wardrobe, but he decided that that would be going too far, so he returned to the chair and began again to concentrate on reading.

3 • Kate returned late in the afternoon, bearing food and notes from her research. "Pizza okay?" she said.

"Great," said Zach.

"Everybody eats pizza. So, did you look around my room?"

Zach panicked. "How did you know?" He glanced toward the postcards that were pinned above her desk to see if he had left any of them out of place, but they seemed okay.

She laughed. "I didn't know. I just guessed, because that's what *I* would have done."

"I didn't look at anything that wasn't out in the open." Zach was distraught.

"Then you're a wimp. You mean you didn't look in my desk drawers?"

"Honestly, I didn't."

She opened the pizza box and took some soda out of the refrigerator. She perched at the edge of her bed, he sat back in the chair, and they ate off greasy paper plates. While they ate, she said, "So, did you figure out what's going on?"

"I think I may have an inkling."

"Tell me about it."

"I'm not sure that I know how to explain this."

"Well, don't keep me in suspense forever. You know, I may not be too sophisticated about political theory, but I'm not that dumb in general."

Zach realized that she was annoyed, but he honestly didn't know how to express the theories that had just begun to form in his mind. "I'll tell you what," he said. "Let me explain about my dissertation. That will give you some of the background you need. I mean, if you don't mind? It's very dull, I realize."

"I can take it. I'm a grad student myself, remember."

Zach explained about Maistre, putting an emphasis on his secret nihilism and public authoritarianism. When he was done, Kate said, "I assume there's something similar going on with these Sternians?"

"Maybe. But obviously they wouldn't just come out and say it in so many words. Otherwise, their writing would be counterproductive; it would just foster nihilism."

"Right."

"You see, Maistre used some very clever stratagems to conceal his actual meaning."

"Such as?"

"Such as giving you all the clues you need to arrive at nihilism, while arguing explicitly for faith and conservative values. That serves a double purpose. On one hand, ordinary readers think, 'He's a conservative, and he's made a strong argument in favor of traditional values. If we don't hold on to those values, we'll have nothing left. There will be no distinction at all between good and evil.' "

"Okay."

"But you see, that's a lousy argument for the *truth* of the traditional values. I mean, it just says that we'd better believe in them, or else. So some of Maistre's readers would actually be converted by him to a kind of secret nihilism. In other words, he would have given them evidence to disbelieve in all values, but at the same time he would have stressed the need for most people to believe in values. So a true Maistre disciple would not announce boldly, 'Nothing is true; all is permitted.' He'd keep that under wraps, and instead tell people they'd better obey the pope."

"But if nothing is true and everything is permitted, as you say, then why should Maistre *care* if people obey the pope? Why is any society better than any other? Why is a conservative system better than anarchy?"

"That's a good question. I'm not sure about that."

"Maybe because it allows Maistre and other intellectuals to survive? Anarchies are dangerous places for nerds."

"Perhaps. Or maybe he just happened to value peace, stability, and order, without thinking that those values were objectively true and good."

"Right."

"Well, in the same way, the Sternians seem at first glance

to be arguing for natural law. Which means they claim that some things are universally true and good because they are 'by nature.' That's obviously a very conservative position."

"I know. They used to talk that way in my period. The Scholastics—didn't they invent natural law?"

"It's an ancient idea, but they revived it, yes."

"So, for example, gays are evil because they're unnatural."

"For example. But actually, what is true 'by nature' is very controversial. You could even say that people are naturally bisexual. That's what Freud said."

"Nature is a pretty fuzzy concept."

"In fact, it's really just a dodge. You say that what you dislike is *contra naturam,* and ergo it's evil, QED. But if someone else says 'No, it's natural,' how do you argue with him? Or her?" he added hurriedly.

"It's probably a him if he's laying down the law from nature."

"I don't know; what about Phyllis Schlafly?"

"A traitor to her gender. But I sidetracked you, I think."

"Well, the point is that the Sternians are big natural-law theorists. And yet they never seem to specify what the natural law *is.* Also, I think I may be on to something even more interesting. I hope I don't sound conceited; it's just that this is one thing I'm really qualified to talk about after all my work on Maistre."

"That's quite all right." She smiled.

"Let me put it this way. What would *you* do if you were a true disciple of Maistre?"

"Are you really asking me?"

"Yeah."

"I'd shoot myself. Or get a lobotomy."

"Okay," said Zach, "but if you were a true disciple of Maistre who wanted to write a book?"

"I'd preach esoteric nihilism. Is that what you're after?"

"Right. But you'd want to make the argument for nihilism very secret. Best of all would be a kind of code that you and your followers could use to communicate the so-called truth that there is no truth, while everyone else got the impression that you were arguing for natural law. You see, the advantage of such a code is, you could recruit new disciples as people read your books and cracked the code."

"Two questions. One, why would you want new disciples? And number two, wouldn't you be afraid that someone sooner or later would spill the beans?"

"The answer to number one is easy, I think. You want new disciples because you think that nowadays a deliberate, constant effort is going to be necessary to sustain the belief in basic values. Science, which is value free, is taking over everything. Historians and anthropologists, not to mention physicists and psychologists, keep telling us that everything is relative. So unless somebody does something, society is going to lose faith—every kind of faith."

He stopped to see if she was following; she looked back impassively, so he continued: "Even belief in science, history, and anthropology will go down the tubes once people agree that everything is relative, as the scientists, historians, and anthropologists keep telling them. Because surely that insight also applies to science, history, and anthropology; those disciplines can't escape the relativism that they find everywhere else. That's why you need to recruit a few good men in every generation to fight back."

"But what about the chance that someone will discover what you're up to?"

"Well, your friend Charles and I made somebody nervous, didn't we?"

"Aha," said Kate. "I thought you were heading in that direction. So now we have a motive. Still, it seems that they were running an awfully big risk that someone would reveal their code."

"Yes, but I think that they were counting on one thing. Anyone smart enough to figure out what they were up to—and I'm not blowing my own horn; I stumbled onto it by accident—would be smart enough to see the necessity of keeping nihilism secret. Anyone who could crack the code would automatically enroll himself in the fraternity of esoteric nihilists."

"Except for you."

"Well, I haven't spilled the beans to anyone but you. Besides, when I was just happily writing my dissertation, I didn't know anything about Stern. My dissertation, which never would have been published anyway, posed no threat to them. At worst, someone might have noticed an analogy between Maistre and Stern—but that someone would have had to track down my dissertation on microfilm. Anyone who was that interested could probably have cracked the Sternian code by himself."

"Have you cracked it?"

"Not yet, so all of this is pure speculation. The code would be the smoking gun, so to speak. But I think I may be on to part of it. How about you; what did you find out about Professor Stern and his friends?"

"And Professor Davies. I looked him up, too."

"Right."

"Well," she said, "there's quite a lot about the Sternians, but it's mostly gossipy. They have a fair amount of influence at some major universities and in Washington among conservatives. Everyone takes them to be right-wingers and natural-law theorists—you're right about that. They publish a lot, but I don't know if anyone reads their stuff. They have quaint customs like celebrating de Gaulle's birthday with secret rites. They're paranoid about being discriminated against in tenure and hiring decisions because they're surrounded by a bunch of value-free social scientists who don't understand their work."

"What about Stern himself?"

She consulted her notes. "Born eighteen ninety-seven in Pilsen, which is now P-L-Z-E-N, however you pronounce that, a Czech town, but was then in the Austrian Empire. Educated in Prague, a very cool place at the time because Kafka, Janáček, everybody was there. Worked with some of the greatest philosophers of the period in Vienna and Germany. Emigrated to the U.S. by way of France after the Anschluss. Taught at various American colleges and universities until he died in nineteen seventy-one. Apparently a nice old Jewish guy, married, I don't know about kids. Gave no interviews. But controversial all along, particularly because he had these crazy, devoted disciples."

"Great. And how about Davies?"

"I like him much less, I must say. Let's see, he was born in nineteen thirty-three in Newport, Rhode Island, to Professor Scipio Davies, would you believe, and Margaret Cabot Davies. Educated at Philips Exeter, Yale, and Oxford on a Rhodes. Lettered in lacrosse. *Who's Who* doesn't say this, but according to a profile in *New England Living*, he was a member of Crypt, one of your awful secret societies."

"You mean, he *is* a member," said Zach. "You don't ever leave those societies."

"Right. Anyway, there's not that much more to say about him. *New England Living* has a photo of him happily sculling down a creek near his palatial Connecticut home; he also has a lovely Maine summer residence and a yacht. You know about his books; they're all on logic. He holds a fancy endowed chair and he's chairman of the department. He has various honorary degrees, but I won't go into that."

"Any political connections?"

"None that showed up in the articles. Although in the sixties, he gave some speeches about how the long-haired radicals were going to bring down the university; how it was the Weimar Republic all over again and he wasn't going to stand for it. That meant opposing coeducation, by the way, among other things."

"Anything about him beating a student?"

"No. He did that?"

"It's probably a myth. He's supposed to have hit some poor kid who was protesting against Vietnam or something. And I don't mean just cuffing him or something; he flogged him with a cane."

"Sounds like him, but I didn't see anything about it."

"I need to do more work on the Stern angle. But I should also prepare for class; I have to teach tomorrow. Can I bring these books up to New York with me?"

"I think so, sure. Where are you teaching?"

"At a state place upstate. For the money, frankly. And it's not going very well, I'm afraid."

"It rarely does."

"So when can we get back together?" Zach asked.

"Thursday, if it's okay by you. Maybe Charles will have turned up by then."

"I hope so," Zach lied.

"Do you want to come back down here? Or I could go up to New York instead if you want to save yourself another trip."

Zach didn't want her to see his apartment. "Down here would be great," he said. "I could make it here by the early evening. Maybe we could have dinner in town and compare notes?"

"Fine. But that raises the question of what I should be

working on in the meantime. I don't have any pressing academic work to do."

"I have an idea," Zach said. "I'm curious about this Crypt connection." Ever since Alice Webster had raised the question of Davies's secret society, it had seemed important to Zach. "How would you feel about doing some research on them?"

"No problem." She got up. "Let me walk you to the dinky. This was kind of fun; if I wasn't worried about Charles, I'd have enjoyed it thoroughly."

Outside, the shadows had grown long and cicadas chattered. The deserted campus was cool and picturesque. They walked toward the Princeton station in silence. The little train waited with its doors open, but it wasn't scheduled to leave for another ten minutes. Kate waved at the conductor and then suddenly said to Zach, "I have an idea. You know, there's only one way that Charles could have left Princeton— on the dinky. And only a few people use it every day during the summer. Hold on a second."

She approached the conductor, a short, middle-aged man. "Mr. Williams," she said, "do you know my friend Charles?"

"You mean this gentleman?" He pointed at Zach.

"No, another friend. Tall, blond, broad shoulders, has kind of a serious, almost pouty expression most of the time?"

"Yeah, sure, I know him. The guy you're with all the time."

"That's right. You know, I'm trying to find him right now, and I was wondering if you'd noticed him leave Princeton on, like, Friday evening?"

"Actually, kind of a funny thing happened with him."

Zach had been hanging back while Kate and Mr. Williams talked; now his interest was piqued and he came nearer.

The conductor explained: "He was waiting here for the train, I think the four oh two, when I pulled in from the

Junction. I said hi, he said hi—we recognize each other although I don't know his name. He gets on the train to wait for us to go. When I come through to pick up the tickets, he's busy talking to this other guy. They're having a real emotional conversation. I ask for their tickets and he says, 'I'm gonna take the next train. When is it?' I tell him four forty-seven; he says okay and gets off with the old guy."

"Did he take the next train?" asked Kate.

"No. I come back in at about four-thirty, right? Your friend and the old guy are there on the bench, still talking. Come four forty-seven, I say we're going; but your friend—Charles is his name?—he says that's okay, maybe the next one. And when I come back at—it would be about five-thirty for the five forty-seven—they're both gone."

"And that's the last you saw of him?" Kate looked at Zach.

"That's the last, I think. Is there some kind of problem?"

"No," said Kate, after a pause for thought. "He's his own man. He *has* kind of disappeared, but it's not like a missing person or anything. I mean, he's only been gone for a couple of days, and it *is* summer vacation. And there's no reason he would tell *me* if he left for a trip or something. I was just curious."

"Would you mind describing the older man?" Zach asked.

Mr. Williams seemed to be thinking about whether it was appropriate to say; in the end, he directed his reply back at Kate. "Yeah. He was an old guy, white beard, shorts, shirt with a collar, sandals, black socks. Looked like a professor."

"Mr. Williams, thanks a lot."

"No problem. Train leaves in about five."

As he left, Kate turned to Zach. "Sound like Davies?" she asked.

"Not at all. Totally different type," said Zach. "If you strapped sandals on Hannibal Davies, it would be like putting Kryptonite on Superman: his vital energy would be sucked out of him and he would die."

"It's creepy, huh? Charles was on his way to see you, somebody met him on the dinky, and then poof, he disappeared from the face of the earth."

The empty campus suddenly started looking less picturesque and more sinister, the Gothic stone buildings and long shadows taking on an almost malevolent aspect. Kate looked back nervously toward the graduate school.

"You want me to walk back there with you?" asked Zach.

"No, I'll be fine."

"Be careful."

"I will. Call me from New York if anything turns up."

She waited on the platform until the dinky pulled out of the station with Zach on board.

4 • On the dinky, the New Jersey Transit train, and the subway, Zach tried to prepare for class, but his mind kept turning back to the day's events. He gave a lot of thought to whether he ought to call Kate when he got home to make sure that she was okay. He'd only known her for forty-eight hours, so it might seem a little strange for him to be taking such an interest in her welfare. Also, it was silly to think that she might be in any kind of danger; and it might just worry her if he were to call. He had made a fool of himself plenty of times before with such gestures. On the other hand, he found himself wanting quite strongly to speak to her again.

He didn't feel like facing his depressing apartment or a decision about whether to call Kate, so he took the subway down to Greenwich Village. He emerged on gritty Fourteenth Street and walked past its shuttered stores and dark office blocks. The upper floors of the buildings reminded Zach of his father's world. It was a David Mamet domain of marginal capitalists: encyclopedia salesmen, book shippers, used-record retailers, importers of camera accessories. Almost all of its inhabitants were white males over fifty, men who blended in with the dust, the card files, the water coolers, the ancient black telephones, and the huge, humming electric typewriters. Zach's father had worked on Sixteenth Street and sometimes used to baby-sit Zach at the office when school was out. Zach would sit on a swivel chair and read mystery stories; at lunch they would grab hot dogs in Union Square.

He turned south on Fifth Avenue and cheered up as he approached the carnival atmosphere of Greenwich Village. He wandered into a book store, thinking that he should check the political philosophy section for Sternian books. Sure enough, there was a new volume by Jules Hausman, among other works. Zach flipped through it for a few minutes, testing a hypothesis about the way Sternians wrote. He checked the back flap for Hausman's biography, but there was nothing very informative beyond a series of glowing reviews from other prominent Sternians. There was, however, a photograph of the author, showing an older man with a white beard, an oxford shirt, and no tie. Zach thought of the man who had stopped Charles at the Princeton station—but of course, every third professor was an older man with a white beard. Still, the discovery gave Zach an idea. He charged the book to his credit card despite its exorbitant price, rushed home on the subway, and let himself into his apartment, which he had all to himself again.

After searching for the right phone number, he called a college friend in Ithaca, New York.

"Can I speak to Andrew?" he asked when a woman picked up the phone. Andrew was now a grad student at Cornell; he and Zach had been pretty good friends when they were both undergraduate philosophy majors. Relaxed, somewhat frivolous, he always managed to have a good time while coasting by on native intelligence. Nevertheless, Zach liked him a lot.

"Zach, dude, what's up?" he said.

"Hey, how's it going?"

"Not bad, hangin' out, endless summer, not a bad deal, you know? What's up with you? Just calling to say hi?"

"Partly. But I also had a question. You know a guy called Jules Hausman? He's not in your department, but—"

"Sure, Hausman, I know the dude. I mean, I know who he is."

"How would you describe him?"

"Oh, typical professor type, you know, like big beard, messed-up hair, bumps into walls probably . . ."

"I know this sounds weird, but can you be more specific? Like what does he wear?"

"I'm picturing him as he makes his way across the quad. Let's see, in the summer, Mr. Hausman might model an ensemble of rumpled shirt, shorts with black belt—not the karate kind—sandals, and the de rigueur black socks. He may accessorize with a briefcase and pens in his breast pocket. In the winter, a large, misshapen black coat covers his professorial form."

"Thanks a lot."

"That's it?"

"Listen, I'll call you back soon and explain all. Is that okay?"

"Hey, anytime. In the meantime, would you like me to compile a reference book describing the wardrobes of the *whole* Cornell faculty? Or how about philosophers of the Ivy League? Would you like a pictorial?"

"That's okay. I can always call you."

"You got it." They said good-bye and hung up.

Now Zach at least had a good excuse to call Kate. She

picked up on the first ring, sounding nervous.

"Hey, it's just me, Zach."

"Oh, hi. I thought it might be Charles, or news about him. But I'm glad it's you."

"I thought I'd call to see if you were okay, if anything had happened on your end. Also, I have a small piece of news myself."

"I'm fine. All quiet down here. What's your news?"

"You know the guy that Charles was talking to on the dinky just before he disappeared?"

"Yeah."

"I think it was Jules Hausman. The conductor's description matches the picture on the back of Hausman's latest book; I also called a friend at Cornell who confirmed that he wears sandals and black socks all the time."

"So do a lot of professors."

"True."

"Listen, I had an idea earlier that might help confirm your theory. I was thinking maybe I'd play back the whole of Charles's answering-machine tape, not just the new messages."

"Good idea. You think Hausman might be on there?"

"Yeah. Hold on a sec. If you want, I'll play it right now and call you back."

She called back in about five minutes. "Guess what?" she said. "There were a bunch of messages from assorted bimbos, an earlier one from Davies—not very informative—and one from Professor Hausman himself, suggesting that they meet in Princeton."

"Any indication of when he called?"

"No. But it was five or six bimbos back on the tape, so I'd say Saturday or Sunday. Unless things are worse than I know."

"I don't know what all of this means, but I think we're

making some kind of progress," said Zach.

"Keep reading and thinking, so will I, and let's figure out a plan when we get together. Okay?"

"Great. I'm looking forward to it."

"Me, too."

"Be careful. Lock your window."

"I'm not going to close my window in this heat."

"Are you sure? There's hardly anyone around in that isolated place."

"You sound like my mother."

"Sorry."

"No, I appreciate it. I'll be fine, though. Thanks for calling."

They said good-bye and then Zach lay on his bed and tried to sleep.

5 • The telephone shocked him awake at 3:12 A.M. He picked it up and muttered, "Hello." A male voice with an excellent French accent said quickly, "La glaive de la justice n'a pas de fourreau."

"What?" said Zach.

The second time it came a bit slower: "Le glaive de la justice n'a pas de fourreau."

"Who is this?"

"Do you understand the quotation?" The man on the other end now spoke with a cultivated American accent.

Zach didn't know how to respond. He thought, "glève"? What the hell is a "glève"?

"Charles Wilson understands." With this, the caller hung up. Zach lay in the dark for a few minutes, trying to decide what had just happened; he even thought that he might have dreamt the conversation. At last he pulled himself out of bed, switched on the light, and looked up "glève" in a French dictionary. There was no such word. Next he looked up "fourneau": it meant a furnace or stove. "The something of justice has no furnace." Zach groaned in confusion and put down the dictionary.

Or was it "fourreau"? A "fourreau," it turned out, was a sheath or scabbard. "The something of justice has no scabbard." Zach asked himself what could lack a scabbard, and immediately recognized the origin of the quotation. Just to make sure, he looked up "sword" in the English-to-French part of the dictionary, and discovered not only the word "épée," but also "glaive." "The sword of justice has no scabbard"—a famous aphorism from Maistre's *Soirées de Saint-Pétersbourg*. In this dialogue, Maistre's stand-in, the Comte, describes an executioner in grisly and appreciative detail. The hangman wakes up, breaks a victim on the rack, hacks off a few heads, and then returns to bed to sleep soundly next to his wife, muttering, "No one breaks people like I do." According to the Comte, the executioner is a hero as valuable as any soldier. Without frequent and painful executions, no society can survive the threat of anarchy and nihilism. Hence the sword of justice has no scabbard; it must always be drawn, always killing.

Zach walked into the common room and made sure that the front door was securely locked. Then he returned to bed and lay with the light still on, listening intently. Finally, he decided that this was ridiculous behavior, that no assailant would be frightened away by a bedside lamp. He switched off the light and lay in the dark, trying to decide what the caller could have meant. After a while, his mind wandered and he started to think about the next day. He suddenly remembered that he had an appointment in the morning with

Alice Webster. Hurriedly he reset his alarm for seven, and
fell back asleep.

Thursday morning was the beginning of another hot day, although the early morning shadows still kept the temperature
bearable. In the daylight, in bustling New York City, the
mysterious telephone call of the night before seemed unreal.
Zach enjoyed riding the subway during the morning rush
hour, a rare experience for him. Although he had to stand in
a hot, packed car, it made him feel like a man of the world
to be out and about at that hour. And best of all, he didn't
have to check himself into an office for the day when the ride
was over. He was an autonomous observer in the workaday
world, like an anthropologist observing the customs of some
exotic subterranean people.

He arrived at Alice's apartment on time but still bleary-
eyed. She greeted him warmly, served him a welcome cup
of coffee and a bagel with lox, and listened as he recounted
the incidents of the previous days. He put as little emphasis as possible on Kate's role, merely mentioning that
Charles's next-door neighbor had let him into Charles's
room. It was not that he wanted to claim more credit than he
deserved for their joint detective work; rather, he found himself too embarrassed to talk about Kate in front of Alice. His
enthusiasm for her would be hard to conceal and might be
misinterpreted, he thought.

Alice listened with interest. When he was done, she said,
"So, we have two suspects, really: Hausman and Davies. At
some point, I may be able to help with Davies. He and I have
been colleagues—though hardly collegial—for thirty-odd
years, so I could easily find some pretext to call him if you
want me to. In fact, we're serving together on the curricu-

lum committee next fall. That will be a mutual delight, I'm sure," she added ruefully.

"Thanks, Alice." Zach was eager for any excuse not to call Davies himself.

"Meanwhile, what's your next step?"

"I'm going to talk that through with Kate tonight."

"Who's Kate?"

"Oh, I guess I didn't mention her name. She's Charles's next-door neighbor, the one who let me into his room."

"Ah. And now she knows all about the mystery of the purloined thesis?"

"Yes. I told her something about it. As a matter of fact, she's been extremely helpful."

"I see. You didn't mention that at first."

"No. I'm not sure why not."

"So, you and she are now working on the case together?"

"Well, she's Charles's friend, and she's worried about him. He *has* vanished from the face of the earth, don't forget."

"Fair enough, if she's nice and reliable. I must say, I feel a bit disappointed to have been displaced by someone younger and no doubt prettier than myself as your chief confidante."

Zach didn't know what to say.

"Just keep me up-to-date, will you?" said Alice. "Don't forget your ancillary aunt Alice. I was finding your adventure interesting, I must say. Not that I took pleasure in your misfortunes, but it was exciting to have a genuine mystery to mull over. Don't leave me out altogether."

"Don't worry about that, Alice," said Zach. "You've been indispensable so far, and you may be even more important in the future."

"Well," she said, rising to signal the end of the conversation, "you have things to do, I'm sure, and I must return to my compulsion: watching those dreadful Senate Judiciary Committee hearings on cable. I can't tear myself away."

"What's happening?"

Alice's face seemed to say that Zach really *should* read the newspaper, but her words did not accuse him. "Oh, he's defending natural-law jurisprudence, which is a device for rolling back everything we've achieved since *Brown,* and the dimwit senators are trying to act as if they knew something, playing to the home crowd of course, and letting him off with the most unspeakable errors of logic and reason. Some of them call themselves liberals. I'd like to mark up their speeches—and his—with a red pen. The worst is their attitude of wisdom and sincerity. They think they're advancing the theoretical debate on rights and jurisprudence, when none of them could get a C in my freshman expository writing seminar." But she immediately regretted her intemperance, adding, "I'm sure they're very clever and professional when it comes to negotiating tax legislation and that kind of thing."

"I know what you mean, though," said Zach. "That's why I stick to political theory. I'm really not that interested in day-to-day political events. That's terrible, I guess."

"Don't you care who sits on the Supreme Court? You should, you know."

"I know." Zach made a perfunctory apologetic gesture, but he didn't feel much regret. In academic life, one was supposed to express one's disdain for politics, apologize for not being better informed about the whole sorry business, and then quickly change the subject back to grown-up, serious matters like literary theory and tenure. Alice didn't challenge his attitude (although her face still registered slight irritation); instead, she just let Zach out with a friendly good-bye and made him promise to keep her informed—"daily, if possible."

6 • Zach had still not seriously prepared for class when he boarded the bus to the state college three hours later. He had expected to find the strength to work as the hour of class approached, but his habits of procrastination were too powerful. During the subway and train trips, he just stared ahead blankly.

By the time he got off the bus, dark clouds had filled the sky and thunder could be heard in the distance. Zach was afraid of lightning, which he could vividly picture striking his unprotected head. He ran through pelting rain across the barren plaza, imagining for an instant that class could be canceled because of the danger of the storm. But the storm's only effect, apart from drenching Zach, was to cut class attendance down to six: the three hair-sprayed women (who needed to be there for credit), Dorothy, fat Freddy the Ayn Randian, and the ever-present, wild-eyed, free-associating Jim.

When he was sure that no one else was going to come, Zach began class by asking: "According to Zarathustra, how did the gods die?"

The anticipated silence fell. "I'll give you a hint," said Zach. "Someone read from near the bottom of page one eighty-five—say, from 'The old gods . . .' Anyone?"

No one met his eyes, so he said, "Dorothy? How about you?"

Without looking up, she began to read in a quiet, serious voice: " 'The old gods long ago met their end, and a very merry, godlike end they had. They did not fade away into twi-

light—that is a lie. Just the opposite: they laughed themselves to death.' "

She continued: " 'This came to pass when an ungodlike
saying was uttered by one of the gods, who said: "There is
but one God. Ye shall have no other gods but me!"

" 'An old wrath-beard god, a jealous god, befuddled himself thus. And all the other gods laughed and quaked with
mirth in their chairs and shouted: ' "Isn't just this godliness?
that there are gods but not God?" ' "

"Thank you," said Zach. "So, what do you make of that?"

There was a pause, and then Dorothy said, "The jealous
god is the God of Israel. Right?"

"Yes," said Zach, "I think that's correct. And he starts out
how? As just another god, right? But then he makes a special claim, which is . . . ?"

"That there is only one God," said Dorothy.

"And what does that do to the other gods?"

"They laugh until they die."

"Literally, yes." Zach surveyed the class in search of
some sign that the humor of this metaphor was being duly
appreciated. In all probability, the women in the back
thought that a grown man who talked about such silliness as
philosophy was always pretty funny; but they were not paying close enough attention to realize that an intentionally hu-
morous passage had just been read. Jim was staring intently
at Zach, his thoughts perfectly opaque. Freddy was just taking it all in. And Dorothy apparently considered the death
of gods a serious matter.

"The gods also say," she added, "that it is godliness not
to have just one God. I don't understand that at all."

"Good," said Zach. "Let's say that every country has its
own gods, and for every virtue and vice they have a different divinity, right? Like the ancient Greeks. That's the sit-

uation before the one jealous god messes things up. What do you think that means?"

"That there are many values in the world, and they should all be able to get along together?" Dorothy suggested, but Freddy snorted with scorn.

With a glance at Freddy, Zach said: "It doesn't sound much like Nietzsche to assert that people with different values all get along well together, does it? I mean, he's always talking about conflict and overcoming. In fact, let me remind you of another passage." After searching briefly for an earlier section in *Thus Spake Zarathustra*, Zach read: " 'No people could live without making values; but if it wants to survive, it must not evaluate as its neighbor evaluates.

" 'Much that one people called good, another called shame and disgrace: this I found. I found much that was called evil here and decked with purple honors there.

" 'One neighbor never understood another: his soul was always amazed at his neighbor's madness and wickedness.

" 'A table of values hangs over every people. Behold, it is a table of its overcomings; behold, it is the voice of its will to power.'

"So," Zach continued, "every country has its own values, which it turns into gods. It actually associates divine beings with the things that it values. But these gods are all necessarily local; otherwise the country or culture would have no way of expressing its identity. For instance, the Greeks had Greek gods who represented their favorite virtues and vices and appeared to spend all their time dealing with Greeks; they even talked in Greek. The American Indians have a different set of deities; and so on. But then along comes this grouchy bearded god who says, in effect, that here is just one God, and He is not created—He is not the product of anyone's values; He is objective, absolute, the Creator."

"I can see why that kills off all the other gods," said

Dorothy, still staring hard at her text. "But why is it godliness for there not to be one God?"

"Anyone?" Zach waited for the requisite ten seconds, then supplied an answer of his own. "Nietzsche thinks that we *do* make our own values; there aren't any objective or absolute ones out there for us to discover. And that process of making values is exciting, empowering; it's the expression of our will to power. On the other hand, if there is just one God and he's forced upon us by virtue of being objectively true, then there's no fun to be had. In a way, *we* stop being gods, or creators; we cede that authority to a higher being. So then there is no godliness on earth.

"We also call that one God the absolutely true, right? So, believing that there is only one God and that He is the Truth, we start studying the world around us, our own beliefs and other people's, as truthfully as we can. We must understand creation in order to understand the Creator; this is what God demands. And what do we discover?"

Again there was silence, but now Dorothy was looking straight at Zach as if she had an answer. "Dorothy?" he said. She shook her head, so he continued: "As we pursue the truth, we develop science, anthropology, and history as tools. And these disciplines discover what? That all the truths of the past have been contingent, the mere products of *our* biological makeup and local values. Above all, it turns out that the so-called discovery of one God, of Truth, was just a product of a certain group of people in ancient times and their arbitrary table of values. So what happens? The God of Israel, the jealous god, turns out to be just our creation, like all the other gods. But now we're in trouble. Because you can only make values if you do not realize that this is what you are doing. For example, if you're an ancient Greek, you can happily retell the myths of your people, not knowing that they are the reflections of your culture's arbitrary values. But once you realize that all values are arbitrary and local, even the value of Truth, then how can you create new values or subscribe to any old ones? Whatever you choose to value will just be as good or as bad as anything else; so you will not be able to value it sincerely.

"Remember the Last Man, from the prologue of *Zarathustra*? Let me read you one more section." Zach again flipped through his text, then read a few paragraphs, skipping sentences that seemed unnecessary: " ' "Behold, I reveal unto you the Last Man," ' " he began.

" ' "What is love? What is creation? What is longing? What is a star?" So asks the Last Man, and blinks.

" 'The earth has become small and upon it hops the Last Man, who makes everything small. Now who still wants to rule? Who obey? Both are too great a burden.

" 'No herdsman and one herd. Everyone wants the same thing and everyone is the same: whoever dissents goes voluntarily into the madhouse.

" ' "Once upon a time, the whole world was mad," say the keenest of them, and blink. They are clever and know all that has happened in the past, so they never stop mocking it. They still squabble, but they soon make up—otherwise they would get indigestion.' "

Zach had finished reading. He said: "Who do you think that the Last Men are?"

"Us?" said Dorothy, after a pause.

Zach let the answer sink in, not saying anything. Finally, he answered: "Perhaps." And then, like one of the distinguished professors at Yale, he closed his book portentously and signaled the end of class.

7 • As his students filed out of the room, Dorothy approached his desk and said: "Professor Blumberg, I'm hav-

ing serious problems with my paper." Zach had assigned a final paper that was due at the end of the following week.

"Can't you find a topic?" he asked, rather brusquely. He was glad that class was over, pleased with his dramatic closing, and not very eager to discuss logistical matters with a student.

"Not one that really works for me."

"Starting is always hard."

"I've written plenty of papers before. I'm just having special problems with this one."

"What kind of problems?"

She sighed. "Okay. In the first part of the paper, we're supposed to explain the arguments for nihilism, right?"

"Right."

"I've got no big problems with that part. I think I understand the whole argument and it seems pretty logical to me. Everything's relative and all that stuff. But then we're supposed to 'state how the argument might apply in real life.' That's the part I can't do. I just don't see how it's relevant to my life, for instance. Like, let's say there's no difference between good and evil, right? So what does that mean for me? I don't depend on any big theory of right and wrong anyway. So if there's no possible theory, then so what? I'm not going to do anything any differently. I'm still going to love my best friend; I'm still going to get satisfaction from helping people."

"I think nihilism makes quite a lot of difference, actually," said Zach, "but *you* have to say why. I can't answer the question for you."

"Okay, I understand that. But can you explain one thing for me?"

"I'll try."

"All right. I came across this part where Nietzsche"—she pronounced it "Neechee"—"says that every time you say something simple and ordinary, like 'it is,' you must be assuming that there is such a thing as an objective world, right? You must also be assuming that there is Truth, I guess. And every time you say 'I am,' you are assuming that you have a self or a subject. So Nietzsche says as long as we use grammar, we are assuming that the soul, the objective world, and even God exist. Right?"

"More or less, yes."

"So the way I understand it—okay?—the idea is that underneath everything we say and do is some big, abstract theory. Like every time I choose to do something, I must be relying on a theory of the Good. And every time I say 'I am Dorothy,' I must be assuming that Being exists, and Truth, and God."

"I follow you." Zach looked, more or less surreptitiously, at his watch.

"Okay. But then Nietzsche doesn't believe in Good or Evil or Being or Truth, does he?"

"No."

"So therefore he thinks we're in big trouble. Because as soon we realize that there is no Truth or Good, we won't be able to make any choices at all."

"That might be oversimplifying it," said Zach, "but I think you're more or less on target. But don't forget the Overman: he can act and make judgments even though there is no truth or justice. That power defines him as an Overman."

"Right. But to me— How do I say this? To me, it doesn't seem like there *is* this big theory underneath everything we say and do. I mean, you can't *see* it, can you? And most people would be pretty surprised to find out that every time they said 'Hi, I'm Dorothy,' they had assumed an objective world and a soul and Being and God and all those other philosophical ideas."

"People don't usually realize what ideas are implicit in

the things they say. That's what philosophy's for: it reveals what we implicitly believe. Sometimes it even turns out that what we've been assuming all along is false. That's what Nietzsche's trying to show."

"Okay. So at least I'm on the right track about him. But making it all sound important or relevant or even believable is hard for me."

"Well, that's the assignment," said Zach. "Try another draft and bring it with you next time, no matter how much you hate it. We'll use it as a starting point, okay? It's difficult for me to advise you with nothing on paper to work from."

She agreed, though not very happily, and they walked out of the building together. In order to avoid walking all the way to the bus stop with her, Zach ducked into the men's room and waited for a few minutes until the coast was clear.

CHAPTER 4

| • On the trip back to New York, Zach no longer had to worry about teaching; the next class was five days away. He was so relaxed, comparatively speaking, that he didn't much mind a forty-five-minute delay at a suburban stop in Westchester County. However, he slowly felt the force of a new anxiety coming on: dinner that night with Kate. He had been looking forward to this a great deal, but he also knew that it would be a struggle for him to maintain his side of an interesting conversation. While the train sat stubbornly in the suburban station, Zach watched the commuters stream out of a succession of northbound trains and thought about possible topics of conversation for that evening. In particular, he tried to remember all he could about Italian medieval art.

Kate was not home when he first arrived at her room, but just as he was beginning to get nervous that something might have happened to her, she came walking up the stairs with a big Styrofoam hamper in her hand. "Zach!" she said, evidently pleased to see him.

"Kate!"

"What do you say to a picnic?"

"Great idea."

"You know the Institute for Advanced Study? They have

some woods on their property and a little lake. I thought we could sit out there and talk while we ate."

"Fabulous."

She wouldn't let him carry the hamper, but she did give him a bottle of cold white wine from the refrigerator to hold. As they walked together down a long avenue, she leaned back slightly to counterbalance the weight of the food. Again she played tour guide, explaining that the institute housing was an early example of Bauhaus architecture in America, describing the portico that had been built so that Einstein wouldn't get rained on, and chatting idly about faculty personalities. Zach discovered that he didn't have to say much.

They found a spot by the lake. She pulled a tablecloth out of the hamper, and they sat on it as they ate fresh mozzarella, baguettes, cold penne with pesto, and tiramisù. "Nothing like living in a yuppie town," said Kate.

"When in Rome . . ."

"It's not quite Rome."

Zach knew that they should talk about their next move against Hausman and Davies, but he didn't want to break the spell of the moment. Neither, apparently, did Kate, who lay contentedly on her side with her head in her hand. They watched swifts glide over the water, deftly scooping up bugs. After a while, she caught him surreptitiously scratching at mosquito bites and said, "Do you want to go back?"

"Only if you do."

"We should."

They gathered their things and stumbled to their feet. The wine and evening sun had made them drowsy. As they walked up a hill toward the institute's main buildings, the sun finally dipped down beneath the horizon. They walked past the institute in silence, then across an open field. Suddenly, Kate stopped and pointed in the distance.

"What?" said Zach.

"Shhh," she whispered. Five or six deer were grazing at the opposite side of the clearing. They were tall and gangly, and their feet were spread wide apart so their heads could dip down to reach the ground. Zach looked over at Kate, who was watching the deer intently. Her face seemed kind and sympathetic to him; he felt profoundly melancholy and wanted to kiss her. But then one of the deer caught wind of them and the herd moved off, quickly but without panicking. They watched them disappear into the woods and then moved on toward the graduate school.

"There are tons of them around here," Kate said, still whispering. "They're almost vermin, really; people are afraid that they spread Lyme disease."

"They're pretty, though."

"Yeah. They're gorgeous."

⅞ • When they arrived back at Kate's room, Zach stood near the door to signal that he was planning to leave soon and would not overstay his welcome. But first he asked whether Kate had made any progress in her research on Crypt, Davies's secret society.

"I worked at it, I really did," she said, "but I'm afraid I don't have much to report. Very little has been written about Crypt that's at all believable, because the members are sworn to secrecy. In the nineteenth century, at least the membership list was public; in fact, it was printed every year in the *Times*. But in recent generations, even that has been a secret. I read some literary descriptions of the society in pre-World War One campus novels—*Bulldog! Bulldog! Rah! Rah! Rah!; Percival Smith, Eli Rough Rider,* that sort of thing—but they weren't very informative, although some of them were pretty funny."

Zach said, "Careful, that's my college you're laughing at."

"Hardly," said Kate. "*You* wouldn't have been admitted back then. Anyway, there was supposed to be a general story about Crypt in a back issue of one of the weekly news magazines, but our copy in Firestone was missing the relevant pages. Maybe we could find it in another library. There are lots of rumors about kinky initiation rituals and some pretty solid evidence about famous members, who include a bunch of senators and governors, a CIA director or two, some bank presidents—you know, nobody important. Seriously, though, they've done pretty well for an organization that only admits a dozen seniors a year. Their endowment is supposed to be bigger than Brown's.

"Like a good art historian, I looked at a picture of their building. It's weird, kind of an eighteenth-century fantasy of a windowless Egyptian temple. Well, I guess you know the building better than I do."

"Only the outside, though."

"I would hope so. I can't see you mud-wrestling in a coffin with a sixty-year-old U.S. senator."

"You underestimate me." He wiggled his eyebrows suggestively; she laughed politely in response. Then she asked: "Have *you* picked up any good rumors about Crypt during your years at Yale?"

"Oh, you know, we grad students are peripheral people. I really don't know much, to tell you the truth. I did read once that Crypt has the biggest water bill in the city of New Haven."

"That's strange. Their building is about fifty feet by a hundred."

"I know. Maybe the city just drastically overcharges them.

Maybe it's an annual bribe. Or maybe they have a water-slide theme park inside."

"Cool!"

She checked her answering machine, but there were no messages. She slipped past Zach into the hallway and knocked on Charles's door, without response. She entered Charles's room with Zach in tow to examine the answering machine, but the display indicated that no new messages had been received.

"You must really be worried about him by now," Zach said.

"Yup. Do you think I should call the police?"

"I don't know. Does he qualify as a missing person?"

"I guess not. They'd say he's probably just off on a trip."

"If we did talk to the police, we'd have to explain why we broke into his room."

"How would they know?"

"For one thing, the answering machine has been played back since Tuesday. And I'm sure we've left other traces of our presence in here."

"To tell you the truth, I feel like just taking care of this ourselves."

"I was hoping you'd say that."

"So," she said, "have you cracked this Sternian code?"

"I haven't had much chance to work on it since yesterday, because I had to teach a class. But I was thinking on the way down here that I could probably figure out a solution if I could just ask a real live Sternian a few pointed questions."

"So why don't we talk to Hausman himself?"

"I doubt that he would consent to a cross-examination if we told him that we were trying to locate my dissertation and your friend Charles—not if he has them both locked up in his attic."

"I'm sure we could figure out an excuse to get him talk-ing," she said. "We're slick and devious people."

They walked back into Kate's room, shutting Charles's door behind them. Zach took up his post at Kate's door; she flopped down on her bed.

"Well, I have a friend in Ithaca who could probably put me up," he said, "and you too, if you want to come. God knows, he's camped out in my place often enough since I moved to New York."

"Let's go, then. Tomorrow, if you can." She pointed at her phone. "Give your buddy a call."

Zach called Andrew in Ithaca and made arrangements for them to stay with him the next night. "How should we get up there?" he asked Kate.

"I can borrow a car from a woman in the art history de-partment who owes me lots of favors," she said. "She has an old yellow Beetle that I've borrowed before. It's missing part of the floor, but it runs like a charm."

"Do you mind doing the driving?" Zach was eager to get this question out of the way. He was the only twenty-seven-year-old, noninstitutionalized Long Island male in history not to have earned a driver's license. When he was eighteen, he had driven into a wall during a driver's test. Then he had gone to college where there was no need for a car, and get-ting a license had just slipped through the cracks. Besides, it made him feel like a genuine Manhattanite to be depen-dent on public transportation.

"Sure. You don't want to drive a sixty-nine Beetle?"

"No, I haven't got a license." Zach paused uncomfortably. "It's a New York thing."

"Oh, then I wouldn't understand; I'm from Illinois."

"That's right; even if you lived in New York until you were sixty, you would never understand what makes us suave ur-banites tick."

"In fact, I didn't even realize that you *were* suave," said Kate with a grin. She called her friend and got permission to borrow the car.

"So, I'll see you here tomorrow," said Zach, hoping that she would offer to save him the trip by picking him up in New York.

"Why don't you stay the night?" Zach's heart skipped, not because he thought for a second that she was inviting him to sleep with her; just because he would be able to spend the rest of the evening with her. "I don't have any stuff with me," he said, wanting to be talked into staying.

"What do you need? You can *buy* a toothbrush. I've got razors if you don't mind a pink handle. And you can hand-wash your shirt and underwear. It's better than making another round trip on New Jersey Transit."

Zach consented, but he was nervous about the prospect of a whole evening during which he would have to keep up his side of the conversation. "Do you want to see a movie or something?" he said timorously.

"Let's see what's playing in town. There probably isn't anything good, but we can at least pick up a toothbrush for you and maybe some frozen yogurt."

They walked through the heart of the campus, which was now almost completely empty. Across Nassau Street was the town of Princeton, a kind of upscale mall with the roof removed and with more or less genuine Colonial buildings instead of fake façades. There were a few essential college-town amenities—a greasy spoon, a T-shirt shop, some bookstores, a liquor store—but the typical Princeton establishment seemed to sell designer scarves or Persian rugs. Store windows contained two or three objects and announced that there were other branches in Beverly Hills, Miami Beach, and Rome. "This is the gold buckle on the commuter belt," Kate explained as they strolled down Nassau Street.

"Every housewife from Metuchen to Hohokus comes here to do her luxury shopping. The name 'Princeton' is highly sought after in the homes of stockbrokers and corporate lawyers. But for us, it sucks. What am I supposed to do if I want a light bulb?" But she was exaggerating, as Zach discovered when he bought his toothbrush and deodorant in a well-stocked drugstore.

The movie house was showing two big-budget summer fiascoes. "Do you want to see either of these?" asked Zach, not really wanting to see them himself (and certainly not wanting to spend $7.50 when he had less than $75 to his name), but desperate for something to do that wouldn't require him to display charm and wit.

"Do you?"

After beating about the bush like this for a few more minutes, each determined that the other was not keen on seeing either *Hard Edge III* or *Terminal Case.*

"How about frozen yogurt, then?" asked Kate. Zach agreed and they each bought a cone. They ate in virtual silence, sitting on a Nassau Street bench and watching the pedestrian traffic of high-school students in desperate search of fun, suburban parents going to the movies with their kids, and a few wan graduate students looking harried and furtive as they slipped back from Firestone Library to their off-campus hovels above storefronts in town.

When they had finished their yogurt, they walked back to Kate's room by a slightly longer route. It was still before eleven when they arrived at her room, but Kate suggested going to bed right away so that they could get an early start in the morning. She and Zach cleared papers, books, and photographs from one six-foot-long area of the floor and spread out a quilt.

It was still hot. In the men's bathroom after his shower,

Zach contemplated his pale and hairless chest, trying to decide whether it would make an unpalatable sight for him to sleep only in boxer shorts. Unfortunately, he did not have anything but his oxford shirt to wear in bed, and that was wet from being hand-washed. He put it back on, walked into Kate's room, and asked for something more comfortable to sleep in. She was reading the newspaper in bed, lit by the soft light of a table lamp, wearing boxer shorts and an oversized T-shirt. Her skin seemed to glow. She gave Zach a Princeton shirt to wear; he slipped into it as quickly as possible. As soon as he got into bed, she switched off the light. Soon she began to snore quite loudly. Zach lay awake for a long time in the dark room, thinking about what they would do the next day.

5 • They awoke at seven, threw some things in a canvas bag, and walked into town to pick up the car. For the first twenty minutes of the drive, they discussed how they should approach Professor Hausman and arrived at a preliminary plan. Then conversation failed and Kate switched on the radio. The local public radio affiliate was carrying the Senate Judiciary Committee hearings live. A senator with a deep Southern accent was saying, "Judge, what is your opinion of homosexuality; is it supported by the natural law, or condemned by it?"

There was a pause. Then the nominee replied, "Senator, my personal view is that it is condemned. That has been the view of wise men throughout history, from Deuteronomy onward."

The senator asked, "But how do you *know* it's against the natural law, Judge? I'm a Baptist, myself, and I was brought up not to be too confident that I understood the laws of God and nature. I do my best to follow my own conscience, but I try not to impose it on others. How come you understand the natural law so well?"

"Senator, perhaps it's not appropriate for me to ask you a question in response?"

"Go right ahead."

"Well, Senator, how do you think the Founding Fathers—excuse me, I guess I'm supposed to say 'the Founders'—how do you think they knew that man was created with certain inalienable rights? Where did those rights come from? Did they just pull them out of their hats?"

"It seems to me that the rights they listed were pretty general, Judge: life, liberty, and the pursuit of happiness. I mean, they left it up to us to decide most of the tough ones. After all, what kind of person would disagree that everyone has the right to life, liberty, and happiness—or at least his best shot at happiness?"

"I think that quite a few people throughout history have denied that those were universal rights, Senator. Certainly the right to liberty has been controversial. And the right to life is a hot topic right now."

"Okay. So where do *you* think the Founders got those rights from?"

"They understood the law, Senator. They understood English common law; but much more importantly, they understood the natural law. That's just another way of saying that they knew what was right. They were men of common sense and heirs to the wisdom of the ages. They had one eye on natural law when they wrote our Constitution; and to understand that document, you have to keep the same immutable truths in your mind."

"So you would base your judicial decisions on the natural law as you understand it?"

"I would base my decisions on common sense and the intentions of the Founding Fathers, who explicitly appealed to natural law in practically all of their work."

"I see."

"Well, what would you have me do, Senator? Flip a coin, read tea leaves? The elected branches can appeal to majority will, but we in the courts are supposed to interpret the law as it was written. And it was written, Senator, with the natural law in the background. You can say 'But natural law is hard to pin down.' Well, so is any kind of truth. On the other hand, if you mean 'There is no truth to be known at all about the natural law,' then you are saying that there is no way to know good from evil. I'm not talking about people's notion of what is good in modern America, but the good in itself. If you seek the good in itself, Senator, then you seek the natural law, the universal law."

"And that is what you would do?"

"Yes, sir."

"No further questions."

At this point, Kate said, "Do you mind if I switch?" Zach had no objection, so she changed to a station that was playing contemporary jazz. For the rest of the morning, they listened to a succession of public radio stations and watched the view, which became quite stunning in the Delaware Water Gap region near the New York border.

They had lunch in a truck-stop diner, served by a friendly, matronly waitress. In keeping with the setting, Zach ordered meat loaf and Kate had a club sandwich. When they had finished ordering, Zach said, "So, you're from Illinois?"

"Yup, Evanston. Just north of Chicago, in the burbs."

"Aha. Did you like it?"

"Yeah. You know, everybody in my high school had professional parents and 'turning out okay' meant going to Northwestern, at least, if not Harvard. I was a good girl, did my homework—did well, actually—went to Bordeaux one summer to polish up my French. My idea of fun was the Chicago Art Institute. Well, it *is* a fun place. By normal American standards I was a social retard, but so were all my friends, so that was no problem. My teachers liked me, adults always praised me, but my peers didn't mind because they got the same thing, most of them."

"Yet there was something missing?"

"Not really, no. Sure, I wanted freedom, adventure, sex, that kind of thing, but I also wanted security, and that I had. Most of the time I felt perfectly willing to wait for the other stuff."

"Where did you go to college?"

"Wesleyan, but I spent my whole junior year in Italy."

"That must have been great."

"Yeah, it was. So then I figured out this art history racket. True, getting a job is no picnic, let alone getting tenure, but once you make it, you can cruise over there any time you want and look at art for free. I may even be able to complete my dissertation in Italy."

"What's it on, again?"

"Giotto. I'm interested in the way he shows concrete human events in a good or bad moral light. I'm comparing his methods to the early humanists, especially Petrarch. I really, strongly believe in art history as a subset of cultural history. None of this connoisseurship and aestheticism for me: I want to talk about *ideas*. You know who my heroes are? Those central European mandarins, the Jewish refugees who used to teach at Heidelberg or wherever, the old guys with classical educations, idealist temperaments, and sweeping theories about Western art and that kind of thing."

She stirred her coffee with a plastic straw, reflected for a moment, and then said, "I even like their lifestyle, although that should be irrelevant, I guess. I like their crowded apartments with overstuffed furniture and trinkets and books piled everywhere, their soft, cultivated accents. You know— Freud, Jaspers, Adorno, Arendt, Panofsky, Popper, those guys. We have some in Chicago; they mostly live in Hyde Park near the U of C. You see them when you go to a Jean Renoir movie or something like that, sitting with their poor, quiet, exploited babushka wives, who were probably communists and feminists in nineteen-twenties Berlin, but now spend their whole time worrying about Karl-Heinrich's blood pressure. Still, where would art history in America be without them? And what would they think of all this recent stuff: critiques of Western values by people who don't know Aretino from Elvis?"

"Otto Stern was one of those guys. Classical training, Jewish, mandarin all the way."

"Yeah, but from what you say, he was into obfuscation. Idealists believe in the Truth, at any cost."

"You know, speaking of mandarins, I should get you together with a friend of mine, Alice Webster."

"You know Alice Webster?"

"Not only do I know Dr. Webster," said Zach with a mock swagger, "but she knows all about my missing dissertation and she even gave me some early advice. If it hadn't been for her suggestion, I would never have put the ad in the *New York Review,* and I never would've run into you."

"Can I meet her? Please?"

"You bet."

4 • As they drove in silence toward Ithaca, Zach thought about Kate's taste in culture and scholarship. He tended to agree with her, but the whole discussion had made him nervous. The very people whom she admired most were the

source of the deepest anxiety for Zach, for he feared professors with encyclopedic minds, fluency in myriad languages, and the wisdom born of suffering and exile.

In general, he felt ignorant and parochial, a young American possessing too many detailed memories of 1970s sitcoms and too few quotations from Plato. He could list everyone on Gilligan's Island, but he still hadn't gotten around to reading *Ulysses*. More seriously, he had to conceal a pair of deficiencies that should have been fatal to his career long ago: he knew neither German nor formal logic. He had become adept at hiding these weaknesses, and could even participate actively in seminars when the German text under discussion was completely opaque to him. He would rely on clues from other students' comments to work out the meaning of key words. In logic classes, he could generally circumvent technical problems by steering the discussion in a more theoretical direction. He would ask, for example, how the most obvious aspect of any theory (the only part he understood) could be defended against extreme skepticism. He congratulated himself on these feats of duplicity, but feelings of deep inadequacy lingered. Since the beginning of his graduate career, he had consistently felt himself to be a bit of a fraud.

They pulled into Ithaca around four in the afternoon, got lost downtown, and finally found their way up the enormously steep hill to Cornell, whose great quadrangles overlook green hills and the wide blue ribbon of Lake Cayuga. It was relatively cool here, and a strong breeze blew off the lake. A rocky gorge that could have been imagined by a nineteenth-century Romantic painter (complete with solitary trees and a raging waterfall) separated the campus from College Town. They nosed their way down a major shopping street, past an assortment of diners and T-shirt stores that would have put Princeton to shame. At last they found the steep side street where Andrew lived. It was lined with frame houses, tightly packed together and slightly seedy. Rock music blared and nearly naked students sunbathed on rooftops.

A bronzed woman in a halter top opened the door of Andrew's house and admitted them to a dark and largely empty residence, with hardwood floors, small pieces of Victorian stained glass, lots of heavy woodwork, and dirty white walls. The long front hall was empty except for a pile of paper bags containing old newspapers. In the parlor, surrounded by stacks of books, was a card table with several folding chairs; a wine bottle on the table held some wilted flowers. The dusty living room contained a TV and a decrepit couch on which sat several more paperback books. A German Expressionist poster was taped to the wall. The kitchen was piled high with cereal boxes, various beans and squashes, beer bottles waiting to be recycled, and unwashed dishes. To the trained eye, this was clearly a graduate-student group house.

The woman introduced herself as Marie, one of Andrew's roommates; she had just graduated from the social-work school and was working as a waitress until she found a job. She offered Zach and Kate beers (which they declined) before flopping down on the weed-infested back lawn to catch more sun. Her guests took up residence in the living room. Kate noticed a copy of the *Cornell Sun* lying on the couch. She pointed to it and said, "Let's get going with our plan."

Zach nodded. He found a telephone and a telephone book, looked up Hausman, and dialed his number, feeling nervous. A man's voice with a faint foreign accent answered.

"Hi," said Zach. "My name is Bob, from the *Cornell Sun*. Is this Professor Hausman?"

"Yes, that is me."

"We're doing a story on the Sternians, and we wondered if you would allow us to interview you for it."

"What kind of story is this?"

"Oh, you know, a general profile kind of thing. I'm just starting out on the *Sun,* so it's no big deal. I don't have any ax to grind or anything. To tell you the truth, I don't really know anything about you guys; my editor just handed me the story before he left at the end of the semester—said we could run it in September."

"I don't usually talk to journalists."

"This is a way to communicate with students, which is what you do for a living."

"But in my classroom I cannot be misquoted."

"We'll check all your quotes with you before printing the story."

"In context?"

"Sure."

"Very well. I will do this."

"Are you free sometime tomorrow, sir?"

"Yes. Tomorrow afternoon will be all right. You will come to my house at noon?" He gave his address, which Zach repeated out loud since he couldn't find a pencil. Zach said good-bye and then gave Kate a thumbs-up sign. "We're all set for tomorrow at noon."

"I can come too, I assume?"

"Sure. You're my partner. It's a joint byline."

"We'd better get our story straight before we go."

They sat on the sticky couch, discussing their cover stories in a desultory way. After about half an hour, the front screen door flew open and in bounced Andrew, dressed in knee-length neon-yellow shorts, a Hawaiian shirt, and sneakers with no socks. He was deeply tanned, with a prematurely receding hairline and small, round, no-rim sunglasses. He was carrying a book and a soft-drink can. He strode toward the kitchen, then caught sight of Zach and Kate in the living room.

"Dude!" he cried in delight. He and Zach shook hands and Zach introduced Kate. The book that Andrew was carrying was a study of current critical theory, in French.

"You have to tell me why you're here," he said. "But first, I am appalled to observe that you are sitting in my house without so much as a beer in your hands. This offends our quaint local customs. What would you like: a gin and tonic, a fine imported beer, some cheap American swill, or a margarita whipped up in my new blender?"

They demurred politely but Andrew began making a complicated mixed drink involving blended ice, fruit juice, vodka, coconut, apples, nutmeg, and celery. "You gotta try this," he said. "By the way, I hope you don't mind, but I'm having some friends over for a barbecue tonight. It'll be a blast, if you're into it. There are lots of cool people here, Zach, including more than our fair share of babes. Or maybe I shouldn't talk about babes?" he said, glancing covertly at Kate. But he continued without pausing for a response: "We'll throw some burgers on the hibachi, chow down on nachos, crank the stereo. Scintillating conversation will naturally ensue, especially with you fine people here to enliven our little community. You know, it's like we're living in one of those movies about British colonial days; we've been exiled to some provincial outpost for bad behavior, condemned to repeat the same cynical stories and drink ourselves into oblivion before finally going native. Actually, it's not so bad. Mostly we hang out, get wasted, teach a section or two, catch a foreign flick, go bowling, pick up undergrads, maybe read for fifteen minutes, get wasted, grade a paper or two, scope undergrads, get wasted, think about our dissertations for ten seconds, get laid, go downtown for sushi, worry about money, get wasted. It's rough, but somebody's gotta do it."

He poured three glasses of the frozen mixture that he had been making, turned up the radio (tuned, of course, to a progressive rock station), and led them outside into the yard, a small, weed-infested plot with four lawn chairs and a large grill. Marie saw them coming and moved silently inside. They sat under the late-afternoon sun and Zach briefly explained why they had come to Ithaca.

"Dude, it sucks that you lost your dissertation," Andrew commiserated. "If I had one, I'd be sorry to lose it. Let me know what I can do to help. I know karate, you know."

Up until now, Kate and Andrew had not spoken directly to each other. Kate lay on the lawn chair with her eyes closed, and Zach hoped that she was not annoyed by his friend. But now she opened her eyes and asked Andrew what he was working on. He told her that the tentative title of his thesis was "Misreading Barthes: The Texts' Struggle to Mis-/Re-interpret Their Author(s)." At some length, he explained his interest in Barthes, psychoanalysis, and the politics of the manufactured self; he brought up Fichte and Adorno and expressed a commitment to the critical theory of pleasure. To Zach's surprise, Kate answered in a rather animated fashion, and soon she and Andrew were engaged in a substantive discussion. Zach tried to interject comments at various points, but found himself unable to say anything useful, perhaps (he thought) because of the effects of the sun and the vodka. After a few failed efforts, he became self-conscious and stopped trying to participate.

After about twenty minutes of this, guests started arriving for Andrew's party. They let themselves into the house and came sauntering into the backyard with various drinks from the kitchen. The guests were of two types: large, tanned, scantily clad people in bright clothes with loud voices; and pale, angry, stringy-haired people wearing all black. Zach found himself between two members of the latter category, who were commenting bitterly on the university's sexual harassment rules. "Well, it's a patriarchal institution, what do you expect?" asked one, a short woman with spiky hair and a T-shirt advertising the band "Dead Roach Carcass."

"That doesn't mean we can't oppose its rituals and structures, including the harassment of women," said the other, a very tall thin man in black jeans. "We can situate ourselves in opposition to it."

"I think any university is *essentially* gendered, though," replied the woman, lighting a powerful cigarette.

"But all gendering is ultimately ambivalent," said the man. "I think your notion of a monolithic power structure is really reactionary. It almost sounds male-heterosexist."

"Don't call me phallogocentric because I oppose exploitation!"

"It's just that your analysis seems to posit a kind of definitive truth about the structure of gender relations here. Isn't that patriarchal?"

"No, I'm just adopting an antagonistic posture toward exploitation."

At this point, Zach ventured a question: "Do you have a big problem with sexual harassment at Cornell?"

They both looked at him as if he were insane. "I don't go here," he explained weakly, but his question seemed to have broken up the conversation: the man and the woman both left in search of more recherché company. Out of the corner of his eye, Zach saw Kate and Andrew still talking and laughing. He thought about joining them, but didn't want to look as if he couldn't fend for himself. He wandered into the kitchen, more to appear occupied than for any other reason. It was full of large, sweaty people in shorts, T-shirts, and bike helmets. Two men and a woman were standing in front of the refrigerator, talking about a 10K race they had run that morning. Zach meekly asked to be let through to the fridge. They paid no attention to him except to let him pass, so he pulled a can of beer out of the refrigerator and walked outside with it, leaving it surreptitiously on a window sill.

By now, hamburgers and tofu kebabs were being roasted on the hibachi. Zach hung around the fire, pretending to be helpful. Looking as if he were having a good time was beginning to tire him: the corners of his mouth hurt from forced smiling. He carried a plate of food over to Kate and Andrew, who were now sitting against the picket fence at the back of the yard, catching the last of the day's sun and trading stories about annoying roommates. They paid little attention to Zach, so when he was done eating, he wandered back inside. There was a game of hearts going on in the living room, with much shouting and laughing. Zach watched for a while, but there was no opportunity to participate. By now it was about nine o'clock and pitch-dark outside, and someone had turned the music very loud. Zach hated the noise and feared that dancing would begin. He walked outside onto the street and away from the party.

The air felt damp and heavy; huge, dark maple trees and frame houses lined the streets, which descended steeply from the college neighborhood toward downtown Ithaca. Zach wandered across a bridge that spanned one of the enormous Ithaca gorges (now just a mysterious black chasm) and onto campus. It was largely deserted, a matrix of massive buildings, trees, statues, paths, and lawns. Continuing off campus in the opposite direction from Andrew's house, Zach found himself in a neighborhood of large frame houses with neatly clipped bushes and lawns. The roar from the falls at the bottom of a nearby gorge could be heard faintly.

He got lost temporarily, but this didn't bother him; he was feeling melancholy and almost reveled in the emotion. At about eleven he found Andrew's house again, but music was blaring out of it so he walked right past. He found a secluded spot under a big tree overlooking Lake Cayuga and sat there for an hour or more, watching the lights in the distance. Passersby invariably said hello in a cheerful voice, which surprised Zach, who was used to Manhattan manners. Finally, fearful that he might be missed, he returned to Andrew's house. With irritation, he heard the music from halfway up the block. Letting himself in the front door, he beheld a room of shadowy forms, swaying back and forth to some kind of rock anthem. He made his way through the crowd in search of Andrew, intending to ask where he could sleep. He finally found his host in the backyard, still standing next to Kate and looking up at the stars.

"Hey," she said, "where have you been?"

"Oh, I just took a little walk."

"Isn't it great up here?" she said.

"Yeah. Hey, Andrew? Where did you want me to sleep?"

"You're not ready for bed?"

"Pretty much. It's been a long day."

"Well, I was going to put you on the couch in the living room, but I think that room's still in use. Why don't you sleep on my bed? It's in the back room upstairs."

"Are you sure that's okay?" asked Zach.

"Sure, man. I'll take the couch when the party breaks up."

Zach took a shower in a dirty upstairs bathroom and lay down on Andrew's queen-sized futon. Andrew's room also contained a desk, several bookcases, posters for French New Wave films, a bicycle hanging on hooks in the wall, and some used beer cans. The noise from downstairs was loud and insistent; the room was muggy. Zach lay on the hard futon with a pillow over his head, but the thumping of the bass would not let him sleep. After a while, he pulled a book from Andrew's shelf—an anthology of film criticism—and began reading. When he could no longer stand the purple prose, he went to the window and looked out. Andrew and Kate were still leaning against the back fence, talking. Zach looked away with a sigh.

CHAPTER 5

1 • The next morning, Zach awoke with bright sun streaming onto his face and realized immediately that he was in a foul mood. He brushed his teeth and walked downstairs. In the kitchen, he helped himself to a bowl of cereal, which he was about to eat in the living room when he overheard voices from the backyard. He stuck his head outside and saw Kate and Andrew sitting in the lawn chairs.

"Hey, sleepyhead," said Kate. "In a second we were going to wake you up."

Zach felt miserable. "What time is it?" he muttered.

"Dude, it's eleven A.M.," said Andrew. "You sleep okay?"

Zach let the question pass.

"Those are Marie's corn flakes," said Andrew.

"Sorry." Zach felt like flinging them in the bushes, but instead he sat down on the back step and ate his breakfast sullenly.

"We have to be at Hausman's at twelve," said Kate. They asked Andrew for directions and then set out on the fifteen-minute walk to Hausman's house. For the first few blocks, they walked in silence.

"Your friend Andrew's a great guy," said Kate to no discernible response from Zach, who was pouting. "He's a little too smooth, maybe," she added, "but he's really funny. How long have you guys been friends?"

Zach wanted to say "Until yesterday," but he restrained himself. "Since freshman year," he said.

"He must have been one happy-go-lucky frosh."

"Yes, he was."

They finished the walk in silence.

Professor Hausman's house was a large green frame building that looked a little like a barn. The wide, crabgrass-infested front lawn was littered with a tricycle, a soccer ball, a plastic baseball bat, a skateboard, and a pogo stick. A screened-in porch covered the front of the house; this contained a random assortment of furniture, logs, cardboard boxes, and a card table piled high with newspapers. The main door was at the side of the house, next to a driveway where a station wagon was parked. Zach rang the doorbell, and he and Kate were admitted by a woman in her thirties with long frizzy blond hair; she wore a knee-length denim dress, a coral necklace, and no shoes.

The interior of the house was dark and cluttered. Like Andrew's house, it had heavy Victorian woodwork and small pieces of stained glass in the Arts and Crafts style of the late 1800's. The walls were lined with books and small Expressionist paintings in a uniform series. Children's toys were scattered all over the floor, cats dozed near the windows, the furniture was old and drab, and there was a funny smell. The woman led Zach and Kate onto the porch and offered them iced tea, which they declined.

After a few minutes a man in his upper fifties emerged; he had a white beard, and his shorts, black socks, and sandals exactly fit the description of Jules Hausman.

Kate and Zach both rose and Zach said, "Professor Hausman, I'm Bob and this is my friend Kate; she's helping with the story."

They shook hands and Hausman sat down with them. Kate and Zach both produced notebooks and pencils. Hausman said, "So?"

Zach said, "Professor, can I begin by asking if you would call yourself a Sternian?"

"Otto Stern was my teacher and beloved friend. When I was lost, facing a kind of intellectual abyss, he helped me to see the way to a solution."

"You did graduate work under him?" Zach asked.

"That is correct. He guided my dissertation. In those days, there was very little normative work in political science— we talked only about how things were, not how they ought to be. This empiricism left me unsatisfied, especially since I had experienced political horror as a very young child in Europe. Statistics and models seemed inadequate to me in the face of evil. Otto Stern taught me how to think about the good, virtue, natural right—such matters. He led me back to a study of the classics, and revealed to me the beautiful treasures that they contain."

"How would you characterize the Sternian philosophy?" Zach asked.

"It is a repudiation of modernity. Modern man, Stern taught, has learned to separate facts from values. He determines the facts through experiment and objective observation, but these cannot tell him how to live. He also studies values objectively, but he finds that they are everywhere different. Furthermore, he learns that he can explain them away. For instance, we obey the law because we have internalized an Oedipal fear of our fathers. Freud, right? Or we value freedom because it's an essential aspect of capitalism, which is the socioeconomic system that determines us. But if these explanations are right, then there are no objective truths about good and evil. That realization, which I had felt so forcefully as a young student in the social sciences, leaves one with no criterion for choosing how to live. It is a source of paralysis and horror. It puts Hitler's regime ultimately in the same category with Pericles' Athens or the United States today."

"What was Stern's alternative?" Zach asked.

"Otto Stern taught that we must return to the great tradition of thinkers who debated the essential things: good, evil, natural right, the role of the citizen, the relations between God and the city. There is no reason to think that moderns are right, with their easy dismissal of objective morality; and if they are right, we must perish, for human beings cannot live without a table of values."

"But where does Stern get his values?"

"From the works of the great tradition."

"Don't those works disagree with each other? I mean, let's say you studied Oscar Wilde, Tolstoy, Jesus, Plato, Marx, Jefferson, and Nietzsche—what consistent lesson could you draw from all of them?"

Hausman seemed surprised by the question. "Well, several of the men you mentioned are moderns who have repudiated the ancient wisdom. But the ancients, those who are wise, all tell the same truths if you read them right."

"How should you read them?"

"Bearing one thing in mind. The truths they tell, being universal, are not likely to conform very well to the local mores of their time, which are always different and often appalling. Therefore, the wise men must write secretly, you see, with a double message. The fate of Socrates is always in their minds; he spoke the truth openly, and was forced to drink hemlock."

"Then how do you decode their true meaning?"

"This was the heart of Otto Stern's teaching. He examined the works of thinkers who clearly had been forced to write secretly: philosophers who lived under repressive theocratic regimes. To his delight, he discovered that they were all saying the same thing and hiding it in the same way. There was a kind of eternal conversation going on, a dialogue of the great men, and we could listen in on it."

Kate interjected a question: "Could you give us a couple of examples of the way these great men hid their ideas?"

"All right. For example, they do not state their true views *in propria persona*—in their own voice. They quote someone else as saying what they really mean. But they use a very compelling and interesting quotation in the midst of much boring material of their own, so that it stands out. Then they state *pro forma* that they disagree with the quotation. Secondly, their own arguments tend to have deliberate flaws built in. For example, they will say that a particular idea could not be true, or else we would have to give up something that we hold dearly, such as belief in a certain god or value. But of course they favor giving up that belief. And thirdly, they place their true views in the precise center of their works, or in some other formally important place, but disguise them by attributing them to some other author."

"That's interesting," said Zach. "Tell me something: how about Stern's works? Can they be read in the same way?"

Hausman looked suddenly alarmed. "What do you mean?"

"Well, I was reading some of his books in preparation for this interview, and I thought I might apply his interpretive techniques to his own work. Correct me if I am wrong, but I found the following things. First, Stern's argument against relativism is that it would be too horrible if relativism were right; therefore it is wrong. He makes that argument eloquently, but it's still not much of an argument. Secondly, he

borrows pithy, convincing quotes from Nietzsche, Max
Weber, and other extreme relativists, only to say in a rather
perfunctory way that of course they can't be right—otherwise we would have no values. Finally, I was trying to find
out what he actually meant by the natural law, what its con-
tent is. I could find no explanation at all, except in one unusual passage where he says that the natural law is always
relative. And where is that passage? Precisely in the middle of his major work."

Hausman looked genuinely distressed. "This is quite a coincidence," he said at last. "You are the second person in a
few weeks to make that case to me."

"Who was the other person?" Kate asked in an innocent
voice, as if she were asking how the weather had been.

"Just another student," said Hausman.

Zach decided to gamble. "Was his name by any chance
Charles?" he asked.

Now Hausman looked startled. "How do you know about
Charles?" he said.

There was a pause during which Kate looked at Zach re-
proachfully: surely he had given away too much. But Zach
continued, "The story we are working on is a little bit broader
than I may have mentioned on the phone."

"Oh?" said Hausman, rising in anger.

"Wait a moment, Professor. It's in your own interest to
hear me out. We're writing a story on the disappearance of
a young Princeton graduate student. At the moment, you are
likely to appear in that story as a prime suspect."

"You must not connect me to him in a published piece!"

"Why not?"

Hausman sat back down again and stared at the floor.
"You say Charles has disappeared?" he said.

"So, it *was* Charles who interpreted Stern the way Za—
Bob just did?" said Kate.

"That's right, it was Charles."

"When and where did he make that case to you?" asked Zach.

"I will tell you the whole story, but on one condition. I must not appear in the article."

Zach and Kate looked at each other and nodded. "Okay," said Zach. "But your story better match what we already know."

"This is the whole story. I had never met Charles until about three weeks ago, when I received a letter from him. Wait, I will show it to you."

Hausman disappeared inside the house and Kate and Zach exchanged excited looks. Zach imagined for a foolish second that Hausman might flee from the house, but he returned in a minute with a letter still folded up in its envelope. He handed it to Zach, who shared it with Kate. She nodded to signify that she recognized the signature. The letter read:

July 15

Dear Professor Hausman:

    I am a graduate student in philosophy at Princeton. I am writing to you because of your status as a leading member of the Otto Stern circle. My dissertation concerns Nietzsche's strategy of esoteric writing—in other words, his deliberately double messages. In the course of this project, I have begun to develop a thesis regarding Otto Stern, namely, that he was an esoteric author whose hidden message was nihilism. I have noted, first of all, systematic allusions to Nietzsche in Stern's work, including especially references to Nietzsche's esoteric style. This discovery led me to apply Stern's hermeneutics to his own writing, whereupon I concluded that he endorses the nihilistic views that he attributes to Nietzsche, Weber, et al. I have not detected any similar double meaning in your books, which appear to be straightforward arguments for natural right. Nevertheless, I wonder if you have any reaction to my thesis that an application of Stern's interpretive methods to his own work reveals—and was intended to reveal—a message of nihilism.

I would be very interested in your response.

Sincerely,
Charles Wilson

"At first," said Hausman, "I paid little attention to the letter, which struck me as thoroughly foolish. I had built an entire career, you see, as a disciple of Otto Stern. This was my life. When it comes to the interpretation of Stern's ideas, I know what I am talking about; I heard it from his mouth. And the idea that he was secretly in favor of all the ideas that he openly despised—it was preposterous.

"Nevertheless, the basic idea in Charles's letter stuck in my mind. I made a mental list of the tactics that Otto Stern used when he decoded the great esoteric works of political thought. Then I took his books down from my shelf and looked again at my tattered, underlined copies. Well, you know what I am going to say. I discovered that Charles's thesis was, to say the least, plausible."

"What did you do?" Zach asked.

"First of all, on a personal level, I was deeply troubled. You see, Otto Stern used to talk about the philosopher's responsibility to guide the city in which he lives. By 'city' of course he meant the *polis,* the society. Since the philosopher's ideas are transhistorical, they are unlikely to find wide favor in any particular society, where arbitrary local norms will hold sway. Nevertheless, they embody the truth, so the philosopher must try to realize them. One method for this is the education of powerful and charismatic young men—gentlemen dupes, you could say—who will rely on him for counsel without necessarily understanding his actual philosophy. Plato tried to bring about the rule of philosophy by becoming counselor to the tyrant Dionysus, but he was not sufficiently shrewd; the wisest philosopher instructs without *revealing* his philosophy. All my life, I had thought of myself as an initiate, a disciple of Otto Stern. Now I had a new thought: perhaps I was a gentleman dupe."

Hausman looked sorrowful. "I must confess," he continued, "that I had even more difficulty in coming to terms with my new suspicions when I reread the work of some of my fellow Sternians. I had thought of us as a kind of intellectual and spiritual confraternity, a replica of the great conversation among the wise philosophers of the past. In addition, we felt like sons of Otto Stern, and therefore like brothers. But now I found that many of their books were like Otto Stern's; read in a certain way, they seemed to reveal a secret message of nihilism. This was not true of my books, however. Added to my feelings of betrayal, of having been left out of an enormously important secret, of having been treated as a dupe, was my deep confusion. Could Stern have been a nihilist? And if so, was it actually true that there was no difference between good and evil?"

Hausman was still looking at the floor, his brow furrowed. "But you wanted to know what I did once I began to entertain these dreadful thoughts," he said. "I wrote a brief note to Charles, not saying much of substance but offering to meet him in order to discuss his thesis in person. I did not characterize his ideas as correct, interesting, or anything else; I just said that I would be happy to talk to him about his work, and that I would be near Princeton at such and such a time. You see, my mother still lives in Philadelphia, where I grew up after the war, and I visit her often. So it was true that I could go to Princeton quite easily; it's more or less on the way."

"Did you see him?" said Kate.

"I saw him twice. The first time was on a Wednesday, three Wednesdays ago. We met in the student center at Princeton and talked at great length about Otto Stern. I came away more sure than ever that Charles was right, although I am still not perfectly certain. He also gave me a copy of his dissertation, which I read with great interest, needless to say."

"And the second time?" Zach asked.

"When I left on that first occasion, I told Charles that he should not hesitate to call and arrange another meeting. When he did call, just a few days ago, I happened to be in Philadelphia. It's summer, I have no teaching, so I go to see Mama frequently. He persuaded my wife to give him the number there, saying it was an emergency. But by the time he called Philadelphia, I was on the road back to Ithaca. Nevertheless, I got his message when I called my wife from York, Pennsylvania, to tell her I was on the way home. Is this too much detail?"

Zach and Kate, still playing reporters, were scribbling down all they could of Hausman's story. They shook their heads to his question, so he continued: "I called Charles from York, since he had told my mother and my wife that he desperately needed to talk to me. After all, I could still stop in Princeton on the way home, although it would make a long drive. He had an incredible story to tell: that his dissertation had vanished completely from his computer and that all the printed copies were also gone. We agreed to meet as soon as I could drive to Princeton, since we both suspected some kind of Sternian conspiracy. It's horrible to say that about my former intimate friends, but this is what we suspected.

"We met again in the Princeton student center, but by now

there had been a new development. Charles had seen an advertisement in the *New York Review* saying that someone else had lost his dissertation. He had agreed to meet this person later that evening in New York City to compare notes. We talked for a while in the student center, then walked together to the train station."

"Did Charles actually go to New York that night?" asked Kate.

"As a matter of fact, no. You see, we had worked ourselves into a bit of a paranoid state by the time we arrived at the Princeton station. Well, understandably, I think. I told Charles that if I were him, I wouldn't just go and meet a stranger in New York City without knowing more about what was going on. He said that whoever had taken his thesis knew where he lived; so there was no greater danger involved in going to New York. But we remembered something else: Charles had given me a copy of the dissertation. In fact, I had it in my car, since I was still carrying it around in my briefcase and rereading certain sections rather obsessively. We could not tell how much these people knew about Charles, but it was clear that they might at least have seen my letter to him in his files. For all we knew, they were aware that we were meeting that afternoon in Princeton. They could, for example, have tapped his phone. I realize that this sounds paranoid. Probably it is, but we were impressed by their thoroughness in rounding up several copies of Charles's work.

"In any case, we agreed that before Charles went to New York, we should hide his dissertation very carefully. That way, if something happened to him, he could always use the extra copy as a bargaining chip. By now, Charles was going to be very late for his appointment anyway, so he agreed to call this man in New York the following day, to reschedule their meeting."

"Did he do that?" Zach asked.

"I do not know, because I left Princeton later that evening and I have not heard from Charles since."

"Did you hide the dissertation?" Zach had to struggle not to appear too excited.

"Yes."

"Where?"

"I think," said Hausman after a pause, "that I should not tell you where. I have told you a great deal already, probably much too much. What if you are not actually reporters; what if you are trying to get that last copy?"

Zach and Kate smiled as if Hausman were joking, but Hausman began to look alarmed again. "Do you have reporters' identification, press cards?" he asked.

They shook their heads. "I have said much too much," he said. "I am an idiot! Sorry, but you must go, please, now!"

Hausman's wife appeared at the door, looking concerned. Kate said, "Thank you very much, Professor. You have been really helpful. I promise we won't print anything without your prior approval." And with that, they hurriedly collected their papers and left through the main door. As they walked down the path to the street, they could see Hausman and his wife watching them through the porch screen.

2 • When they were two or three blocks away from his house, Kate said, "Poor guy! As soon as we can, we should write him a letter to explain what we're really up to. We're actually on his side, and it might make him feel better to know that."

"Do you think he was telling the truth?"

"I think so. All the details seemed to fit. And he was so sad."

"I trust him, too. So that means that Charles disappeared

sometime between his talk with Hausman and noon the next day, when I showed up at his door. Did you try to see him before then?"

"Yes, I think I knocked on his door sometime that morning, but there was no answer."

"So that narrows the period when he disappeared to about twelve hours. Of course, he could easily have gotten up the next morning and gone somewhere on his own steam."

"But Mr. Williams would have seen him if he had taken the dinky."

"Does Mr. Williams run that thing all day long? Anyway, there are always borrowed cars, rental cars, buses—"

"True. You know, I bet if we went back into his room, we might be able to figure some things out. For instance, did he take his suitcase and toothbrush with him? Is the letter from Hausman in his files?"

"We should have done that a long time ago."

"Let's do it as soon as we can."

"Good. Let's grab the car and hit the road." Zach was eager to get out of Ithaca.

"I wonder if Andrew would want to join us. I mean, this is kind of fun."

Zach fervently hoped not, but stifled the urge to say so. They arrived back at Andrew's house and rang the doorbell, but no one answered. The door was wide open except for a screen, so they let themselves in. Zach suggested leaving a thank-you note and departing immediately, but Kate wanted to stay until Andrew returned. She wandered into the backyard to wait in the sun; Zach, still resentful, remained in the living room.

Having nothing better to do, he switched on the old black-and-white television. There were soap operas on the networks, but the public station—fuzzy but watchable—was carrying the Senate Judiciary Committee hearings. The same

Southern senator who had been asking questions the day before was again speaking. He was an elderly gentleman with
half-moon glasses and brilliant white hair. Mindful of Alice
Webster's reproach, Zach decided to watch for a while: it was
his civic duty. The senator was saying:

"Judge Frye, I think your membership in a selective, secret society whose membership list is undisclosed is *perfectly*
relevant to our deliberations. Does this club admit minori-
ties?"

The nominee replied: "Yes, sir." He looked angry and was
tapping a pencil against the table in front of him.

"How about women? Does it admit women?"

"No, Senator, not at this time."

"I see. And do you approve of that policy?"

"I think that my views on that matter are irrelevant, Senator. It is a private club. It does not receive or solicit federal
monies. It is not engaged in interstate commerce. I was fully
a member only when I was a senior in college, which was a
very long time ago. Several of your colleagues were also
members, as is well-known."

"Let me rephrase the question. Do you now, or have you
ever belonged to one or more associations that deny admis-
sion to females?"

"I have, Senator. Haven't you?"

"Yes, I have, Judge, but I resigned from them upon growing wiser and more sensitive to matters of sexual discrimi-
nation. Nevertheless, membership in such organizations
would hardly constitute sufficient cause, on its face, to defeat
your nomination. It is simply something that this committee, and the American people, ought to be able to consider.
Now, you say that you are no longer a member of this secret
society?"

"I did not say that exactly, Senator."

"Then you remain a member?"

"My full, active membership ceased when I graduated from Yale."

"Yet you have been on that campus for a substantial part of your adult life, have you not?"

"I had the honor to serve as a professor in the Law School, yes."

"And during that time, which ended only two years ago when you were appointed to the bench, you had no further contact with the club?"

"I did not say that."

"Then what was the nature of your contact?"

"I am not at liberty to say, sir."

"What do you mean, not at liberty? Club rules forbid it?"

"That is correct."

"You would rather obey the rules of an elite and secretive society than answer a question before the United States Senate?"

"I invoke my right to silence, Senator."

"A right that you tend to construe narrowly, Judge."

"Nevertheless, it is the law of the land."

"All right. No further questions."

With the television still on, Zach started looking around the house for a newspaper. For the first time, he actually read a series of articles on the Frye nomination. When he had satisfied his curiosity, he walked into the backyard and announced, "Wendell Frye was in Crypt."

"What?" Kate had been lying on a lawn chair with her eyes closed. She opened them and looked at Zach with a puzzled expression.

"Davies's secret society at Yale? Wendell Frye, the Supreme Court nominee, was in it."

"I guess a lot of powerful, famous people have been in Crypt."

"True. It struck me as a coincidence, but I guess it isn't

much of one. Probably half of the U.S. Senate was in Crypt."

Just then, Andrew arrived. "Dudes, how'd it go?"

Kate gave him a brief account of their conversation with Hausman. "So now we're going back to Princeton to rifle through Charles's stuff. How about joining us?"

"Sounds like a blast," said Andrew, to Zach's dismay. But he continued, "Unfortunately, I've got too much stuff to do around here. There's a party at my place tomorrow night, for one thing. Also, I should probably do some reading. You guys want to join me for a picnic this evening?"

"We need to go," said Zach.

"One extra night wouldn't make a lot of difference," said Kate.

"I think we should get a move on."

"We could leave first thing tomorrow morning."

"I really want to go."

"Okay. Let's go."

Kate looked displeased, and Zach immediately felt guilty. Nevertheless, he didn't want to jeopardize his victory by re-opening the topic. He quickly went upstairs to collect his toothbrush, razor, and comb. When he returned, Kate was collecting her things; he noticed that they had been stacked in a corner of the living room. Zach shook Andrew's hand good-bye, with Andrew arguing all the time that they should stay another night. Andrew and Kate hugged and then she and Zach got into the car and drove away while Andrew waved from the sidewalk.

ʒ ● The atmosphere inside the car was tense. They drove down the hill into Ithaca without a word. Finally, Zach said, "Look, let me buy you a late lunch at that veggie place. It's supposed to be great."

"I thought you were in a big hurry to get to Princeton."

"I'm sorry about all that. We can stay here another night if you want."

They were waiting at a stop sign on a quiet Ithaca street. Kate apparently decided to forgive him. "You must be very worried about your dissertation," she said. "I totally understand that. If all my work for three or four years suddenly vanished, I'd go out of my mind. It's just that I was having a good time here and I wanted to stay, but that was selfish of me."

"Here's an idea," said Zach, "a compromise. Let's drive back to Andrew's place, pick him up, and have lunch together, the three of us."

After a moment's reflection, Kate answered: "I'd rather have lunch just with you."

"You would?"

"Yeah."

As they cruised through downtown looking for the restaurant and a place to park, Zach's elation was mixed with misgivings. Was she eating with him out of pity? Did she know that he was jealous of Andrew? Had he been grouchy? Had she *noticed* his bad mood? Had she noticed his mood the night before? Zach was extremely good at inventing such questions, but not very good at finding peace from them.

So late in the day, he and Kate were the only two customers in the restaurant. A hearty, friendly woman served them cold avocado soup and piping-hot lasagna while chatting about their hometowns, what they thought of Ithaca, the virtues and drawbacks of Cornell students, the availability of fresh eggs in upstate New York, and layoffs in local industry. An atmosphere of comfort and well-being pervaded the place; Zach's misgivings faded and a feeling of contentment settled over him. He ordered a cheesecake and cappuccino despite the price. Kate drew buildings on the paper tablecloth with crayons provided for doodling. When they were done, they quarreled good-naturedly over the bill, and ended up splitting it.

They were back on the road by four in the afternoon. But they missed the access ramp to the right highway and ended up driving north along the shore of Lake Cayuga instead. "It looks pretty up there. Why don't we check it out?" said Zach on a whim.

"You *really* don't care about getting back to Princeton, do you?" She sounded reproachful.

"I think we should get there tonight, that's all," Zach said defensively. "I say 'we' assuming you want me to go there with you. If you prefer, you can drop me at the train and I'll head home late tonight. That way you won't have to go out of your way."

She kept driving north without comment. Soon they had left the city behind and found themselves on a two-lane road through piney woods; the lake appeared now and then on their right, fifty yards or so below them. After a few miles, a clearing opened up and the broad expanse of the lake came into view. They were in a state park with a little lakeside beach on the right and trails into the woods on the left. Still saying nothing, Kate parked and got out of the car. Zach, feeling guilty again, followed meekly behind as she walked down to the shore. They watched the lake in silence; the Gothic towers of Cornell could just be seen in the distance, and the sunlight glittered off a skyscraper in Ithaca. Several brightly colored sailboats seemed to be racing. A few hundred yards away, two toddlers played in the gentle surf under a woman's supervision; otherwise the park was deserted.

Zach sat down on a large rock and watched Kate, who stood pensively at the water's edge. After a few minutes, she started skipping rocks. On her sixth or seventh try, the stone skimmed over the water for a very long distance, leaving behind a neat little trail of circles. "Seventeen," said Zach, having counted them meticulously.

"Are you a little jealous of Andrew?" she said, without looking back at him.

"Probably."

"You shouldn't be." She took off her shoes and waded into the lake up to the level of her shorts, then tipped over face-first into a breaststroke and swam a few yards away. She swam back toward the shore and emerged shivering, her arms crossed to cover her breasts under her wet shirt. "It's freezing!" she said.

"Are you okay?"

"Fine. The sun feels great. You should go in, too."

He shook his head. "You know what, though? It would be nice to have another picnic here."

She nodded noncommittally and lay on a boulder to warm up. Zach wandered down to the shore, smiled benevolently at the toddlers, and contemplated the view. Out of Kate's sight, he practiced skipping stones, not doing too badly after a few tries. He sensed that going back to her right away might be intruding, so he sat down on a rock a few hundred yards away and brooded, his chin in his hand. A small fish came to the surface to catch a mosquito; a dragonfly cruised over the water's surface. He looked up to see Kate standing a few feet away.

"I don't want to drive too late," she said. Her voice was neutral, neither reproachful nor very warm.

Zach looked at his watch and calculated their likely arrival time in Princeton. "I guess we should go," he said. Even if they left right away, they would still be driving after midnight.

"Do you need to go back to New York tonight?"

"Not really."

"Then why don't you stay with me again?"

"That would be great."

The drive to Princeton took about seven hours, most of which they passed in silence. Dusk was beautiful in upstate New York, shadows filling the valleys while the top of the hills remained warmly lit; but Zach appreciated the privacy that came with night. They both watched the mesmerizing pattern of headlights and road markings, lost in their own thoughts. When they got out of the car in Princeton, it was as if they were leaving a movie theater; they spoke hesitantly and in whispers.

"Thanks for driving," said Zach.

"Thanks for coming with me."

"Are you sleepy?"

"Very."

Once inside the graduate student dormitory, Zach took a shower in the men's bathroom and then knocked on Kate's door; she shouted that it was fine for him to enter. She was lying in bed, staring at the ceiling with only her bedside lamp still lit. As soon as Zach had found his way to the futon, she switched the light off. It took Zach a long time to fall asleep, and all the time he knew that she was still lying on her back, wide awake.

CHAPTER 6

1 • They awoke the next morning to the sound of someone knocking at the door. Zach remained in bed while Kate, dressed in men's boxer shorts and a T-shirt, peered through the peephole. She opened the door to reveal a thin, middle-aged black woman with a short-cut Afro and a business suit.

"Dean Sheehy," said Kate.

The dean looked past Kate into her room, saw Zach, and said, "Katharine, can I talk to you privately for a second?"

Kate said "Sure" and closed the door behind her, leaving Zach alone on the futon. He could hear them talking, but too quietly for him to make out their words. They talked for five minutes, then ten, then fifteen. Zach had to go to the bathroom, but he didn't want to interrupt by passing them in the hall. He put on his clothes and sat on the chair to wait, growing somewhat irritated as twenty minutes passed, and then twenty-five. His mouth was still gummed shut from sleep and his hair was sticking up in the back.

Finally the door opened and Kate came back in alone. Zach could see the dean walking away down the stairs in the background. Kate sat down on the edge of the bed and buried her face in her hands.

"Are you okay?" said Zach. Kate remained motionless

and silent. After a few minutes, he got up and said, "I'll be right back." He took his time in the bathroom, brushing his teeth and combing his hair slowly, all the time pondering what could be wrong. He returned to find Kate in the same position as when he had left her.

She looked up and he could see that she had been crying. "What's the matter?" he said softly.

"Charles," she said.

"Where is he?"

"They found him in a motel in Virginia. The doors and windows to his room were locked from the inside. He had bought the gun himself the day before, also in Virginia. He still had the receipt and the store clerk remembered him. There wasn't any note or anything. The wound was, as they say, 'consistent' with suicide. One shot through the roof of the mouth. No signs of a struggle."

"I'm so sorry."

"I'll probably feel sad later, I guess," she said, forcing a smile. "Right now, I'm more scared than anything."

Zach sat down again. "This is getting serious."

She nodded and he said, "You really aren't involved, you know. They're not interested in *your* dissertation. Why don't you just take a week off, go to Illinois or Jamaica or something, put this behind you?"

"No. I want to get to the bottom of it. Let's search his room."

"Now?"

"Yeah. I'm sure the police will be coming to look around soon, or the university. Let's get in there first." Her expression was grim and determined.

They had left the door to Charles's room unlocked. His answering machine showed no new messages. Zach looked out of the window, glad to see that the front door of the dormitory was in clear view. "Stay there," said Kate. "I'll pass you some files, but keep an eye out for cops."

"Should we be touching stuff in here, do you think?"

"We've left our fingerprints all over the place already. What difference will a few more make?"

Kate opened Charles's desk drawer and pulled out some overstuffed manila envelopes, which she handed to Zach. "When you're done, I'll give you more," she said. Meanwhile, she opened Charles's closet door. "Most of his clothes seem to be here still," she said. She peered under the bed. "But no suitcase, no toothbrush or shaving stuff that I can see. He must have packed to go away for a few days. There's certainly no sign of a struggle." Her voice sounded strained; her face was drawn.

The files that Kate had given to Zach contained memos from the philosophy department, course listings, and financial-aid information. He handed them back to her and she gave him another set, which turned out to contain bank statements, bills, and the previous year's tax forms. Charles, he could see, had significant income from a trust fund and a large taxable scholarship: presumably the Austin. Zach exchanged the financial files for a thick one containing notes on legal-sized yellow sheets. Charles's handwriting was difficult to read and much of the material was in German; nevertheless, it was clear that these were Charles's notes on Nietzsche scholarship and related topics, consisting mainly of quotations and page numbers. There were also some photocopied sections from books, including Jung's work on Zarathustra, Jaspers on Nietzsche (in the original German), and some contemporary German scholarship on the intellectual origins of Nazism.

Zach traded the folder of notes for another file containing personal letters in no discernible order. Kate paged through still more files while Zach looked at the letters, keeping one eye on the front door as he read.

One whole folder bulged with letters from Charles's mother in Greenwich, Connecticut. Zach skimmed them rapidly, finding nothing of special interest. Charles's parents were still together, apparently, but only his mother seemed to write regularly, bearing news of social events and the accomplishments of his siblings. Another folder contained letters from former professors at Yale, inquiring about Charles's career and expressing high admiration for him. There were also postcards from friends, mostly women, none very revealing or intimate in tone. Zach noticed a postcard from Kate, which he read covertly. It had been mailed from Venice and it said:

March 5

Caro Carlo,

Having a great time in the *serenissima repubblica*, which really is pretty serene—but cold as heck—in the off season. Very romantic: the whole place looks like it was filmed through Vaseline. Miasmas from the lagoon and all that.

I miss you. Not sure where we stand after that weird time in New York, but ready to start again, pick up where we were, just be friends, whatever . . .

Love (?), Kate

Zach glanced at the author of this postcard, who wore a somber expression and was rapidly flipping through a folder of business correspondence. He wondered what had happened between her and Charles in the months since March.

The next interesting letter that Zach found was signed by Jules Hausman and typed on department stationery using an old-fashioned typewriter that drove each fuzzy character deeply into the paper so that the reverse looked like braille. It read:

Dear Mr. Wilson:

Thank you for your interesting letter. I would be willing to meet you to discuss your ideas—perhaps in Princeton, for I will be nearby on several occasions this summer. Please contact me at the above address to set up an appointment.

Otto Stern was a complex man. I doubt that any uncomplicated interpretation of his ideas would do him justice. Nevertheless—we should meet.

Yours sincerely,
Jules Hausman

Zach showed this letter to Kate while he continued to page through the file. She handed it back with a nod and said, "What do you think of this?" She showed Zach a letter written on a small sheet of notepaper. At the top of the page, in fancy cursive calligraphy, was the single word "Crypt." The letter, from the Crypt treasurer, informed Mr. Charles Wilson that he still owed twenty-four dollars in battles, which he should pay at his earliest convenience. The envelope was made of the same elegant paper, but it carried no return address.

"What are 'battles'?" said Zach.

"God knows."

They finished looking through Charles's files and tried to return everything to its original condition. After looking around carefully one last time, they closed the door behind them, leaving it locked.

"What next?" said Zach.

"I've been invited to a memorial service in Connecticut." She still looked grim.

"When?" said Zach.

"Tomorrow. His parents didn't know who to invite; they

asked the dean to talk to his friends. I was the only one around, I guess."

"When did they find out?"

"I don't know. A few days ago, I guess."

"I have to teach tomorrow," said Zach. "But I'll tell you what. My college is not very far from the Connecticut state line; why don't we go that far together? That way I can keep you company most of the way to the service. Would you like that?"

"You don't want to go to the service itself?"

"I didn't know him at all."

"I'd like you to come with me. Please?"

⅛ • They went into town to buy breakfast. Neither of them spoke much on the way there or while they ate, until Zach said, "How about if I leave you alone until tomorrow morning? You can pick me up in New York."

"Am I being a drag?"

"No. I just thought you might like—as the pop psychology books say—some space."

"I'd rather have company, to tell you the truth. But you're free to go, of course."

Zach shook his head. However, he wondered what they could do to pass the time until they left for Connecticut the next morning. He didn't feel up to sitting silently across a table from her all day. "How would you like to meet Alice Webster?" he said.

"Not today."

"The thing is," said Zach, "I wonder if it's such a good idea for us to hang around here. Say the police come to Charles's room, figure out that somebody broke in, and we're just sitting around next door? It might be better for us not to have to answer any questions right away. Why not get out of town, preserve our freedom of movement?"

"I wouldn't mind leaving, anyway."

"Right. So I thought maybe we should go to New York."

"Can we stay in your place?"

"It's a dump and my roommate will be around."

"That's okay with me, if he doesn't mind."

They took the next train out of Princeton, after Kate had packed a few things in a book bag. Since she did not seem to want to talk, Zach opened an Otto Stern book that he had brought along. He didn't feel like reading, but he had to admit that the prose was very forceful and compelling, if somehow slippery. Kate looked out of the window, hardly moving. For a short time, she wept quietly.

They got off the train at Penn Station, which came as a shock after the tranquil affluence of Princeton. Few approaches to the great cities of the world can be as unwelcoming as Pennsylvania Station, which is totally devoid of signs, attendants, and maps; the people who don't try to push you out of the way generally want to steal your bags. Zach led them through a network of packed subterranean tunnels, trying to seem as if he were more sure of his way than he really was, while Kate followed silently. He was sorry that she had to be in such a hostile environment. Rows of men and a few women slept on the floor; garish signs announced discount electronics and fast food; people streamed by in angry torrents. Zach was relieved to see a set of stairs to street level, which deposited them on Eighth Avenue.

"What would you like to do?" he said.

"I don't know." She shrugged.

"Something to take your mind off—things. A film? A museum? A walk?"

"You decide." Her eyes were downcast.

"All right. How about a walk? Are you up for a long one?"

"Okay." She didn't seem enthusiastic, but Zach didn't know what else to do; he certainly didn't want to go to his apartment until they absolutely had to. He led her back down into the subway. On the platform and in the train they remained silent, Zach apprehensive about the day ahead. They got off the train at Brooklyn Heights, the starting point for his favorite walk. They had to navigate carefully through the highways and the hot, inhospitable public spaces of downtown Brooklyn until they reached the pedestrian entrance to the Brooklyn Bridge. It rose quickly like a steep hill, and all around them a lattice of cables soared to Gothic heights. Beneath, the river broadened into a vast harbor, and the tops of the downtown Manhattan skyscrapers sprouted above the summit of the bridge like the towers of a medieval fortress. What Zach liked best about this walk was the way the skyscrapers seemed to grow in front of you as you climbed, while the pattern of the cables shifted rapidly like a kaleidoscope.

Near the midpoint, Kate pointed to a bench and they sat down together, silent for several minutes. Zach fervently hoped that he hadn't done something inappropriate by bringing her to the bridge; he hadn't known *what* to do. Suddenly, she said, "He was a jerk, you know."

"Who?" said Zach, just to make sure.

"He really wasn't very nice. I don't know why I was so into him. Now I'm mad at myself for feeling that way, mad at him—I don't know. At some level, I'm glad to be free of him. He was arrogant, he was self-obsessed. He was basically unfair to me, too."

Zach's face was a mask of sympathy; underneath, he was quite pleased to hear this.

"It's a stage of grief," he said. "That's what you're going through."

"No it isn't! I was only half–worried when he disappeared—basically, I thought I *should* be worried. The fact is, I had gotten my life entangled with his, and now it's cut free. I'm sorry it happened in such an—awful way, but now it's over. I mean, my relationship with him is over. As for exactly what happened to him, who knows?"

They descended from the bridge into lower Manhattan and Zach took Kate to his favorite Chinese restaurant, a Cantonese lunch place with roast ducks hanging in the windows and everyone ate at top speed, seated at tables with complete strangers. Kate and Zach ended up facing each other across a narrow table that they shared with a Chinese woman and her small son.

"Why do you think he went to Virginia?" said Zach.

"Guns are easy to buy there. Isn't that where the New York crack dealers go to buy their weapons?"

"I don't know; probably. But surely there are easier ways to— I mean, if you can get a car, you don't need a gun."

"What do you think, then?"

"Where was Wendell Fry when Charles was in Virginia?"

"Being grilled by the Senate, I guess. In Washington."

"Which is right nearby, isn't it? And both of those guys were Crypt men."

"So is Davies."

"Right. Furthermore, Frye's nomination is controversial because of his reactionary political theories. Charles was writing a dissertation about political reactionaries when he died. And Davies's opinions are definitely right-wing."

"What do we know about Frye?"

"Not much. But we could find out. The New York Public is open."

3 • They decided to walk part of the way there. They crossed the mobbed bazaar of Canal Street, where cheap electronics, pornographic videos, and Chinese vegetables are all sold on the same sidewalk and the crushed cardboard boxes underfoot bear labels from around the world. From Canal they walked north through the narrow streets of SoHo with their cast-iron buildings and chic postmodern window displays, and into Greenwich Village. At Washington Square Park, they decided that they might as well walk all the way, so they continued up Fifth Avenue, growing somewhat weary in the heat as they passed through the dull commercial district below Forty-second Street.

At last they arrived at Zach's home away from home, the public library on Forty-second Street. A *Who's Who* in the reference section gave them the basic information they were looking for:

> Frye, Wendell Eli. Fed. judge, auth., prof. b. 1934, Boston. Fath. Rev. Thaddeus Frye (episc.); moth. Natalie Leclerc Frye. Educ. Boston Latin Sch.; Yale College (BA, 1956), Phi Beta Kappa, summa cum laude; ed., *Yale Daily News;* Yale Law School (J.D., 1959), ed., *Yale Law Review.* m. Christina Solomon Frye, homemaker (1957). S. Wendell Frye II., b. 1959, atty. U.S. Navy, 2nd lieutenant, 1963–65. Clerk, U.S. Supreme Court (1965–67); Fulbright Scholar, University of Paris (1967–68); Associate, Bower & Chadwick (1968–70); Assistant Counsel, Committee to Re-Elect the President (1971–72); Assistant Secretary of State for Planning and Evaluation (1972–73); Assistant

Prof., Yale Law School (1973–75); Associate Professor, Yale Law School (1975–77); Centennial Professor of Jurisprudence (1977–1982); Fed. judge, Second Circuit (1982–present). Auth. *The Natural Law Tradition* (1974); *The Commands of Reason* (1979); *Law and Justice* (1983).

"Nothing too surprising here," Zach said.

"But his mother must be proud."

"Yes, hasn't he turned out well?"

"Hold on a second." Kate tapped the page with her forefinger. "This is the same book I used to look up Davies. Something rings a bell. Didn't they both graduate from Yale in nineteen fifty-six?"

This turned out to be true. "That means they were both in Crypt the same year," said Zach.

"So they're probably blood brothers."

"That's right; I bet they swore eternal brotherhood over the corpse of a virgin or something. Interesting."

Kate looked up recent press reports on Frye, of which there were many, while Zach requested copies of his books. The books turned out to be in use (and there was a long waiting list for them), but Kate found a profile in a weekly magazine.

"Nothing about Crypt in here," she said.

Zach was sitting across a long reading table from her, waiting to see what she found. "I think his membership has only become news in the last two or three days," he whispered.

"Right—and this is last week's issue."

"What was he doing in Paris?"

"Let's see." She skimmed for a few minutes, then said: "He was studying philosophy with Emanuel Bourlieu, apparently. Is he a Sternian?"

"Quite the contrary. He's a rabid poststructuralist, a mem-

ber of the generation of sixty-eight, a radical of both the epis-
temological and the political variety. He has likened truth
to copulation with a hermaphrodite—he's famous for that."

"What does it mean?"

" 'What does it mean?' How naïve! Its meaning is radi-
cally indeterminate, of course, like all meaning. It eludes any
definite sense."

"I see. These philosophical crazies are your turf, not mine.
Why do you think an American conservative would be studying with a French po-mo revolutionary?"

"He was a young man in 'sixty-eight. Paris was an exciting place; philosophy grad students were staring down de
Gaulle, and the general blinked. Maybe, when he got home
and got a real job, he just grew up."

"On the other hand," said Kate, "correct me if I'm wrong,
but following up on what you said about Stern, could Frye
be a *secret* postmodernist and a public conservative?"

"You think he picked up the gospel of nihilism in France,
but decided to hide it when he got home?"

"Doesn't that make sense? Bright guy, goes to Yale in the
sixties, picks up wild ideas, but then decides they're dangerous, so he ends up working for Nixon. Ultimately, he gets
himself appointed to the Supreme Court, where he can
really keep an eye on those deconstructionists who want to
say that there's no fixed meaning in the Constitution."

⊣ • They could not find much else in the New York Public
Library, in part because books and articles relating to Judge
Frye were in such heavy demand. That left them with the late
afternoon to fill, and Zach still wanted to delay going home.
They sat on the front steps of the library and looked through
Zach's *Times* to see if there was anything to do.

"Do you like opera?" he asked.

"Some of it."

"How about Mozart, *The Magic Flute*?"

"I *love* that. Why?"

"It's at Lincoln Center."

"Isn't it incredibly expensive?"

"Not if you get standing-room tickets. You can usually move to a seat by the second act."

"I'm not dressed very well for it." She was wearing white canvas sneakers, shorts, and a blouse; Zach was dressed at about the same level of formality.

"That's fine," he said. "Let's strike a blow against the philistines. If you're there for the music, who cares how you're dressed? And if other people care, just consider whose side Mozart would be on."

"You've convinced me."

They walked toward Lincoln Center: Zach always tried to save money by walking everywhere in Manhattan. But Kate looked tired, and after a few minutes she stopped and asked if they could take a taxi. They hailed a cab; Zach watched the meter nervously as they cruised up Sixth Avenue, along Central Park South past the liveried doormen, and across Sixty-third Street to Lincoln Center. He and Kate split the fare, reducing Zach's entire worth by about ten percent. Then they bought tickets and walked to a nearby Burger King to eat: another blow against philistinism. Meanwhile, Zach calculated that he had all of sixty dollars left in the world, and a rent check to pay on September first. What was he doing at the opera? He bought the skimpy $1.99 special.

In the theater lobby before the performance, Zach decided that he and Kate were the only members of the audience truly dedicated to Art: young, badly dressed, poor, and prepared to stand—it was a state of grace. The usher showed them to their places behind a felt-covered lectern at the back of the auditorium, meant for holding scores. They read their pro-

grams while the orchestra tuned up. Then the familiar chords
of the overture were heard and they were transported out of
Manhattan, graduate school, and the modern world altogether.

At the intermission, while they split a seven-dollar soda,
Kate said: "Sarastro's temple looked a bit like the Crypt
building at Yale."

"You know who Sarastro is, don't you?" said Zach. She
shook her head. "It's Italian for Zarathustra, Nietzsche's
main character. Aka Zoroaster. Mozart was a Mason—in
other words, a member of a secret society. I think that's why
The Magic Flute caught my eye in the paper; it's been in the
back of my mind lately."

"Why were Mozart and Nietzsche interested in Zarathustra?"

"Up until the end of the eighteenth century, it was widely
believed that Zarathustra was a real guy who had known
many important things and had passed them on to posterity.
He was identified with one of the Magi in the Bible. Leibniz
believed that he had written the *I Ching;* Newton thought he
knew all about physics. In other words, he was supposed to
be one of the founders of the perennial philosophy, the core
truths that are known to all wise men, starting with Adam;
but after the Fall they have been transmitted secretly from
one generation of philosophers to the next.

"This was a mainstream theory in the eighteenth century.
By Mozart's time, it was already a bit of a joke: it's hard to
tell whether he's serious or not about Sarastro and his secret
society. By the nineteenth century, the whole idea of a perennial philosophy gets dropped by professional academics,
but it gets picked up by believers in occult and magic, New
Age enthusiasts, and so on. Typically, they're also into Rosicrucian and Masonic ideas. The Crypt building clearly feeds

on those ideas, though whether seriously or not—who knows?

"But you asked why Nietzsche was interested in Zarathustra. Because Zarathustra was an antidote to modern historical relativism, which Nietzsche feared and hated. But also because Nietzsche was interested in secret writing, in circles of wise men who know the truth and propagate simple, consoling messages for everyone outside."

During the second and third acts, Zach forgot all about philosophy and secret cults. He knew the music so well from playing his ancient record that lately he had stopped really hearing it; but the experience of concentrating on it alone and seeing it come alive on stage reawakened him to its magnificence. They were still standing during the third act, for the house was full. During some spoken dialogue, Zach whispered, "Are you still okay standing?"

She turned to him with a warm smile and her eyes reflected the light from the stage. "Great!" she whispered.

Just then the music from the last scene began and Tamino and Pamina began their solemn trials of fire and water. Zach and Kate were still looking at each other, alone under the eave at the back of the auditorium. The music turned joyful as the trials ended and the hero and heroine were joined in eternal bliss. Zach realized that he was grinning like an idiot; but so was Kate. Suddenly, without making a conscious decision, without knowing who was responsible—without thinking at all—Zach and Kate kissed.

The house lights came up, the curtain came down, and the applause began. Zach and Kate pulled away (Zach felt a bit foolish), and then they stood facing the stage and clapping. They avoided making eye contact as they walked out of the theater and into the plaza of Lincoln Center, but near the fountain they bumped up against each other, perhaps accidentally, and kept walking that way. They took a Broadway bus uptown and got off in Zach's neighborhood.

"My roommate will be there," he said.

"That's okay."

Zach was always nervous entering his building, which lacked a doorman to guard its long, ominously dark passageways. They shared the elevator with a small old woman and her dachshund, neither of whom posed any threat of violence, although the dog looked decidedly unfriendly.

Judah was indeed home, working on his computer. Zach introduced them and led Kate into his area of the apartment, behind the row of bookcases.

"Can I get you something?" he asked in a near whisper. She shook her head.

"You got a message," said Judah loudly. "It's still on the machine."

Zach played it back. It was from Zach's supervisor. "Ah, hello, Zachary? This is Professor Mollendorff. I am waiting to see your thesis. Please give me a call back as soon as you can."

Zach looked at his watch and saw that it was too late to call back. "That's my advisor," he said. "Sooner or later I'm going to have to tell him that there is no thesis anymore."

"Maybe we'll find it."

"Maybe. Do you mind if I prepare a little for class tomorrow? You can make yourself comfortable, read any of these books—"

Zach hoped that Judah would go to bed, but he remained at his computer, clicking away at the keyboard. Silence reigned in the little apartment, as Zach halfheartedly read Nietzsche, Judah typed, and Kate browsed among Zach's books, settling at last on an edition of George Bernard Shaw.

"I think I'll read a play," she said. "Plays are nice and short."

"Go ahead. That book's left over from freshman English."

At midnight, Kate announced that she was tired.

Zach whispered, "You sleep there, in my bed. I'll take the couch." Kate made a face as if to say "Are you sure?" and Zach nodded decisively. They took turns getting ready for bed in the bathroom, and then lay down, separated by the bookcases. After half an hour, Judah went into his section of the apartment, which was divided from the living room by a doorway and a curtain. He switched off his light and the three of them lay in the dark.

After a long while, Zach decided that his two companions must both be asleep. He began to shift around, trying to get comfortable on the couch while he thought about all the confusing events of the past few days. Suddenly, he saw Kate pad into view from behind the bookcases. She approached and bent over him; he signaled for her to be quiet, but she kissed him lightly on the forehead. Then she disappeared around the corner again. His heart racing, he lay still on the couch.

After what seemed like another ten minutes, he got up and went into her area of the apartment. She was lying on top of the sheets because of the heat and her eyes were wide open. She gave him a warm smile. He knelt down beside her and whispered into her ear: "Do you mind if I lie next to you? It's not too comfortable on the couch. I promise I—"

She nodded and he climbed into bed. They faced each other and kissed gently; Zach's hand, shaking slightly, rested on her waist. She kissed his eyes and then he lay with them closed, pretending to be falling asleep, although he was far too excited for sleep. When he opened them again, he saw that she was still awake and looking at him. He couldn't decipher her mood. She seemed to have been crying, but she had also kissed him. She had lost a friend that day, but she had smiled at Zach affectionately. Suddenly, without premeditation, he was kissing her passionately on the lips. After a long while, she pulled away and buried her face in his chest. She stayed still for a long time, but Zach thought that he could hear gentle sobbing. At last she fell asleep; Zach, however, remained still and sleepless and increasingly uncomfortable until dawn.

5 • When the sun rose, he got up, left Kate snoring in bed, and returned to the couch so that Judah would find him there when he awoke. He finally dozed off at about eight in the morning, only to be awakened at eight-thirty by Judah, who was eating breakfast in the kitchen alcove. Zach took a shower, got dressed, and ate some cereal while trying to concentrate on notes for his class. After a few minutes, he stuck his head around the corner to look at Kate, but she was still sleeping and he was afraid to wake her. Instead, he dialed Professor Mollendorff's number in New Haven.

"Hello," said his advisor. "Who is calling?"

"Hi, Professor Mollendorff? This is Zach."

"Good morning, Zachary. Where is your thesis?"

"To tell you the truth: it's gone. There's been a computer—error, and I've lost almost everything." For some reason, he couldn't bring himself to say simply "everything."

"Ach, computers. I told you to stay away from them. Technology and philosophy should never mix; they are mortal enemies. How can a *machine* help you to write?"

"They can be quite helpful, actually. But in this case—"

"Les choses sont contre nous, Zachary."

"Thanks for the advice." Zach's words might have

sounded bitter, but he was actually not paying a great deal of attention. His mind was on Kate and the day ahead; his dissertation seemed like a trivial exercise from long ago.

"In any case," said Mollendorff, "the setback is not that significant."

"Why not? Was my work totally *in*significant?"

"That's not what I mean. I mean that you can simply get a copy of the last draft that I gave to the chairman."

"You gave my work to Davies?"

"Certainly. He asked for it."

"When?"

"Perhaps two weeks ago."

"That's amazing. Thank you."

Zach hung up and saw Kate standing across the room in her T-shirt and shorts, her hair disheveled and her face still marked with lines from the pillow. He felt great affection for her, but also a tinge of fear as he remembered the previous night. He wondered how she would feel about him in the cold light of day.

"Who was that?" she asked, smiling at him when Judah looked away.

"My supervisor. Get this: he's been giving copies of my dissertation to Hannibal Davies."

"That's great. Then there's hope that you can get it back."

While Kate showered, Zach called the philosophy department at Yale and asked for Professor Davies.

"The chairman is not available," said the familiar and forbidding voice of Mrs. Stephens, the department secretary.

"Mrs. Stephens, this is Zach Blumberg. It's kind of an emergency; I really need to see him."

"Professor Davies is not holding office hours at this time."

"Nevertheless, I think he'd really want to talk to me."

She snickered ironically, then said: "I cannot say whether

the chairman would *want* to speak with you, Zach. However, I *can* say that he has left New Haven for his holiday. He is not here at all in July or August."

"Well, can you tell me where he is?"

"Certainly not."

Zach flushed with irritation. Then he took a deep breath and spoke in a calm, even voice like someone instructing a child: "He's supposed to be the chairman of my department. That's an administrative job—did you ever think of that? Professor H.P.T. Davies, despite his name, his pedigree, and the fancy title, is an *administrator*, an employee of the university. That means he works for me, since I'm a tuition-paying customer. He gets paid; I pay him. Furthermore, I'm a philosopher, a graduate student in his department, recipient of his advice and counsel, fellow toiler in the groves of academe. Now I would like to talk to him, just briefly, on a matter of great importance to us both. Do you think, therefore, that you could JUST TELL ME WHERE HE IS?"

"Are you finished, Zachary?"

Zach fell silent, amazed at his own performance.

"Would you like me to take a message for the chairman, which he can pick up in September?"

"Okay. Just tell him I'd like a meeting with him. It's about my dissertation."

"Very well, I will tell him."

Zach cradled the receiver in his hand after Mrs. Stephens had hung up, considering the injustice of it all. Kate emerged from the bathroom. "Where's Davies?" she said. "Did you call him?"

"He's in seclusion," said Zach bitterly.

They had to go upstate so that Zach could teach, then to Greenwich for the memorial service. Zach also wanted to go to New Haven to see if they could find Davies. To visit three towns in one day seemed difficult by public transportation, so Kate suggested renting a car.

"To tell you the truth," Zach said, "I have about thirty dollars in the bank and change from a twenty in my pocket. I'm waiting for my stipend. That'll come in September—unless they throw me out for lack of a dissertation, which could happen. So, to be frank, I'm not sure I can *afford* a car."

"You poor thing," said Kate. "All those expensive meals you bought, courting me."

"I only paid for my half."

"Still. From now on, it's all on me."

"How are you doing for money?"

"Compared to you, I'm Ivana Trump."

"I don't think it's fair—"

"Oh, be quiet." She gave him a twenty-dollar bill out of her purse. "Spending money," she said. "Use it wisely, and you can have more. Squander it, and I'm cutting you off."

"I'll pay you back in September."

"Good."

6 • They rented a car at a Midtown company and then drove north out of the city, arriving at the state college by noon. Zach enjoyed the novelty of arriving by car instead of public transportation, and with a woman at his side. He hoped that someone he knew would see them, but the campus was largely deserted. He left Kate at the library while he taught his class, which went fairly smoothly except for a brief conversation with Dorothy, who again stopped at his desk on the way out of the room. She stood there silently, and Zach said, "Have you made any progress with your paper?"

"Not really." He was glad, since he didn't want to look over a draft. He said, "It's due next week, you know."

"I know. I'm having awful problems with it, though. Nothing looks right when I put it down on paper."

"If you'd brought a draft with you, we could have gone over it." Zach felt sorry for his reproachful tone, since it was completely hypocritical.

"I'm sorry. I didn't want to show you what I'd written."

"You'll *have* to show me what you've got next week, or I'll be required to give you an F."

She nodded, and Zach left her to join Kate in the library. It was a small building with an impressive glass-and-steel atrium, but not very many books. Zach found Kate in the periodicals section, a gloomy, windowless area in the basement with concrete walls and gray steel furniture. He felt a twinge of pleasure at the sight of her: she was squinting as she tried to read a microfiche, and the light from the machine illuminated her face. She was dressed up for the memorial service, wearing a dark cotton dress.

"Hey," he said softly, as he approached her from behind the machine.

"Oh, hello." She peered around the microfiche reader and adjusted her eyes to the relative gloom. "How was class?"

"Not too bad. What are you looking at?"

"Crypt stuff. You want to hear something strange? Remember that article that was missing from the library at Princeton? Well, the same issue is missing from this collection."

"Maybe someone checked it out because of the fuss over Judge Frye's membership."

"No, it doesn't circulate. Somebody ripped that issue out of the binder and took it away with them, or threw it out."

"Weird. I doubt very much that there are any Cryptites— or Crypties? Cryptheads? Cryptmen?—whatever you call them, I doubt that there are any around here. This is not their kind of place. For one thing, it's open to the public."

She shrugged. "Ready to go to Greenwich?"

7 •   The drive took less than an hour. On the way, Kate asked, "You know what you said about the Sternians? How they put their real ideas in the exact middle of their books?"

Zach nodded.

"How do you know what the real middle is? I mean, let's say one of these esoteric writers—give me an example."

"Maimonides."

"All right. Let's say he writes out his books on papyrus or whatever, and then they get copied by one scribe after another for hundreds of years, and translated, and printed, and reprinted, and stored on CD-ROM probably—well, how do we know where the middle was originally? I mean, do you have to count words in the original language?"

"As far as I can tell," said Zach, "the recent authors literally put their esoteric meaning on the middle page. That's how it works for the Sternians' own books. I guess they don't expect their works to go through many editions after their deaths, or to be translated. As for the classics, most of them are divided into parts, the parts into chapters, the chapters into sections, or some such arrangement. For instance, Nietzsche's *Genealogy of Morals.* Do you know it?"

"I read it in college. But I guess the answer is no."

"Well, you might remember that it purports to tell the history of our distinction between good and evil. It turns out that this distinction is arbitrary, the mere result of certain people's political victory at one point in history. That's why we are now able to go *beyond* good and evil, right?—because we know that the distinction is merely arbitrary."

Kate, watching the road, nodded to show that she understood. Zach continued: "But it also turns out that even our idea of history relies on the distinction between true and false, which itself depends on the separation between good and evil. So there is no true or false, and therefore Nietzsche's so-called history of morals is no history at all. Well, where do you think that self-destructive part of the argument comes in? Ignoring the preface, there are three books, each divided into sections. Look at the middle section of the second book, and voilà. You can do the same kind of thing for *Zarathustra*."

They arrived in Greenwich too early for the service, but not too early to be greeted by the minister, a tall Episcopal priest with a chalky complexion and beaked Roman nose.

"Welcome," he said sonorously, and led them to a pew near the altar. The program had been elegantly printed on parchment: there were to be several eulogies, some music, and then refreshments in the sacristy. Zach looked around at the sunlit interior, wondering if it was really Colonial or just Colonial-revival, and thinking it odd that an Episcopal church should be so plain and unadorned; there was no stained glass and just a simple cross on the altar. Obviously, the New England Puritan tradition was stronger here than the heritage of high-church Anglicanism. "What do you think?" he whispered to Kate. "Eighteenth century? Nineteenth? Early twentieth?"

She gave the building a professional inspection and finally pronounced it circa 1910. "The timbers are too straight for genuine Colonial," she said, "and the construction techniques are modern if you look closely—screws instead of nails, for example."

"You're good," said Zach.

"Just doing my job."

People started filing into the church. Only in movies had Zach seen such beautiful clothes and such picture-perfect people. Almost everyone was over fifty except for a band of twenty-something men in dark blazers and silk ties who entered together and sat in the back.

"Crypties?" whispered Kate, and Zach nodded, although he wasn't sure.

A Bach prelude and fugue emerged from the organ, played slowly to make them seem mournful. Then the priest took the pulpit and read passages from Isaiah and First Corinthians. He spoke briefly of Charles, remembering the soccer star and the Christmas Charity Drive volunteer, the fine student and role model. He concluded with some remarks about the special burdens borne by those who receive God's greatest gifts, the grave problems faced by today's youth, and the infinite mercy and wisdom of the Lord.

Charles's father was the next speaker. He walked stiffly to the front of the aisle and turned with military precision to face the congregation, his expression a mask of formality that barely concealed his profound grief and confusion.

"Charles's mother and I," he began, "received a letter from Charles yesterday. His last letter, sent from Virginia apparently. Because I do not know what else to say—about what has happened to my son and to all of us, I thought I would share it with you, his closest friends and his beloved family. He writes:

" 'Dear Mom and Dad'—" At this point, Charles's father's voice faltered and he briefly lost control of his countenance. Regaining command, he continued, " 'Dear Mom and Dad, Please forgive me for what I am about to do. This is perhaps impossible, but I beg your forgiveness nevertheless.

" 'I cannot explain to you the basic reasons for my decision, and in any case, it is better that you should not know them. It is true that I have suffered a setback in my career recently, a frustration, but this is not the reason that I do what I do. Nor does my conscience bear any sin that should cause you anxiety. Rather, although this sounds pompous and certainly counter to the spirit of our times, I have chosen to die because of an *idea*. Perhaps I am insane, certainly I am eccentric, but whatever the cause, I have let certain patterns of thought connected to my philosophical work lead me to a despair from which there is no escape but death. I ask only that you take this seriously, at face value, and do not succumb to the temptation to psychoanalyze me and attribute my decision to some contingent cause such as depression or guilt or, worst of all, your parenting. For better or for worse, I act freely. I wish you both strength, happiness, and love.'

"Charles," said his father. "We do not understand you, son, but we forgive you without reservation."

The next speaker was one of the young men in blazers, a blond, baby-faced man of about twenty-five. Taking his place at the head of the aisle, he began to speak: "I knew Charles before senior year, but just well enough to say hi to; I really got to know him in our last year at Yale. Well, in this company it's no secret that Charles was a Cryptsman, and so am I, and so are his brothers in this room. *Novus ordo*, Charlie boy.

"Many of the things we do together in Crypt are secret, although they're far less outrageous than you might imagine. But one thing that's well-known, I guess, is the tradition of telling your autobiography. To be honest, I wasn't really close to Charles, but in your autobiography, you tell all. I cannot say that I remember everything that Charles said, but

I remember the general impression. Listening to what Mr. Wilson just read, I felt very sad, but I must say I was not totally surprised. Charles was a serious guy, seriously into philosophy and what it meant for his life. That's what he talked about the whole time in his autobiography, and apparently that's what killed him.

"It is a tragedy. It's unfathomable, and our hearts go out to Mr. and Mrs. Wilson. But we owe it to Charles, I guess, to say that maybe he was a better man than all of us; he faced up to *his* truth, the facts as he saw them, and he did what he thought was necessary. God bless you, Charlie."

The service ended with more organ music, a hymn, and a benediction. Kate and Zach filed past the bereaved parents: Mr. Wilson still wearing an expression of somber formality, his wife clinging to his arm in bewilderment and grief. The sacristy contained a long table laden with cheese and fruit; glass cabinets held ornamental crosses and vestments. Here's where they keep the high-church stuff, Zach thought.

The Cryptsmen gathered around the table, trying to keep their expressions somber but barely stifling their habitual good humor and high spirits. If Charles had had close friends, these were not among them. Zach helped himself to crackers, cheese, and kiwi-fruit slices, suddenly feeling exhausted from his sleepless night. Meanwhile, Kate approached Mrs. Wilson, and Zach could see them together; he admired Kate's moral stamina, but spent his own time carefully avoiding anyone who might be authentically grief-stricken. The priest also seemed to be avoiding conversation, and he and Zach found themselves leaning against the window ledge, observing the company.

"Were you a friend of Charles's from Yale?" the priest asked.

"No. To tell you the truth, I had never met him. I'm here with a friend." Zach gestured toward Kate with his cracker.

"Pity. He was a *fine* young man. If *only* he had sought some kind of help, whether spiritual or psychological. These things *pass,* you know."

"Yes," said Zach, but he thought of Charles's last request in his letter. He also wondered whether the note was genuine.

"Did you see the letter, Reverend?" asked Zach, wondering whether that was the proper form of address to use with an Episcopal priest.

"Oh, yes."

"This is probably an inappropriate question, but can you tell me: was it handwritten or typed?"

"Typed," said the priest, raising his eyebrows. "Typed rather neatly."

"I thought so," said Zach. "I could see the back of it from where I sat."

"Why do you ask?"

"Just curiosity."

"An odd thing to be curious about." The priest moved away abruptly.

Kate joined Zach by the window ledge. "I'm ready to go when you are," she said.

"You're a good person, talking to Mrs. Wilson."

She shrugged. "You would have done the same thing if he'd been your friend." But Zach doubted it: his personal reservoirs of cowardice ran deep.

⸿ • They left the church as soon as others had begun to do so, got back into the car, and found their way to the interstate in the direction of New Haven. On the way, Zach said, "Charles's suicide note was typed."

"So?" Kate shrugged.

"How do you think he got access to a typewriter in a motel?"

"You think he would have just written the note by hand?"

"Yeah. And if he had, then his parents could have examined the handwriting and verified that he actually wrote it."

"Whereas this way—" said Kate. But she lapsed into silence.

They sailed right past Yale on I-95, missing the tiny sign that marked the correct exit. The university's Gothic towers looked small and out of place amid New Haven's industrial landscape. They left the highway at the next exit and Zach was able to navigate their way through the city streets toward Yale—not without difficulty, since like most students, he rarely left the campus. They parked near the science area in a neighborhood of attractive old houses and tree-lined streets, and did some planning while they sat in the car.

At a nearby public telephone Zach called Information and asked for Davies's address; not surprisingly, he was unlisted. In a classroom building they found a campus directory, but that too omitted Davies's home number and address.

"Is there anyone you could ask?" Kate said.

Zach shook his head. "They'd have his phone number in the department, of course, but not for distribution to mere students."

"Could we sneak a look at it in the department office?"

"It's a tiny little place, watched over zealously by Mrs. Stephens in the morning and Mrs. Piore in the afternoon. I'm sure information on Davies is in the desk drawer, and neither secretary is going to let me rifle through there."

"I have an idea," said Kate, and they began to discuss it in some detail.

The philosophy department occupied part of the ground floor of a Colonial building in the heart of the Yale campus. Zach entered the office and, after saying hello to Mrs. Piore, started looking through the junk mail in his pigeonhole and reading notices on the board. Another graduate student, a first-year man whom Zach knew just slightly, was also in the room. He was about five-feet-two, bald, with a beard and wire-rimmed glasses: the philosopher's uniform. Zach procrastinated until the first-year student wandered out, then yawned and stretched, raising his hand ostentatiously as he did so. He stood in clear view of the windows, although he did not look directly out of them. A few seconds later, the telephone rang.

"Philosophy Department," said Mrs. Piore in a bored voice. "What? I can't . . . Well, all right." She looked up at Zach. "All right, I'll be there right away."

She hung up. "I'm going to have to close the office for a second," she said, shaking her head in annoyance. "They want me to go over to campus police to pick something up."

"You want me to go over for you?"

"No, they want me to go." She rose from the desk and lumbered toward the door.

"Why don't I watch this place?" said Zach. "That way you don't have to lock it up."

She looked at him doubtfully. He said, "I don't mind; I'm not doing anything special today, anyway. What if Saunders or Pinnock or somebody comes by and wants his mail? I might as well stay here and let them in. I can also answer the phone—remember, I used to do that on Monday afternoons my first year?"

"Okay," she said. "I'll be right back. Keep your eye on things."

She moved slowly out of the room and left the door partially ajar. Zach waited a few seconds, then walked nonchalantly over to her desk and sat down, as if to cover the phones. Watching the office door, he examined the desk. A gray metal card file that was almost hidden beneath some papers looked promising. Opening it, he found index cards filed in alphabetical order, including one for Hannibal Davies complete with his home address near New Haven. Zach wrote this down and put the box back in place. Then he looked carefully at the desk surface, which was covered by a glass pane under which lay several cartoons about the annoyances of office life, a university schedule, and a small piece of paper that read: "HPTD, 7/20–8/30." On the next line, there was an out-of-town telephone number, ending with "room 1231." Zach wrote these down, then quickly pocketed his notes as the office door opened and Mrs. Piore trudged back in.

She held a plain manila envelope in her hand; her name was written across the front in large block capitals. "Never seen anything like it," she wheezed. "There's a girl there handing out these envelopes—to department managers, I guess. Let's see, what's in here?"

Zach got up and let her take her chair. She examined the contents of the envelope. "Look at this!" she said, showing Zach a campus map with locations of emergency phones marked in black ink. She was irate. "Now why did I have to go all the way over there for *this?* They could have stuck it in campus mail, or I could have sent my bursary student over. I don't know—it's unbelievable. They want us to do everything these days."

Zach made a sympathetic face and left the office as quickly as he could manage. Kate was waiting for him near the campus police office, and they exchanged high fives. Zach showed her his prize. From a public telephone, using Kate's calling card, they called the long-distance number. She said, "Hi, is Professor Davies still in room twelve thirty-one? . . . No, there's no need to bother him. It's just that I was going to send him an express-mail package?—and I wondered if he was still there. Will he be there tomorrow, do you know? Great, great. Thanks . . . Hey, one more thing? Could you give me your mailing address?"

She hung up and turned to Zach. "The Ambassador Hotel, Washington, D.C.," she said. "He's been there for a couple of weeks, apparently, and he's booked for another week."

CHAPTER 7

1 • They drove back to New York in time to drop the car off in Manhattan before closing time. After Kate paid the bill, they walked around midtown looking for an affordable place to eat dinner. Zach felt irritable from his lack of sleep, and nervous about the evening ahead. They finally chose an Afghan restaurant near Penn Station where they were the only customers. The combination of the unfamiliar menu, the quietness of the restaurant, the over-solicitous service, the fact that Kate was paying for the meal, and the need to offer entertaining conversation all combined to make Zach increasingly tense. There was also the small matter of where they would sleep that night and how he was supposed to behave. Skirting the issue, they spoke intermittently and in near-whispers.

They left the restaurant and walked toward Herald Square and Macy's. Rowdy crowds flowed in the opposite direction, toward a concert at Madison Square Garden. The night air was thick and hot; some of the late commuters looked just inches away from fury or despair. Dodging three boisterous, tattooed teenagers, Zach stepped between parked cars and said, "Where to now?"

"We don't want to go to Washington until tomorrow, do we?"

"No."

"Your place was fine."

"But kind of crowded."

"Are you inviting yourself to my place, then?"

Zach blushed.

"Well, are you?" She stopped and looked him right in the eye. Finally he mumbled, "It might be a good idea."

"It *might* be?"

"I'm sure it would be a very good idea," said Zach, peering over her shoulder to make sure that no one could hear him.

They rode a nearly empty commuter train to Princeton Junction, with Kate resting her head on Zach's shoulder; and then they held hands on the deserted dinky. It would have been nice if the campus had been bathed in moonlight; unfortunately, the night was still muggy and overcast. Nevertheless, they enjoyed the walk through Gothic quadrangles and leafy avenues toward Kate's room. Perhaps they lingered a bit out of nervousness, and deliberately chose a meandering route. When they finally arrived at Kate's building, Zach tried to distract himself by worrying about a possible ambush by Sternian conspirators. Kate allowed him to slip upstairs first in order to check out the room; when he had determined that everything was safe, she joined him on the landing, looking suddenly apprehensive and close to embarrassment. They slipped inside her room, locked the door, and without switching on the light they embraced and stumbled in laughing, clumsy tandem toward the bed.

The next morning, Zach awoke before Kate, got dressed, and slipped outside, leaving her a note to say where he had gone.

When he returned with coffee and stale croissants, she was sitting in bed with her hair in disarray and the sheets pulled up to her neck. She smiled affectionately and he felt a sense of deep contentment.

When she had finished breakfast, she asked, "How shall we get to Washington?"

"If it were just me, I'd take New Jersey Transit to Trenton, SEPTA to Philly, a bus to Baltimore, and the MARC train to D.C."

"You really know your commuter rail services."

"From Bay Area Rapid Transit to the Long Island Railroad, I've done 'em all. It's the fate of those who can't drive and don't want to pay Amtrak fares."

"Well, I suggest we take Amtrak, and you can try to pay me back when you get your stipend. As for accommodations, my sister works in D.C.; she's an environmentalist type. Let me call her and tell her we're coming."

Washington's Union Station is the very antithesis of Penn Station in New York: elegant, marble-lined, quiet, lofty, full of expensive boutiques. Kate and Zach tried not to gawk as they walked across its vast lobby. Outside, the streets were broad and strikingly empty compared to New York; a few cars and taxis and a tourist bus passed by, but there were virtually no pedestrians in sight. The Capitol dome, just a few blocks away, shimmered under the intense sun.

They found the entrance to the Metro and then tried not to look like tourists as they examined the map and figured out how to buy a ticket. Again, the contrast with New York was striking. The silent Metro cars, with their carpeted floors and cushioned seats, seemed like toys or observation cars in a theme park. The customers were a far cry from riders on the New York subway: three or four people in the car with Zach and Kate were dressed in expensive, conservative suits;

two wore sparkling white naval officers' uniforms; and the rest belonged to families of blond tourists in shorts. Everyone spoke in subdued voices, as if they were in a museum.

They got off the train at Farragut North and found the building where Kate's sister worked. The air-conditioning in the pink-marble lobby hit them like a bucket of ice. Feeling shabby in their sweaty student clothes, they made their way past the security desk and up to the fourth floor, where a large chrome sign above the receptionist's desk announced that they had arrived at CLARC, the Clean Air Research Council.

The receptionist called Suzanne, Kate's sister, who emerged a few minutes later and hugged Kate tightly. She turned to Zach and examined him (somewhat critically, he thought) while she shook his hand. Then she gave her sister a key.

Kate and Zach caught a bus at a stop nearby and rode it through several blocks of dreary office buildings and then up Sixteenth Street, past an eerie Masonic temple built in the shape of a windowless ziggurat. Sixteenth Street was broad and lightly populated, like many Washington arteries, and the architecture that lined it included some relatively seedy embassies and prewar apartment buildings. Following Suzanne's instructions, they got off the bus at Columbia Road and walked into the Mount Pleasant neighborhood. Here the main streets were dominated by Central American immigrants, who lived in apartment buildings, shopped in bodegas where only Spanish was spoken, and worked hard to escape to the suburbs. But the back streets, steep, crooked, and tree-lined, belonged to yuppies: the younger ones living four or five to a house, the older ones bringing up their families in clapboard homes with front porches and small back gardens. Without too much difficulty, Zach and

Kate located Suzanne's little house on a steep street not far from the National Zoo.

They let themselves in and dropped their bags in a large front room equipped with a television set, VCR, CD player, beanbag chair, futon couch, and a large Earth Day poster. There was no air-conditioning, but the interior of the house was dark and relatively cool. No one seemed to be home, so they explored the downstairs, finding a sparsely furnished dining room and a sunny, modern kitchen overlooking a tiny garden. The refrigerator door was covered with postcards, recycling rules, and ads for local bands.

They conferred, consulted a map, and then ventured back into the heat. The Metro took them to Dupont Circle; then they walked to the Ambassador Hotel on Massachusetts Avenue, near some of the city's finest embassy buildings. Liveried doormen stood outside, calling taxis with brass whistles. There was almost no foot traffic and absolutely no restaurants or shops on the broad avenue, but a stream of cars and busses passed by noisily. Zach and Kate walked inside past the footmen and adjusted their eyes to the plush crimson interior. There was no obvious public space in which to sit and wait for Davies, so sheepishly they walked outside again and sat at a bus stop on Massachusetts Avenue.

It was sweltering under the translucent dome of the bus shelter. Zach's shirt was drenched with sweat, and salty perspiration kept stinging his eyes. They idly watched the front door of the hotel and waved to let a series of busses pass by without them. By four o'clock, they felt as if they had been broiled alive. Dark clouds started to gather and the wind picked up, spinning leaves and dust in little circles. Just ten minutes after the first cloud had appeared in the sky, lightning was crashing down and rain was pouring on the shelter like a waterfall. Zach made a brief foray into the rain to cool down, feeling as if he had just stepped under a warm shower; but he jumped back under the shelter again as a lightning bolt lit up the sky and thunder roared almost simultaneously. Through the back of the rain-drenched shelter, they could just make out the doorman under the Ambassador's marquee. Another lightning bolt struck and illuminated the hotel for an instant. Zach thought he saw a man in a long black raincoat and with an umbrella waiting for a taxi to pull under the marquee. Between flashes of lightning it was difficult to see through the back of the shelter, so Zach stuck his head around the corner. Through the rain, he could see the man fairly clearly, but not his face, which was obscured under a peaked cap. Another lightning bolt struck and lit up the man's face. "It's Davies!" Zach shouted.

"What's he doing?" said Kate, peering through the Plexiglas wall of the shelter.

"Waiting for a cab."

"Let's follow him," Kate yelled, just as Davies climbed into a taxi.

Zach ran out to the street corner and looked both ways in search of another cab. The rain came down so hard that the drops bounced off the sidewalk, and Zach's clothes were sodden. Davies's cab pulled out into Massachusetts Avenue, turned into the opposite lane, and then drove back toward Dupont Circle, stopping at a red light less than one hundred yards from where Zach stood.

Kate joined him at the curb and they frantically waved at four or five passing cabs. One pulled over and the driver asked them where they were going. There was an elegantly dressed woman in the back seat, and apparently she didn't mind sharing the taxi. Zach didn't want to say that they were trying to follow another cab, so he waved this one away. Meanwhile, Davies's taxi pulled away as the light turned green, only to stop again at another red light. They could barely make it out in the distance, its signal light indicating that it was going to drive around Dupont Circle. Zach watched it while Kate stood in the street under the pouring rain, trying to flag down a taxi.

Just as the light in front of Davies's cab turned green, a taxi pulled up next to Kate. Zach kept his eye on Davies, meanwhile climbing into the taxi with Kate. Their driver was a West African immigrant with a broad smile. "Where are you going?" he said.

"We're following a cab that just pulled around Dupont Circle," said Kate.

"You want me to catch him?"

"To follow him, yes," said Zach.

"No problem," said the driver, and he stepped on the accelerator, crossing the nearest intersection just as the light turned red.

"Where did he go?" he asked.

"Around the circle," said Zach.

"Do you know which street he turned into?"

"No."

"There are at least eight streets going out of Dupont Circle."

Zach cringed as they careened around the circle. Davies' cab had disappeared in heavy traffic.

"I tell you what," said the driver. "I assume he takes Mass Ave, okay?"

"Go for it," Kate agreed.

They turned into Massachusetts Avenue on the opposite side of Dupont Circle from the Ambassador Hotel. The driver said: "Three years in Washington, and you are my first spies." He laughed heartily; it was clear that he did not think that they were real agents.

"I think that's him," said Zach as they raced down Massachusetts Avenue, weaving their way through the other traffic. There was a cab ahead of them and Zach could barely make out Davies in the back seat.

"He will not see us," said the driver, pulling skillfully behind another car. They drove through an underpass, around another traffic circle, and farther down the avenue past the Washington Convention Center and an area of blighted buildings and empty lots. The rain stopped almost as suddenly as it had started and the sun came out again; steam rose from the wet sidewalks. There was a point at which traffic was diverted off Massachusetts Avenue, and as they waited at the corner of a numbered street, they found themselves directly behind Davies's cab. Zach and Kate ducked down in the back seat, and their driver laughed, saying, "He is the bad guy, I hope. I hope I have the good guys in my taxicab. I do not want to assist the bad guys."

They started moving again as the light changed, and the driver said, "You can come up again." They raised their heads and watched Davies's taxi as it turned down a numbered street and into an area of massive federal buildings. Their cab followed at a discreet distance, turning onto Pennsylvania Avenue, past the fortresslike FBI building, and on toward the huge glazed wedding cake of the Capitol at the end of the avenue. They turned onto Constitution Avenue and finally stopped in front of a vast white building in a modern minimalist style. Davies was getting out of his cab, so Kate paid and thanked their driver and then they exited on the street side of the taxi, watching Davies from behind.

He entered the building through a large tinted-glass door. They followed, trying to stay directly behind him, and noticing as they entered that they were walking into the Hart Senate Office Building. Inside was an airport-style security gate, through which they passed hurriedly, keeping an eye on Davies. Once past the gate, they followed him into a huge marble atrium with a Calder sculpture standing in the middle that was perhaps one hundred feet tall. They felt chilly in the air-conditioning, perhaps because their clothes were so wet. Davies walked across the hall at a brisk pace, swinging an umbrella in one hand while in the other he carried a cardboard portfolio. A regular briefcase would have been too bourgeois for Professor Davies, Zach thought.

He seemed to know where he was going. Past the Calder, he turned down a corridor and then climbed up a short flight of steps. There were few people in the cavernous building, so Zach worried that Davies might see him. "I'm going to drop back a bit," he whispered to Kate. "He knows me but he's never seen you before."

She nodded and followed Davies up the stairs. Zach waited for a few seconds and then followed Kate, keeping only her in view. At the top of the first flight of stairs, she stopped climbing and entered a long corridor that led out of the Hart Building and into an older, somewhat dingy building lit with fluorescent lights. Zach waited at the end of the corridor, which was so long that the other end was almost invisible, and watched Kate follow Davies into the distance. When she began to grow small, he started walking behind her. Suddenly, she turned around and walked back to join him.

"He went into an office," she said.

"You couldn't follow him inside?"

"No, it was a tiny place, very formal, with a receptionist at the desk."

"What was it?"

"The Committee on the Judiciary."

7 • It appeared that Davies had gone into the committee's staff offices. Farther down the hall was the hearing room, where Wendell Frye was being questioned. A long line of

people sat outside the door waiting to be admitted. Television cables, klieg lights, and other paraphernalia of the mass media were strewn outside the room. Kate and Zach joined the end of the line, not because they wanted to attend the hearings, but because they could keep the door to the staff office in view from there and yet remain inconspicuous.

The line was not moving at all. People—mostly young tourists and students—sat against the wall and read newspapers or talked in low voices. The door to the hearing room was jammed with visitors who craned their necks to get a view, and a Capitol police officer tried to keep a passage open for those who wanted to leave. Someone had a radio tuned to a station that was covering the hearings live, but from where Zach and Kate sat, it was impossible to make out much of what was being said. It sounded as if a single senator were giving a long, tedious speech. Two law students next to them discussed the meaning of stare decisis.

They sat like this for over an hour, moving only two spaces closer to the hearing-room door when a couple of reporters left. Then Kate pointed at the entrance to the staff room: Davies was coming out in the company of another soberly dressed, middle-aged man. He and his companion walked right past Kate and Zach while Zach tried to conceal his face by turning toward the wall. Then the two men walked farther down the corridor into the heart of the Dirksen Senate Office Building, with Kate and Zach in tow, Zach a few paces behind Kate.

Davies and his companion turned the corner onto another immense hall—the proverbial corridors of power, Zach thought—and stopped at a bank of elevators. Huddled by a water fountain, Zach and Kate kept their eyes on the two men. A bell rang, a door opened, and Davies and his partner entered an elevator that was going down.

Zach and Kate hurried over to the elevators. Again a bell

rang and they were about to get on the elevator when they
noticed an illuminated sign above the door: Senators Only.
From inside, two elderly men with blow-dried hair looked at
them suspiciously, so they took the stairs instead. One flight
down, Kate vanished through heavy wooden doors, gesturing to Zach that he should search the floor below. He ran
down the steps three at a time and timidly stuck his head
through a door marked "exit." Davies and his companion
were walking down a long corridor toward a security check.
Zach looked behind him to see if Kate was nearby, but apparently she was still upstairs, so he followed Davies. He
walked quickly and caught up with the two men as they approached an X-ray machine near the exit. He turned his face
to the wall and walked a few paces behind them, trying to
overhear their conversation. He thought he heard Davies say,
"Saved by the bell, then, eh?"

His companion nodded and said, "Looks that way." They
passed by the security gate and through a revolving door onto
the street. Standing near the curb under a bright sun, Davies
raised his hand to flag a taxi and then the two men shook
hands good-bye. Zach looked back down the corridor for
Kate, but she was nowhere in sight. He contemplated finding a cab to follow Davies again, but he had hardly any
money in his wallet and he didn't want to split up from Kate.
Davies's companion walked back up the stairs and past Zach
into the building; Zach followed him through the X-ray machine and went in search of Kate.

4 • It took them a while to find each other: Zach walked upstairs while Kate took the elevator down to the floor that he
had just left; and then they switched places again. They finally crossed paths near the committee room.

"No luck," said Kate.

"I was luckier," said Zach, and he told her what he had heard.

They decided to go back to Davies's hotel and confront him. Zach would demand his thesis; if Davies refused, then they would accuse him of participating in a conspiracy. Their evidence was circumstantial at best, but they could threaten to make trouble for Davies by trying to associate him with two missing dissertations, Charles's death, and the nomination of Wendell Frye. They could threaten to approach administrators at Yale, police in Virginia and Princeton, Charles's parents, the *Yale Daily News,* the *New Haven Register,* the *New York Times,* the American Philosophical Association, senators opposed to Judge Frye, investigative reporters for various alternative papers, and anyone else who might listen to them.

They caught the Metro at Union Station, and soon they were standing outside the Ambassador Hotel in the early-evening sun. They entered the lobby, once again feeling shabby and underdressed. A severely beautiful woman behind the counter asked them if she could help in some way: obviously, people dressed as they were could not be looking for a room. Zach cleared his throat and said that they wanted to see Professor Davies, who was staying at the hotel. The attendant called his room, spoke with him briefly, then cupped the receiver in her palm and asked Zach for his name.

"Zachary Blumberg," he said. "From Yale."

She spoke on the telephone again, and Zach thought he heard Davies bark, "Get rid of them." Then she hung up. "He does not recall your name, sir. Perhaps you would like to leave a telephone number?"

Zach shook his head and then he and Kate moved a few feet away from the desk to confer. They decided to sit down on a velvet-covered bench near the hotel elevators and wait for Davies. The woman behind the counter watched them as they took their seats. Two or three minutes later, a man in a dark suit approached them, covertly revealed a hotel detective's badge, and asked them if he could help them.

"No, thank you; we're just waiting for a friend," said Kate.

"Is he or she a guest at this hotel?" asked the detective in a polite but firm voice.

"That's right," said Kate genially, while Zach grew increasingly nervous. The words "house dick" kept running through his head.

"Did you call his room?" asked the security man.

"Yes," said Kate, but Zach said "No" almost simultaneously. He shut his eyes in dismay.

"This bench is for patrons only," said the security man. "I'm going to have to ask you to move along."

They beat a humiliating retreat to the bus shelter. It was still rush hour, so a large crowd waited for busses up Massachusetts Avenue. They got on the end of the line and kept an eye on the front door of the hotel. However, as they discussed the situation in whispers, they realized that Davies was unlikely to emerge immediately, and that if he did come out, he would probably leap into another taxi. Furthermore, they noticed that the hotel security officer was standing under the marquee, watching them.

Zach suggested another plan: communicating with Davies by mail. They decided to go back to Suzanne's house and compose a letter, which they could hand-deliver to the hotel the next morning when a new shift of receptionists and security people would be on hand. Kate called her sister to get directions to her house, and then they rode a bus back to Mount Pleasant.

Suzanne had a computer in her bedroom, and as soon as Zach and Kate arrived, she left them alone to compose a letter on it. Her room lay under the back eave of the house: it contained a small desk piled with cosmetics, papers, and a computer; a futon; and a freestanding rack of clothes. Kate flopped down on the futon while Zach sat at the terminal. Together, working slowly and discussing strategy at length, they composed the following letter:

August 21
Washington, D.C.

Professor H.P.T Davies
Ambassador Hotel

Dear Professor Davies:

    I have been informed that you are in possession of a fairly recent copy of my dissertation, which concerns the Comte de Maistre. All my other copies have been lost, or—as I believe—stolen, so I would very much like to get this copy back from you. Please call me at your earliest possible convenience.

The letter closed with Suzanne's telephone number and Zach's signature. When they had finished writing it and had printed a copy, they lay down together on the futon, glad for a moment's peace and rest.

    After four or five minutes, Suzanne knocked on the door and asked them if they wanted any dinner. Kate shouted that they had eaten, but that they would join her downstairs. Zach, disappointed, made a face, but he dutifully followed Kate down to the kitchen, where Suzanne was preparing an elaborate salad.

    Her house was full of roommates coming and going. Another woman, about twenty-five years old and dressed in a business suit and sneakers, was making pasta in the kitchen.

Two men of about the same age drank beer and watched the news on cable television in the front room, their ties loosened and their shoes kicked off. A third young woman had just arrived on a bicycle and was nervously preparing to go to a community meeting. These people were about the same age as Zach's classmates in graduate school, but the mood here was entirely different. Entry-level workers in white-collar offices had a much more realistic estimation of their own importance to the world than graduate students, who were paid—if poorly—to think about great issues of metaphysics and global history. Instead of brooding about the politics of critical theory or gynocolonization, Suzanne's roommates concerned themselves with whether or not the next membership mailing would go out on time; and they enjoyed their evenings and weekends with a pleasure that was only tempered by thoughts of Monday morning—or so Zach inferred after an evening in their company.

He quietly nursed a bottle of beer while Suzanne and Kate caught up on news and Kate told her sister the story of their recent adventures. They seemed comfortable and relaxed in each other's company—an unfamiliar experience for Zach, an only child. He felt somewhat out of place and would have excused himself, but he wasn't sure if there was anywhere else in the house where he could go and not be in the way.

In the kitchen, one of Suzanne's roommates chatted on the phone for over an hour, while the two guys in the living room watched a baseball game and argued loudly about hitting and fielding statistics. They spoke in a college argot that was familiar to Zach from his undergraduate days, full of expressions like "dude" and "from hell" and "way cool"; whereas students in Zach's doctoral program spoke an entirely different dialect, peppered with ironic allusions to trendy theorists. The other female housemate returned at around nine o'clock and vented her anger at the way the community meeting had gone. Apparently, the city was unwilling to do anything about broken lights on some nearby streets, despite a recent rape. Zach watched the whole scene with interest, wondering whether his chosen career really was the best for him.

At last people started going to bed. Zach and Kate were assigned the futon couch in the living room. It seemed very exposed to the rest of the house, so they slept with T-shirts and shorts on, but it was good to be alone together in the darkness.

ʃ • Suzanne had agreed to deliver Davies's letter on her way to work, so the next morning, Zach and Kate watched all the housemates eat their hurried breakfasts in sequence and then rush away to Metros and busses. Once they were alone, they settled down to wait for Davies's telephone call.

Zach switched on the television and found the Frye hearings on a cable station; senators were cross-examining a series of academic lawyers who were offering their opinions of Frye's qualifications. It was all fairly tedious. Kate read the newspaper and then started cleaning the kitchen as a favor to her sister. Zach offered to help but was turned down. When she finished, they took a shower together—an exciting first—and then lay down in Suzanne's room. The telephone rang once at about eleven and Zach ran downstairs (wrapped in a sheet) to answer it—but it was only a long-distance telephone company soliciting their patronage. They spent the rest of the morning dozing off, talking idly, and raiding the refrigerator.

By three o'clock in the afternoon, it was clear that Davies was not going to call. Kate called the Ambassador Hotel and asked for his room, but he was not answering—nor had he checked out. The receptionist also told her that Professor Davies had picked up his mail earlier that morning. They decided to compose another letter, which they could deliver that evening if Davies still had not called.

The letter, which they again composed jointly, read as follows:

August 22
Washington, D.C.

Professor H.P.T. Davies
Ambassador Hotel

Dear Professor Davies:

Since I have received no response to my letter of August 21, I feel that I have no choice but to make the following accusation. Earlier this month, my dissertation was erased from my computer and numerous copies of it were stolen from several cities in the Northeast. The same has happened to a graduate student at Princeton, Charles Wilson. He and I both were encouraged (or coerced) to choose our respective dissertation topics by you; and each kept in touch with you thereafter—he directly, and I through Professor Mollendorff. Moreover, our dissertation topics were both relevant to interpreting the covert philosophical theories of Otto Stern.

Charles Wilson has since been found dead in a Washington-area motel. I have learned that you possess a copy of my dissertation, but yesterday you refused to talk to me about it. Meanwhile, in the same city where Charles died, you have been residing for the last few weeks and consulting with staff members of the Senate Judiciary Committee—a body that is considering the nomination of Judge Wendell Frye to the Supreme Court. Judge Frye, Charles Wilson, and you were all members of a Yale secret society, Crypt, and Judge Frye appears to hold views consistent with those of Otto Stern. You could be expected to know about these views, since you were presumably present when he confessed his private thoughts to his fellow Crypt members in 1956.

This does not amount to a case against you for theft or murder. Nevertheless, it surely warrants an investigation, which in itself might damage your reputation. I do not state this as a threat, because even if I had no personal animus against you, I would still feel duty-bound to approach the police, the Yale administration, and the media. I will take these steps immediately, unless you contact me with an explanation for your behavior and a copy of my thesis.

I will be standing in the rotunda of the Jefferson Memorial at eleven o'clock tomorrow morning if you wish to meet me.

Sincerely,
Zachary Blumberg
Yale Philosophy Department

They had decided to offer to meet Davies in person, since he might not want to speak candidly on the telephone. In case they were dealing with a murderer, they thought it best not to meet him in his hotel room; and the Jefferson Memorial was a public spot that they both knew from movies and books. They rode the Metro to Dupont Circle and delivered their letter to the Ambassador Hotel, relieved to see that the receptionist and security guard had changed from the day before.

The evening passed slowly, feeling like the night before

an exam. Zach was nervous about a possible meeting with
Davies the next day, but perhaps more apprehensive that
there would be no meeting. If Davies did not appear, Zach's
hopes of getting his dissertation back would be extremely
slim. He, Kate, and Suzanne rented a movie and watched it
in the front room, interrupted repeatedly by telephone calls,
people at the front door, and shouted conversations up and
down the stairs. Zach found this all rather irritating. In addition, he felt reasonably sure that Suzanne did not like him.
Nevertheless, the evening passed without any outright un-
pleasantness, he slept well, and at about ten in the morning,
he and Kate made their way downtown on the Sixteenth
Street bus.

They got off the bus near the White House, which Zach
had never seen before except on television, and walked past
it to the Mall, which looked like a vast desert of dry grass
stretching from the Lincoln Memorial to the Capitol. Tourists
trudged by, almost all of them looking grumpy, and the heat
shimmered off the white marble buildings. They crossed the
Mall, skirting the base of the Washington Monument (which
reminded Zach of the Egyptian imagery favored by Masons
and Rosicrucians), and then sprinted across a highway
through a break in traffic. The white Palladian dome of the
Jefferson Memorial stood across the Tidal Basin from them.

They walked around the Tidal Basin under the Japanese
cherry trees, which looked rather scrubby with their blos-
soms gone. The memorial itself was built on a shiny white
platform jutting into the water: on one side was a highway
and the broad Potomac; in the other direction stood the
Washington Monument and, behind that, the White House.
They ascended the marble steps into the relatively cool interior of the memorial, overseen by a thirty-foot bronze statue
of Jefferson. In silhouette, his jutting chin and military bearing made him look resolute, incorruptible.

The interior of the building was embellished with some of Jefferson's most famous lines. "Almighty God hath created the mind free," said one inscription; another read, "I have sworn upon the altar of God eternal hostility against every form of tyranny over the mind of man." Zach pointed at the inscriptions, which were written in unpunctuated Roman capital letters, and said wryly, "Old Jefferson had no problem with cultural relativism and the haunting specter of nihilism. 'We hold these truths to be self-evident.' Now what would Nietzsche say to that?"

It was ten minutes before eleven. A U.S. Park Police officer, a tall black woman with a steely expression, stood near the front of the building. Zach appreciated her presence, which reduced the chance that they would be abducted. There were a few Asian tourists at the base of the monument, and a group of bored Boy Scouts sat on the side steps receiving instruction on Jefferson's greatness.

Eleven o'clock came and went with no Davies. Zach and Kate sat down glumly on the front steps, watching the White House in the distance. It was intensely humid and Zach could again smell pollution in the air, but there was an intermittently refreshing breeze from the Potomac and it was quiet near the memorial except for the cries of the sea gulls and the faint sound of traffic.

"What do we do now?" said Zach.

Just then they heard the sound of someone clearing his voice behind them. They both turned around and immediately saw a man in a dark suit emerge from inside the pavilion. They rose and approached him; his face was concealed in the deep shadow cast by Jefferson's statue, but he looked as if he could be Hannibal Davies.

"Mr. Blumberg?" he said.

"Yes." Zach's voice broke a little as he spoke.

"Follow me."

Davies crossed the pavilion and descended the steps past Kate and Zach. They exchanged shrugs and decided to follow him, with Zach looking around to see if there were any potential witnesses in sight. He was happy to see a group of slow-moving retired tourists who were disembarking from a bus marked "Mercy Christian Church, Scranton, PA."

Davies walked briskly down the two flights of steps, then around the perimeter of the monument, across an access road and a parking lot, and on toward the highway. Zach and Kate caught up with him near the edge of the road.

"Where are we going?" Zach asked.

"We are endeavoring not to be observed or followed."

At the edge of the highway, Davies flagged a cab. Kate said, "I'm not getting in there with him."

Davies said, "Suit yourself. If you want to talk, come with me."

Zach and Kate looked at each other doubtfully, silently decided to take a chance, and got into the back seat with Davies holding the door for them. He barked, "Twenty-first and M, northwest, please." The cab pulled a U-turn during a break in traffic and then swung past the Tidal Pool and around the base of the Lincoln Memorial. Long vistas opened up in every direction, replete with the symbols of imperial power and official culture: the Capitol, the Founding Fathers ensconced in their respective classical monuments, the National Cathedral above them on a hill, Arlington Cemetery just across the river, the National Gallery of Art, the Kennedy Center. The nation's capital betrayed no sign of metaphysical angst, no knowledge of the death of God.

Davies sat bolt upright in the cab, looking straight ahead like a soldier on parade. Zach, seated next to him, mostly stared at his hands, while Kate looked out of the window. They left the Mall and turned north, until they pulled up at the corner of M Street, where they were surrounded by of-

fice buildings and crowds of workers. Davies paid and exited the cab, then walked briskly down the block with Kate
and Zach in tow; he certainly seemed to have taken them to
a safe and public spot. However, he next turned into a wide
alley that had been converted into a small shopping center
and marched quickly through it to the next block. At Twentieth Street, he hailed another taxi. Zach and Kate exchanged
puzzled glances, but they got into the cab as Davies again
opened the door for them.

This time he barked: "Take the Arlington Memorial
Bridge."

Thinking of Charles and feeling a fit of panic, Zach said,
"Where are we going now?"

"We need a private place." Davies didn't look at Zach as
he spoke. Their taxi drove back to the Lincoln Memorial,
then across the broad and placid Potomac on a bridge that
was virtually empty of traffic. Gold, fascist-style statues of
men with horses guarded the bridge. At the other side of the
river, Davies said, "Keep going." The expression on his face
was grim. They crossed a highway at a traffic light, then drove
up a long ceremonial avenue lined with military monuments.
Behind them stood the mock–Roman temple that housed
Lincoln's brooding statue; directly ahead was Robert E.
Lee's Doric mansion and the National Cemetery. At the huge
gates of the cemetery, Davies said, "This is fine, driver." He
paid the fare and the cab pulled away, leaving them alone
before the cemetery gates.

Davies looked around carefully and then, apparently satisfied, he began leading them up the hill toward the Lee Mansion, past thousands of white tombstones arrayed in military
formation.

"Who is the young lady?" he said.

"I'm a friend of Charles's," Kate replied.

"Your letter claims that Charles is dead." Davies looked only at Zach when he spoke; otherwise, he stared straight ahead.

"So that was news to you?" said Zach, skepticism obvious in his voice.

Davies stopped and turned on him. "It certainly was. Have you proof of this—that he is dead?"

Kate said: "We were at his memorial service. There's been an inquest. He's dead; that much we know."

"Where?" said Davies. "Where did he—die?"

"Here in Arlington," said Zach. "In a motel."

"And the cause?"

"Allegedly, suicide."

"I mean the efficient cause: poison? a gunshot? what?"

"A gunshot," said Zach. "Fired at close range. But surely you know more about this than we do."

"Surely not. I spoke with Charles late last week. He was depressed, distraught even, but I certainly expected to see him again. Then he disappeared and—now this."

"Why was he depressed?" said Zach.

"And what were you doing talking to him?" Kate asked.

They were walking along a steep path broken by occasional flights of stairs that ran parallel to the Potomac. The grand sweep of Washington gradually came into view above the field of tombstones. Zach and Kate trailed a few steps behind, unwilling to follow Davies into a trap; but a few tourists were visible in the distance, so they decided to proceed.

"It seems to me," said Davies, "that we are being hindered by a certain amount of mutual mistrust. You appear to believe that I stole your dissertation, murdered poor Charles, and so forth; and I have my own suspicions about you. You certainly seem to have acquired a great deal of information

about me by underhanded methods. Mr. Blumberg, can I see
some identification?"

"You know who I am."

"I have an unusual degree of difficulty remembering faces,
unfortunately. My mind does not produce internal images,
as other people *say* that their minds do. Not wanting to go
by your word alone, I would prefer to see some identification, please."

Zach showed him his university ID card. "Very well," said
Davies. "That at least establishes that you have a clear and
relatively benign motive for snooping around. When did you
say your dissertation vanished?"

"Almost two weeks ago."

"You had several copies, and all of them disappeared simultaneously?"

"That's right. But you also have a copy, and I would like
it back, please."

"I *had* a copy, yes, as I had a copy of Charles's work. But
no more, unfortunately."

Kate said: "So, you're claiming to be a fellow victim
here—is that what you're getting at? I'm sorry, but I don't
think that will wash, Professor."

Davies scowled; he was not used to being addressed this
way. Nevertheless, he replied in a calm enough voice: "Very
well. I can understand your skepticism. You have blundered
into fairly deep and shark-infested waters, you have lost a
friend and a great deal of work; and I am, I suspect, a rather
mysterious figure in all of this. So why not proceed as follows? In the letter yesterday, you revealed some or perhaps
all of your cards; now let me show you my hand."

"Fine," said Zach. They stopped at an intersection of
paths near a small grove of trees that surrounded the tomb
of one of Lincoln's children or grandchildren. Davies stood
against the sun so that it was difficult to see his face clearly.

To Zach's right lay the panorama of the Mall and the federal buildings of Washington. There was no one else in sight.

Davies began to speak, still addressing Zach alone: "Many years ago, as you have inferred, I met Mr. Wendell Frye and became acquainted with his views. I did not take them very seriously at the time. As you know—or ought to know—it is my firm belief that facts are available to scientists alone and that philosophy can at best help to clear up some conceptual issues regarding methods of reasoning. Everything else is pure speculation, metaphysics, and therefore nonsense; and that includes morality, aesthetics, politics, and so on."

He stared directly at Zach, apparently demanding an answer. To Zach, all of this was anathema, but he nodded to indicate that he understood. Davies continued: "The meaninglessness of all ethical claims has never troubled me in the slightest. In my professional work, I deal with logic, with the a priori; otherwise, I conduct my personal life with dignity, I believe, but I do not concern myself much with how other people choose to ruin *their* lives. However, my friend Wendell was more sentimental, I suppose: more susceptible to fears and worries about nihilism, moral degeneracy, that sort of thing."

He turned and started walking farther uphill; Zach and Kate walked alongside. After a moment, Davies continued: "This aspect of Wendell's thought was nothing unusual, no reason for any special worry; I did my work, he did his, and when we met at a faculty party or something of that nature, we talked mostly about academic politics. On the other hand, it did not escape my notice that Wendell had fallen in with a rather odd group of so-called philosophers, to whom you allude in your letter: the followers of Otto Stern."

He stopped walking and paused for a moment, looking in the direction of the Capitol dome. Then he said, "This especially came to my attention when Wendell tried to con-

vert a promising young student of mine to Sternian views. As
you have correctly concluded, Frye, Charles Wilson, and I
are all members of a senior society at Yale. At society meet-
ings, dinners, and so forth, I overheard a number of interesting conversations between Wendell and Charles. On other
occasions, I did my best to disabuse young Charles of the
foolish worries and weak logic that Wendell was trying to im-
part to him."

"You mean you tried to persuade him that Stern was
wrong?" said Kate, still skeptical.

"That's right. Indeed, I believe that I succeeded in convincing Charles—who was, after all, an exceptionally bright
young man—that this Otto Stern was barking up entirely the
wrong tree. In the process, however, I became perhaps more
concerned about the whole business than I ought to have
been. You see, in general, I do not give a damn how other
people lead their lives. But one thing bothers me—it gets
under my skin—and that is when someone who claims to be
a philosopher engages in obscurantism. Call it professional
pride, I suppose, but I believe we philosophers are seekers
after clarity, and I don't want to see my colleagues betray that
goal."

Zach thought that this was somewhat hypocritical, given
the impenetrability of Davies's own prose; but he said nothing.

"Now," said Davies, "here was Frye: a lawyer, admit-
tedly, and not a professor of philosophy, but nevertheless
philosophically trained and rapidly rising in his profession
on the strength of a theory that was built on *lies*. This disturbed me—offended me, I suppose—and caused me to
abandon my usual posture of armed neutrality with respect
to political events. Generally, my attitude is: don't prevent
me from doing my work, which is serious and sound, and I
won't pay any attention to you. My only previous foray into

politics had occurred when some long-haired baboons tried to block me from teaching, late in the sixties. But here I was concerned with the career of a respectable political figure, a judge. The point is, you see, that I didn't care what in hell he thought; I just didn't like his obscurantism and sophistry. Do you understand me?"

Zach and Kate nodded.

"Very well," said Davies, turning to walk uphill again. "It came to my attention through Crypt sources, who are extremely well placed in this town, that Frye was more or less a shoo-in for the Supreme Court. His party had put him on the federal bench, you see, so that he could sit there for a few years, and then they could claim that he had judicial experience when they nominated him for the high court. I should have washed my hands of the whole affair and gotten back to work—but clearly, I didn't. Instead, I decided to attack old Wendell in print, reveal him for what he was."

Kate was shaking her head, and Davies, noticing this, looked at her briefly. Then he shrugged almost imperceptibly and continued to speak, looking only at Zach.

"In this effort to discredit Frye, Charles was my guide and informant. He still went to Sternian convocations, acted like an initiate, and picked up what information he could. It soon became clear to us that the Sternians not only had a secret doctrine of so-called nihilism, which I had known about all along from overhearing Frye, but that they revealed their duplicity in their texts, predominantly by means of allusions to such thinkers as Nietzsche, Maistre, and Heidegger. Now, I knew nothing about these maniacs: Nietzsche and his ilk represent the antithesis of everything I stand for, mad Germans with obscure meanings and high-strung temperaments. On the other hand, Sternian books seemed quite innocuous unless you recognized that they were duplicitous, and that could only be proved by showing that they alluded to Nietzsche and similar figures. This much you have discovered on your own," he said to Zach.

Zach muttered, "Yes."

Davies said, "I had no time, and frankly little inclination, to read obscure Germans, but Charles was willing to carry out a study of Nietzsche, and I found him a graduate scholarship on which to do it. We also wanted to cover Maistre, so I had you do that. We were not sure that Maistre's work was relevant at all, but we thought that a nice, workmanlike general study would be helpful; and Mollendorff told me that you could probably handle it. If any of your findings interested us, I could ask Mollendorff to have you pursue whatever lines of inquiry I chose."

"That was very convenient for you," said Zach.

"Well, one uses the resources that one has available," said Davies. Kate glared at him, but Davies continued: "In due course, Frye was nominated for the Supreme Court. I had hoped to have published an article against the Sternians by then, but our work was moving too slowly. It was difficult, you see, to pin old Stern down; and Frye's own work seemed to be completely devoid of Nietzschean allusions. Presumably, it had been judged too risky for him to spread the gospel of secret nihilism; they left that task to his academic allies, while he just acted like a straightforward conservative."

Zach muttered that he had guessed the same thing. Then Davies said, "Although I had no hard evidence, I approached the Senate Judiciary Committee staff through my Crypt contacts and gave them what information I had. Because I was acquainted with several of the senators on that committee, the staff listened to me. Indeed, their lawyers and I tried to work out a line of questioning that could get Frye into trouble. The difficulty was that we would have to force him to admit that he was a Sternian, *and* trick him into revealing that Stern had been a secret nihilist, *and* prove that Frye knew this about Stern. You can see that this would not have been easy."

Again, Zach and Kate both nodded.

"Then two things happened in rapid succession. First, Charles called me in Washington, very excited, to say that he had discovered a much more straightforward way of proving that Stern was a covert nihilist. It would not be necessary to show any allusions to other writers; Stern's texts contained an internal clue to their real meaning. However, Charles could not elaborate this hypothesis on the telephone, since it was rather complicated and depended on reading the relevant texts in a certain way. In any case, he wanted to confirm his theory first by speaking to a Cornell professor who was a Sternian. Charles wanted to approach this fellow because, although he called himself a disciple of Stern, he did not seem to be a duplicitous or obscurantist author. He thought that the fellow might be a kind of dupe, who would know a great deal about the Sternians without actually belonging to the secret inner circle of the sect."

Zach and Kate looked at each other; Kate gave a nod as if to say that Davies's story was plausible. Davies continued. "The next thing that happened was that Charles called again, this time to tell me something extraordinary: all of his important notes and every copy of his manuscript had disappeared, as if spontaneously. He wanted me to send him my copy of his dissertation, you see. But when I looked around my hotel room, that copy was gone too, and so was your thesis, I'm afraid to say."

For an instant, Davies looked almost sympathetic. But then his face resumed its usual resolute expression. "It seemed clear that somehow the Sternians were on to us, that they had become worried by Charles's recent discovery, and that they wanted to stop us however they could. Charles promised to come down here as soon as he had met with his Cornell friend, who might still have a copy of his thesis. Meanwhile, I continued my work with the committee counsel, but it was difficult to proceed without any evidence about Nietzsche or Maistre, nor any word from Charles."

Davies paused for a moment, as if considering how to proceed. Then he said, "Finally, Charles called me. He had retrieved his thesis from the Cornell professor and had hidden it securely. However, he had also been approached by another Sternian acquaintance, and they had had a long conversation about the need to keep nihilism secret, and such poppycock. I demanded that Charles tell me about his new method of decoding Stern, but he hesitated, refused point-blank to tell me where he was staying, and merely promised to call me back. He had obviously been persuaded once again that nihilism was a real concern and that obscurantism was the appropriate response to it. Meanwhile, the Frye nomination was hurtling toward a vote. And that was the last I heard of him."

Davies had stopped talking. He turned and stared out toward the Capitol.

"I know what clue Charles must have used to unlock Stern's code," said Zach, after a pause.

"Don't tell him," Kate warned.

"It doesn't much matter if you tell me or not, at this point," said Davies. "I admit that I am curious, but I can understand why you might still be suspicious of me. My story is coherent, but coherence is a weak test of truth, as we know."

"If you were telling the truth," said Zach, "then you would let me meet directly with the Senate staff people who are working to oppose the Frye nomination. You would let me make the best case I can against him."

"I'm not sure that they would want to meet with you at this point, now that confirmation appears certain; they have a great deal of work to do. However, I have no objection to trying. It has been my consistent goal to defeat him."

CHAPTER 8

Several hours later, Zach and Kate were once again on the road, this time driving north in a rented subcompact car. They left Washington by way of New York Avenue, a tawdry urban highway lined with motels that rented rooms by the hour, fast-food joints, used-car lots, and check-cashing establishments ("No ID Required"). The setting sun cast a warm, superficially benign light over the neon, tarmac, and refuse. Zach locked his door and wished that Kate would do the same.

She said, "So, what did you think of the meeting?"

"I thought it went okay." Zach looked at Kate's face to get an idea of what she was thinking, but she watched the road intently and he could only see her silhouette. "What did you think?" he said.

"They weren't exactly overwhelmed by our information."

"Would you have been? Our evidence is pretty circumstantial, you know. And what is it evidence of, anyway? Malfeasance? No. Criminal behavior? No. Sexual peccadilloes? Hardly. We're accusing the guy of holding a position that he doesn't really believe in. So what else is new in Washington? If some senator went on national TV with our material, and it didn't seem relevant or important to viewers, he'd look like an idiot."

"I guess you're right."

"Actually, I thought it was nice of them to agree to a short delay. They wouldn't have done that if we hadn't been with Davies."

"Yeah, but I think they'll only postpone the end of the hearings for as long as they can make the delay look like a genuine scheduling problem. As soon as it starts to look like they're procrastinating deliberately, they'll quit."

"Well, how could they defend a postponement? By saying that the nation has to wait because two young grad students are making a desperate trip to Ithaca to see if they can track down the last copy of a missing dissertation that might contain something that could possibly sink the nomination? I don't think that would sound too great on the evening news."

"On the other hand, if we can find Charles's thesis, it might really contain something good. Remember, they killed him, but they haven't even *tried* to kill you. So maybe he was on to something that applied directly to Frye. Maybe that's why he went down to Washington."

"That's great. So I'll find it and they'll kill me, too."

"We'll be okay." Her voice did not carry a great deal of conviction.

They reached the Capital Beltway, beyond which hardworking, common-sense, no-nonsense American citizens were said to dwell. Kate said, "You're supposed to be navigating. How do we get to Ithaca?"

Zach began to unfold the map in the near darkness, but before he could find the right section, Kate had had to make some rapid decisions in heavy traffic, and soon they were heading northeast toward Baltimore—not the most direct route to upstate New York, although they still managed to cross the Pennsylvania border by eleven-thirty. As they drank coffee at a fast-food franchise near Wilkes-Barre, Kate said, "Why don't you call Andrew now? I guess it's okay to invite ourselves to stay with him, but we ought to give him at least a few hours' notice."

"I was thinking, why don't we just stay at a motel?"

Kate made a face. "On your expense account?"

"That's true." Zach suddenly felt crabby. "It has to be your money, so it definitely should be your decision."

"I wouldn't mind spending the money for a good reason, say to avoid making a nuisance for Andrew. But I don't feel like laying out forty bucks so that you don't have to be jealous for a night. Plus, motels are depressing."

A pimply teenager mopped the floor by the molded-plastic booth where they sat. An obese couple munched loudly nearby. Zach observed them while he considered how to continue the conversation without further hostilities. He decided that he would rather stay at Andrew's place than fight about it.

"I'll call him," he said. He got up slowly, intending to look for a telephone.

"Does he annoy you?"

She was still sitting in the booth; he stood a few feet away and said: "Sometimes. He's too slick."

"You shouldn't be jealous."

"I thought you liked him."

"I like anyone who likes me."

Zach pouted again. He thought, So that's why she's involved with me. Then he thought, And she did like Andrew; and he liked her. While he walked away in search of a phone, he tried to decide which of these facts was the more depressing.

Finding a telephone near the men's room, he began to make a call with his charge card, wondering how he could possibly pay the bill at the end of the month. Just as he was giving Andrew's telephone number to the operator, he felt a hand gripping his wrist; he jumped with fright and turned around quickly. It was Kate. She pushed the receiver back into its cradle as the operator's voice faintly repeated, "Sir? Sir?" Then she hugged him hard, and they held the embrace for a long time while the sounds of the mop and the slamming men's-room door played in the background.

Finally, Zach grinned and said, "Let me call him now."

"You sure?"

"Yeah."

2 • They reached Ithaca shortly before three o'clock in the morning and drove uphill to Andrew's house. They saw just one other car on the silent Ithaca streets: a dark Lexus sedan that left the highway with them and drove behind their car to College Town before heading onto campus. Lights were still on in Andrew's house, and as they walked onto his porch, he emerged, wearing a T-shirt, boxer shorts, and a bathrobe. He and Kate exchanged European-style kisses on the cheek; he and Zach shook hands; and then they all went into the kitchen to drink herbal tea. They spoke in low voices to avoid waking his roommates, but Andrew himself seemed perfectly wide awake. He had been smoking, eating Concord grapes—the seeds lay in piles on the wooden surface of the kitchen table—and reading Baudrillard.

"So, what have you two intrepid sleuths cooked up to do next?" he asked, after he had heard them describe their adventures in Princeton, Connecticut, and Washington.

"We're going to try to talk to Hausman," said Kate. "He knows where the last copy of Charles's dissertation is hidden."

"Sounds good," said Andrew. They finished their mugs of tea and then rose from the table. Andrew said, "Zach, are you okay sleeping in my room upstairs?"

Kate put her arm around Zach's waist and said, "Andrew, I'm with Zach now."

"No kidding? Dude, congratulations! You two may sully my futon together, then." Beneath Andrew's bravado, Zach thought that he could detect a hint of regret; and so he felt renewed goodwill toward his old friend.

3 • The next morning, they woke up relatively early and walked across campus toward Hausman's home, intending simply to ring his front doorbell unannounced. It had rained just before dawn, and now the sidewalks were steamy under the morning sun. The big old frame houses near campus looked comfortable and secure amid their lawns and maples and box hedges. From one point on the hilly campus, they could see Ithaca spread out below them; it looked more like a forest than a city, so few glimpses of buildings appeared between the trees.

They turned onto Hausman's street and approached his house. Zach felt apprehensive, thinking about the hostile way in which their previous conversation had ended. He was considering how to begin a new discussion with Hausman when Kate suddenly grabbed his arm and stopped him. She pointed farther down the street toward a dark green Lexus that faced away from them, parked opposite the Hausmans' residence.

"See that?" she whispered.

"Is that the car we saw last night when we first got to Ithaca?"

"Yeah, I'm sure of it. I started watching it in my mirror when it pulled out of the parking lot in Wilkes-Barre behind us."

"He followed us from Pennsylvania?"

"From D.C., presumably. He had D.C. plates."

"No kidding?"

They couldn't see the license plates from where they were standing. They crouched down behind parked cars and approached the Lexus from the rear. When they were about a hundred feet away, Kate peered around a minivan that was parked outside a big, barnlike red house. She turned around to face Zach, who stood behind her out of sight of the Lexus, and whispered: "D.C. plates; two guys sitting in there."

They retreated back to the end of the block and then moved securely out of sight onto a nearby street.

"Should we go into the house with those guys sitting there?" Zach had a habit of asking the obvious question in times of crisis.

They exchanged shrugs. Then Kate said, "What if we got backup?"

"What do you mean?"

"What if we just brazenly walked up to the front door and rang the bell, right? But meanwhile, Andrew and a couple of his more macho friends, if he has any, drove down the street and parked somewhere out of sight, ready to respond if we needed them. Would that work?"

They decided to give it a try. They returned to Andrew's house and found him still sleeping on the living-room couch, so they roused him and explained the situation. "At last, a chance to prove my mettle," he said, going upstairs to his bedroom to make some calls to his burliest friends. He returned in a few minutes to say that they could put their plan into action at about noon.

At five minutes to twelve, Zach and Kate once again walked down Hausman's street, passing the Lexus without appearing to notice it. They walked up Hausman's driveway, past rain-soaked tricycles and skateboards, and rang the doorbell. The wooden door was wide open, but the screen was shut and it was difficult to see into the dark interior of the house. Soon a boy of about six walked into view, barefoot and wearing a Lords of the Cosmos T-shirt and Cornell shorts.

"Is your daddy home?" Kate asked.

The boy wandered away without a word, but after a minute they could hear him shout, "Mom!" Zach and Kate backed away from the door and thought silently about what to do if only Hausman's wife turned out to be home. She arrived almost immediately and opened the screen door, again wearing a long sleeveless denim dress and a coral necklace.

"Oh," she said, "it's you two. My husband was very upset after he spoke to you last time. He has a lot on his mind and it's not good for him to be upset at his age."

"Ma'am, we really think he'd like to hear what we have to say," said Kate.

Hausman's wife looked at them dubiously, but then Professor Hausman himself came into view behind her. "What is it, darling?" he said, in his faint European accent. He was wearing khaki shorts and a blue oxford shirt with patches of sweat under each armpit. He saw Zach and Kate and said angrily, "What do you want?"

Zach began, "Professor—"

"You are not really journalists, are you?"

"Sir, we have news that you really will want to hear," said Zach.

"It'll just take a minute," said Kate, adopting what Zach considered a slightly patronizing tone.

"All right. All four of us, then. On the porch." Hausman turned to lead them inside; his wife, scowling, watched them enter. To her son she said, "Ivo, play with your tricycle, okay?" The grown-ups walked through the dark hall to the porch, and everyone found somewhere to sit, either on a piece of rusty lawn furniture or on a cardboard box. There was a moment of silence during which Zach and Kate exchanged looks; then Zach said, "Professor, have you heard what happened to Charles?"

Hausman shook his head. In a slow, deliberate voice, Zach said, "Professor, he is dead."

Hausman looked angry rather than sad. "What is this?" he cried. His wife stood up and walked behind his chair, resting her hands on his shoulders.

"It appears to have been suicide, in a Washington motel," said Kate. "Professor, we came here on false pretenses last time, but that was because we didn't know whether or not we could trust you. Really, we're on the same side as you and we want very much to help. I was a friend of Charles's; in fact, I was briefly—well, I was his friend." She glanced apologetically at Zach. "That's my motivation in this whole business: to find out for sure what happened to him and to see that those responsible are punished. And Zach here—Zach Blumberg is his real name—he's the other guy who had his dissertation stolen. He's the guy that Charles was going to see in New York just before he disappeared."

Hausman looked very skeptical, but Zach said, "Sir, perhaps you would be able to judge us better if we told you our whole story. Would that be possible?" Hausman did not reply, so after waiting a minute, Zach began a brief summary of everything that had happened to him since his dissertation first vanished. As the story progressed, Hausman's face seemed to relax and he began to listen more sympathetically. He even started muttering "ja, ja" softly to himself and nodding. When Zach had finished, he said, "So, I think I believe you. What is it that you want from me now?"

Kate said, "First of all, we wanted you to know what's really going on. You have a right to know."

"Also," said Zach, "we want you to consider helping us. We understand that you know where a copy of Charles's dissertation is hidden." Hausman stiffened visibly, so Zach continued as quickly as he could. "We're not asking you to give it to us. If we could just see it, or see a *copy* of it. You see, we want to expose these Sternians so that we can keep Judge Frye from being confirmed. And for that, we need to know exactly what Charles was writing; it's a crucial piece of evidence."

Hausman shook his head almost imperceptibly and glanced up at his wife. She stared dubiously at Zach, who said, "Look, let's say that we're lying and we're really Sternian conspirators. What benefit would we get from seeing a copy of the dissertation? We'd already have the original, right?"

"Actually," said Hausman, "I believe you. Your whole story, I believe it. The problem is, I am not sure that I want to expose the Sternians. Have you thought about the consequences of this? Perhaps you don't understand: you are young, and as Americans, you are naïve. But I have seen a total breakdown in values. I have seen what happens when no one believes in good and evil. It is what Nietzsche forecast: the long fulfillment and cycle of breakdown, devastation, wreckage, and catastrophe that is now hanging over Europe because of nihilism and the death of God."

"You really think a few philosophy professors have had any influence on our culture?" said Kate. Hausman's face did not reveal what he was thinking, so Kate added: "And what about democratic values? Aren't they worth something? Lying to the public is kind of a betrayal of those values, isn't it?"

"Right," said Zach. "But I know what you're thinking, Professor: democratic values are no values at all. You can't just say 'What the people believe shall rule,' because first they have to decide what to believe. And if they're all nihilists, then what is there for them to believe in? But Professor, if you want to prevent nihilism in this country, the way to do that is not by importing a bunch of sophisticated European philosophy professors who try to insinuate themselves into the federal government. It would never work. The best way is to recognize the robustness of our own, weird, American values, which include the belief that public officials shouldn't systematically deceive the public."

"I have been thinking about those questions since before you were born," said Hausman. "The reasons for and against what you say are long and complex. I have reached a sort of stalemate, I suppose; I cannot decide what to do. But I know what I *want* to do—I want to hurt those bastards somehow." He smiled wryly and his wife squeezed his shoulders. Zach and Kate began nodding and smiling rather foolishly. Then Hausman said, "All right, why wait? You want the thesis, let's go and get the thesis. We will stop those charlatans."

He rose and led the way to the front door. "You want to take a drive with me?" he asked. "We will get the dissertation right now; then we can make a copy at my department and you can use it as you see fit."

Zach and Kate agreed, and then the three of them went outside and climbed into the Hausmans' huge old station wagon, which was parked under a carport at the head of the driveway. Hausman's wife remained in the house, holding her son's hand. Hausman backed the car down the driveway. Zach noticed that the Lexus began to move as they drove by it. At the corner, they passed a severely dented 1970's American gas-guzzler that belonged to one of Andrew's roommates. Zach saw Andrew in the front seat of that car, giving a covert thumbs-up sign. This is going to be a little convoy, Zach thought.

As they drove through the steep, tree-lined streets of Ithaca and neighboring Cayuga Heights, Hausman said, "I told Charles to mail the manuscript to a friend of mine in Anthropology who's on leave this year at the University of Costa Rica. Their next-door neighbors' children pick up their mail and stack it on Dennis's desk, so Charles's dissertation should be there. I have a key because I agreed to go over to Dennis and Sara's house once a month or so to check for important mail. The forwarding to Costa Rica is no good, apparently."

Zach nodded and peered surreptitiously into the rearview mirror at the Lexus, which followed about a block behind. Andrew's car was nowhere to be seen.

They descended on a steep road toward the lake, then took a sharp right turn and climbed back up the palisades on a densely wooded road. As they drove uphill, Hausman said: "There's something that I haven't told you yet, but it may prove quite important. I didn't tell you about it until now because I didn't trust you fully. But when you see Charles's dissertation, you'll see what I'm talking about."

"What is it?" said Zach. "Tell us now."

"Charles had—or claimed to have—more than merely circumstantial evidence about Otto Stern's secret doctrines."

"He had worked out the code, right?" said Zach.

"More than that. His dissertation contains quotations from unpublished manuscript documents in Stern's own handwriting. These were obviously meant to be secret documents, because they gave explicit instructions to insiders about how to preserve the secret truth of nihilism, what political steps to take, how to recruit followers—that kind of thing."

"Did you see the documents?" said Kate, from the back seat.

"Not the originals. I don't think that Charles trusted me enough to show them to me."

"How about copies?" asked Zach.

"He had photocopies of the actual pages from which he had quoted sentences. He showed one to me so that I could verify that it was in Otto's handwriting."

"Which it was?" said Kate.

"As far as I could tell. I'm no expert, but it looked like Otto."

"I wonder how he got those manuscripts," said Zach. "Did he say?"

"No. I asked him, but he wouldn't say."

At last they turned onto a driveway and approached a big modern redwood house with solar panels on the roof and expanses of glass on every side. The house sat in the middle of a substantial wooded lot, although neighboring homes were visible in each direction.

Hausman parked under a basketball hoop near a two-car garage. They got out of the station wagon and approached the house; no other cars or people were in sight, but a dog barked in the distance. Hausman took out a key and opened the front door. They stepped inside to find a high entrance room with rafters and skylights, hung with Central American rugs and masks. Hausman led them past a large dining room whose panoramic windows faced the garden, and then into a study lined with books, mostly paperbacks in Spanish. A large redwood desk supported a computer, a laser printer, a telephone, and a tall pile of packages and letters. Hausman began sorting through the mail while Zach absentmindedly examined the books and Kate discovered a little stone statuette of a well-endowed man in a state of high excitement.

She wiggled her eyebrows suggestively, and then Hausman said, "Here it is." He held a large manila envelope in his hand. He ripped open the package and looked inside, then pulled out a thick manuscript. "This is it," he said, flipping rapidly through the pages.

Just then they were startled by a voice from behind them. "Professor Hausman?" A young man had spoken; he was blond and dressed in casual but expensive-looking clothes. A companion, also young and blond, stood next to him, holding a briefcase in his left hand.

"Who are you?" said Hausman. Zach backed away and looked for an exit. There was a large window, but it did not look as if it would open easily.

"We're friends," said the man with the briefcase, but he did not smile. He had an American accent and reminded Zach of many Yale students. "It seems that we have arrived just in time to persuade you not to make a serious mistake. You don't want to betray everything that Otto Stern stood for, do you?"

"What did Otto Stern stand for?" said Hausman. "I used to think I knew."

"You still know perfectly well."

"I wasn't aware that he was interested in playing political games. I thought he kept his mind on higher, more permanent things."

"Well, the philosopher has to go back into the cave now and then to keep things from getting out of hand, doesn't he? And if Stern wouldn't do that himself, well, he's passed away now. We're his students' students, and we're ready to put the great man's ideas into practice."

"Weren't you at Charles's memorial service?" Kate asked suddenly.

"Oh, yeah," said the man who was not carrying the briefcase. "I remember you." He smiled flirtatiously.

His companion seemed displeased by this exchange. He addressed Hausman, saying: "Don't give them the manuscript."

"Why not?" said Hausman. "There is no good or evil, right? So I might as well do what gives me pleasure for a change. And nothing would give me more pleasure than to drive you and your friends right out of the universities of this nation." Hausman handed the package to Zach.

"You're Zach Blumberg, right?" said the man with the briefcase.

Zach nodded, and the man continued, "Perhaps, if I cannot talk Professor Hausman out of giving you the dissertation, I can persuade you to give it to me."

"What do you mean?"

"Well, which one would you rather have, Charles's manuscript or your own?"

"You have my dissertation?"

"Yup, right here in this briefcase. So it seems we ought to be able to work out a deal. We'd rather you didn't see Charles's manuscript, for obvious reasons. But surely you'd rather have your own manuscript back. All you have to do is polish a few footnotes, hand it in, and you've got a PhD. The chairman of your department is a heavy hitter, he loves you now, so you're a made man. Harvard, here you come."

"You want me to trade manuscripts?" said Zach.

"Don't do it," said Kate.

"I certainly won't," said Zach. "Why should I? I'll just make a quick phone call to the Ithaca police and have you arrested for possession of my stolen property. Then I'll have *both* manuscripts." He began to move toward the telephone that sat on the desk near the computer.

"I wouldn't touch that phone if I were you," said the man with the briefcase. His other hand now held a small automatic pistol. "Besides, I don't think that the police in a hick town like Cayuga Heights, New York, could detain us for long. How do you think we stole all those copies of your dissertation? We had a little professional help from some friends of ours who work in, let's say, the intelligence community. Those kinds of friends can come in very handy in situations like these."

Zach let his hand drop to his side. He looked at Kate for guidance, but she just shrugged.

Then the man who was holding the briefcase and gun said, "Well, we had hoped not to have to use such crude methods. But now that the gun is out and threats are being exchanged, I'm afraid I'll have to ask you for that package." He gestured toward Charles's manuscript, which Zach was still holding. "Since we've already broken the law, we might as well clean house," he added, apparently for his companion's benefit.

Zach looked at Hausman, who made a gesture of resignation. He looked at Kate, who was staring directly at the gun. And then, slowly and reluctantly, he began to hand the package over.

Just then, they heard a man with a familiar voice say, "Not so fast, gentlemen."

The man with the gun began to turn around, but behind him the new intruder said, "Freeze." Andrew came into view, holding a shotgun somewhat awkwardly in his arms. Simultaneously, another man appeared at the picture window, this one older and wearing a plaid flannel shirt and baseball cap over a mop of long hair. He too held a shotgun.

"So, gentlemen," said Andrew, "the jig is up. I suggest you put that gun down very slowly."

The man with the briefcase slowly lowered the gun to the ground.

"Zachary, collect that weapon," said Andrew. Staring right into the eyes of the man with the briefcase, Zach reached down and picked up the gun. He had never held a loaded weapon before. It felt potent and charged, as if a slight squeeze anywhere on its surface would cause it to go off with a bang. He pointed it at the two intruders and sighed deeply to calm himself. Then he looked quickly at Kate, who was grinning broadly and staring at the weapon in his hand. She gestured as if to ask for it. Realizing that she was much more collected than he, he carefully handed her the gun. She accepted it and adopted a posture like a television police officer, with her legs spread and both hands on the trigger. "Don't give me an excuse to get even for Charles," she said. "I'd take it."

"So, gentlemen," said Andrew. "All we'll be needing now is that briefcase. Then you can be on your way and all's well that ends well."

Kate barked, "You! Hands away from your pocket." The man without the briefcase let his hand fall to his side. "Both of you," she said, "hands on your heads. That means, drop the briefcase. All right." She grinned as the briefcase fell to the floor with a thud.

"You want me to call the police now?" said Zach.

She shook her head. "No. We don't have time for all that."

"So how do we get rid of them?" said Zach.

Kate addressed the two Sternians: "Just turn around nice and slow and start walking toward your obnoxious, yuppie car. Remember, I'm jumpy as hell. One little move and this thing goes off. So walk nice and slow."

Andrew stepped out of the way as the two blond men filed out through the dining room. The Lexus was parked near the end of the driveway next to Andrew's eyesore of a car. He and Kate walked slowly down the driveway with the two Sternians marching in front of them, clasping their hands over their heads. When they reached the car, Kate told them to get in slowly, one at a time, and to keep their hands constantly in view. Zach, Kate, Andrew, Professor Hausman, and Andrew's friend all piled into their two cars as fast as they could and drove back toward Ithaca.

Andrew, who was driving, said, "This is Mr. Murkowski. Stan Murkowski, may I introduce Zach Blumberg." Murkowski was seated in the front passenger seat, and he showed no signs of wanting to shake anyone's hand. In the back seat, Zach held the two dissertations on his lap. Andrew explained about Murkowski: "He owns a farm about twenty miles outside of Cortland where me and some of my friends go to buy—well, certain hard-to-find fungi and weeds that he grows himself, organically. When he heard a friend of mine might be having a problem with some goons from Washington, he said he'd be happy to show up with a pair of shotguns, assuming that these guys weren't from the FBI or DEA. I'm glad I didn't have to use my gun, though. I don't really know how it works."

"I'da been happy to show ya," said Murkowski with apparent regret.

"Where to?" asked Andrew as they drove along steep, wooded roads, catching glimpses now and then of the lake below them.

"Are those guys following us?" Zach tried to spot them through the rear window. Kate and Hausman were right behind in Hausman's car.

"Yup," said Andrew, looking in his mirror. "About fifty yards back." He took a sharp right turn down a narrow road, then the next left, but the Lexus could still be seen not far behind them.

"Pull over," said Murkowski. All three cars stopped. The blond men got out of the Lexus and each crouched behind one of the front doors. It was difficult for Zach to see them clearly through the back window of the car, but one of them appeared to be holding a handgun.

Murkowski grabbed his shotgun from under his seat and opened the door. Zach ducked instinctively, but then he raised his head again out of curiosity. Murkowski started walking slowly toward the Lexus, holding his shotgun loosely in one hand.

One of the Sternians shouted, "Stop where you are."

Murkowski stopped but raised the shotgun to firing position. He said, "Back me up, guys. Andrew!"

Andrew, in the driver's seat, had the other shotgun. Looking pale, he stepped outside and walked toward Murkowski.

Murkowski cocked his shotgun and asked Andrew, "Got 'em covered?" Andrew mimicked Murkowski's action with his gun, and then pointed the cocked weapon toward the Lexus. Meanwhile, Zach climbed out of the car unarmed, not wanting to be the only one to stay inside with Hausman.

Murkowski shouted, "Now listen to me. I'm gonna have to shoot your front tire out. I'm not shootin' at you. But I've got the other barrel, so don't try to fire back. We've got two shotguns to your one revolver, and I've been shootin' deer since I was seven. You hear me?"

His voice echoed slightly. There was no response. "Ready?" he asked Andrew. Zach couldn't see Andrew's face, but he could see him give a quick little nod. Andrew's firing arm was shaking visibly.

Zach jumped right off the ground as a shot broke the silence. Murkowski had fired, and the impact was clearly visible on the front left wheel of the Lexus.

"All right," said Murkowski. "I can put the other round right in one of your chests, if that's what you want. If not, let the gun drop to the ground and get back in."

For a few seconds, no one moved. Then the driver of the Lexus dropped his gun onto the side of the road. With their hands clearly in view, the Sternians climbed back inside.

For the second time, Zach was startled by the report of a

gun. Again, it was Murkowski who had fired, and the other tire of the Lexus blew out. "Two for two," he muttered as he reloaded.

"Uh, that'll do it, I think," said Andrew, obviously worried about where Murkowski might put a third and fourth round.

"I know, I know," he said, offended.

They backed toward their car, climbed in, and drove away as quickly as possible with Kate and Hausman following in the station wagon. They took two sharp lefts and finally turned onto a private access road leading to a Cornell research facility. They drove through densely wooded property until they were hidden from the main traffic route, then pulled over and stopped the cars. A low, windowless brick building was barely visible farther up the road. They all got out and began to discuss what to do next.

Hausman said: "Can I see the dissertation, please? Charles's, I mean."

Zach handed it to him. Hausman removed the document from its envelope and began thumbing through it. "You see?" he said. "It's this kind of quotation that I was referring to."

He pointed to a passage and held the dissertation so that Zach could see it; Kate looked over his shoulder. It read as follows:

It is, of course, always dangerous to attribute systematic irony to a text, even when one has been able to identify as many internal clues to an author's duplicitous intent as we have recognized in Stern's writings. To those who find contextual evidence more convincing, quotations from Stern's unpublished writings may lend weight to our thesis. For example, Stern told one of his followers: "Contrive as many ways as you can to communicate the truth that there is no truth, for you must recruit acolytes down through the ages. But be careful: your means must be deeply cryptic. Although most of our fellow men are fools and cretins, the passage of time will increase their chances of uncovering our meaning through sheer chance. If that happens, then woe be unto them and to all men, for they will be unable to bear the message that good is no better than evil, and we shall have storm troopers and cruelty and wars and death."[93]

"What does the footnote say?" Kate asked.

They turned to the back of the dissertation, where notes ran on for scores of pages. Note number 93 to chapter six read "Stern MS, author's trans., Aubrey VI, 2, p. 92."

"What's Aubrey?" Kate asked Hausman, but no one seemed to know. Murkowski got out of the car, paced, and looked at his watch. Andrew said, "We have to make a plan here."

Zach said, "What other references does he give?" They found a few more quotations in the main body of the manuscript, then looked up the relevant notes. All referred to Stern manuscripts that were each identified by a proper name, a Roman numeral, an Arabic number, and a page citation. The proper names were either "Aubrey" or "Harmondsworth."

For several minutes they discussed how Frye might be linked to Charles and Stern, why Charles had been killed, and what they should do next. Finally, Murkowski opened the door and got back into the front seat, saying, "So?"

"Where should I take us?" said Andrew, turning the key in the ignition.

"Safety first, I think," said Kate. "Zach and I have got to

get back to our car and drive out of town with the dissertations. Then we can plan our next move."

"All right," said Andrew. "They might know that you're staying with me. So I'll drop you somewhere downtown, and later my roommate Marie or I will deliver your car to you. We won't come unless we're sure we're not being followed. I'll bring Professor Hausman home after I've left you downtown."

4 • An hour later Zach and Kate were waiting at the appointed meeting place, a used bookstore in downtown Ithaca. Given the situation, it was difficult to concentrate on books about Aquinas's concept of the beautiful, or political theory in postwar Yugoslavia. Still, they must have appeared to be serious book shoppers as they thumbed through musty volumes and stared silently at the ceiling, deep in thought. A grandfather clock in the main room ticked loudly, a cat slumbered on the rug, and the proprietor, an elderly bald man with a conspicuous Adam's apple, watched them hopefully. When Kate began to examine a multivolume Ruskin collection, he said, "I've got an excellent deal on that one. Can't beat eleven bucks a volume for a book that old. The underlining stops halfway through volume one."

"Yeah," said Kate, "but thirty-seven volumes?"

"I'll take any reasonable offer."

At that moment, Marie entered the store, caught Zach's eye, and approached him. She whispered, "It's around the corner to the right, outside the drugstore. I didn't see anybody watching the street or following me, but better be careful."

She handed Zach the car keys. "How will you get home?" he asked.

"Oh, Ithaca Transit."

"You sure?"

"No problem."

They said good-bye to a disappointed store owner, then walked around the corner, where Zach and Kate got into their rented car. Marie curtly wished them good luck and went away in search of a bus stop. Kate drove the car out of town along the shore of the lake. It was the middle of the afternoon and hot. In the front passenger seat, Zach thumbed through Charles's dissertation, looking for something directly relevant to Frye. Although he soon began to feel nauseous from reading in the car, he managed to glance at every page. Frye's name never appeared, nor were there any further surprising revelations. Zach also paged through his own thesis, delighted to see his work safe again.

"Where am I supposed to be taking us?" Kate said.

"If we stopped and called Davies, we could find out when the committee is likely to vote."

"Yeah, and you could ask him if he has any idea where those Stern manuscripts are. Maybe Charles told him where the Stern archive is. Or maybe he knows what Aubrey is, and—what is that other name?"

"Harmondsworth."

"Right."

"You know," said Zach, "it's weird that Davies didn't mention the existence of the secret Stern manuscripts. He must have known about them if he was reading Charles's stuff."

"That is weird."

"Anyway, I can call him and find out what's going on in Washington. I could also call Alice Webster. It's possible that she would recognize Aubrey and Harmondsworth, since she has a vast amount of experience in library research all around the world."

"Good idea."

Ten miles out of Ithaca, they passed a gas station with one forlorn pump, a little convenience store, and a pay phone outside. They pulled up next to the telephone and Zach placed a call with his phone card while Kate stood at his side and listened.

He reached the Ambassador Hotel in Washington and asked for Professor Davies. There was no answer in Davies's room, and Zach decided not to leave a message. He called Alice Webster, but she too seemed to be out. Her answering-machine message suggested that callers try reaching her at her Yale office, which Zach proceeded to do with no success. He and Kate conferred and decided that they might as well travel south, since either New Haven, Princeton, or Washington was likely to be their next destination. This meant turning around and driving back through Ithaca, then out of town in the opposite direction. As they drove, Kate said, "Where would a Stern archive be housed?"

"Stern taught at several American colleges during his postwar career. But I doubt that he would have bequeathed his secret papers to a university library that's open to scholars—at least, not the papers where he confesses that everything he ever published was a lie."

"True."

They drove toward Binghamton on back roads, passing dairy farms that were spread like quilts over rolling hills. Every time they reached the top of a hill and looked down into a new valley, they saw clusters of quaintly dilapidated silos, barns, and farmhouses. The little towns through which they drove all had names drawn from classical antiquity; their main industry seemed to be selling the contents of local attics in antique stores.

Zach and Kate listened to a public-radio affiliate as they drove. At four o'clock, a concert of baroque organ music ended and there was a news briefing, which included a short item about the Frye nomination. They were eager to hear the latest word about Frye, but it was unpleasant to be dragged back into political reality after being lulled into a sense of peace by the rustic beauty of central New York. According to the radio report, there was no news yet about when the hearings would end, but a loose coalition of advocacy groups had held a press conference in Washington at which they had called for the nomination to be defeated because of some decisions that Frye had made as a federal judge. In particular, he had ruled that a prison guard who had raped a woman in the penitentiary had not violated her civil rights. Meanwhile, some conservative senators were beginning to complain about the slow pace of the confirmation process.

Kate stopped the car in one town that was not much more than a row of houses and stores strung out along the county road; she peered in the window of a junk shop while Zach looked for a public telephone. He found one outside the post office and began to dial Davies's number again as Kate joined him.

This time he was successful: Davies answered the telephone in his room.

"Professor Davies? Zach Blumberg."

"Ah, Zach. Any luck?"

"Yes, as a matter of fact. We found Charles's dissertation. We had a little run-in with some guys with guns; I guess they were Sternian types. But we ended up with his thesis and mine too, as a matter of fact."

"Excellent. Anything interesting in it?"

"I think so. Charles refers to some manuscripts in Stern's handwriting that openly discuss esoteric nihilism."

"That's interesting." Davies did not sound particularly surprised.

"You hadn't seen this part of Charles's dissertation?"

There was a pause. "No. No. He never showed that part to me."

"I see. He never mentioned using Stern's personal papers at all?"

"No."

"I wonder why not."

Davies suddenly sounded irritated. "Well," he said, "I can hardly speculate about that, can I?"

"No, sir. It was a stupid question, I guess. But let me ask you this: how much time have we got before the Senate vote?"

"The chairman is willing to postpone a committee vote until someone on the other side makes an issue about the delay. As soon as that happens, he will give up, since he has no public rationale for stalling."

"When do you think someone will complain about the delay?"

"The danger is, you see, that Frye will get wind of your activities and complain to the White House about the holdup, in order to get the hearings over with. It's not that the President's men know anything about a conspiracy, of course. But if Frye urges them to demand a quick vote, they may comply."

"I see what you mean."

Davies said: "You realize that Frye may deny knowing anything about Stern's secret doctrines, at which point our whole strategy will collapse."

"Of course."

"So what do you propose to do?"

"We'll find a stronger link between Frye and Stern. For instance, we'll find the original Stern manuscripts and see if they mention Frye directly."

"Charles's dissertation doesn't discuss Frye, does it?"

"No, but why would it? It's a scholarly piece about esotericism in Nietzsche, Stern, and some other political philosophers; it's not about Supreme Court nominations. Charles could have seen papers linking Stern to Frye, but chosen not to include them in his thesis."

"True."

Kate was mouthing the word "Aubrey." Zach said, "Do the names Aubrey and Harmondsworth mean anything to you?"

Davies's answer was immediate: "No."

"No?"

"Nothing."

"I see. Well, we'll call you again when we know more."

"Where are you?"

"On the road. We're trying to hide, quite frankly."

"Well, call me as frequently as you can."

"Thank you, sir. I will."

Zach said good-bye and hung up. After he had recounted the conversation to Kate, he said, "I guess I'll try Alice again." She was not at home, but she did pick up the telephone in her Yale office.

"Alice, it's Zach."

"Zachary! Where are you? Have you forgotten all about your auxiliary aunt Alice?"

"No, I haven't forgotten about you at all. Far from it: we desperately need your help and wisdom."

"Flattery will not excuse your failure to call me. Nevertheless, tell me what you and your femme fatale have been up to, and I will try to help."

Zach attempted to tell Alice an abbreviated history of their adventures since he had last talked to her, but she demanded amplifications and clarifications at every step, so it took him fifteen minutes or more to finish the story. He ended by asking, "So, do the words 'Aubrey' and 'Harmondsworth' mean anything to you?"

"Of course they do, and you ought to recognize them as well. Don't you ever go to concerts at Aubrey Hall? And what about the Harmondsworth Lab?"

Zach had indeed attended chamber music recitals at Yale, but he hadn't noticed the name of the concert hall. As for the science facilities, those might as well have been located in Kazakhstan for all he knew about them. He said: "I don't see any connection between two Yale buildings and the Stern case, do you?"

Alice sounded somewhat impatient. "Well, for whom do you think those buildings are *named*, Zachary? John Adams Aubrey was president of Yale in the eighteen sixties; Harmondsworth had the same job just before the First World War."

"I guess I should have known that."

"Whether you know about Yale history is unimportant; there are more significant topics to study, God knows. But Davies: he must recognize those names. After all, his grandfather was a Yale president too, and he's completely steeped in college lore."

"So why would he lie to us?"

"May I suggest something, Zachary? The obvious answer is just one syllable long: Crypt. Davies is a Crypt man, so it follows that his grandfather was one as well: they always pick legacies. At least a third of all Yale presidents have been Cryptsmen; the rest have come from the other two chief secret societies. I strongly suspect, although I can't prove it, that Aubrey and Harmondsworth were selected by Crypt to be presidents of the university."

"Which Davies must have known."

"Must have known, but could not say. Haven't you heard

that if someone even mentions Crypt, a Cryptsman must leave the room? Davies would be breaking solemn oaths if he divulged to you that Aubrey and Harmondsworth were Crypt brothers. More than that: they were the men secretly chosen by Crypt to govern Yale in their respective generations."

"We cannot be sure of this."

"I'd bet my rent-controlled apartment on it. Look, don't let Davies off the hook. I suspect he's torn between his silly blood oaths of silence about Crypt and his desire to fight the Sternian conspiracy. Call him back, put the case directly to him, and tell him it's time he acted like a grown-up and not a frat boy. He must confess everything he knows about the connections between Crypt, Stern, and Frye. This is serious business; the future of the nation may be on the line."

"I'm not sure I can talk to Davies quite that way, Alice."

"I don't care how you do it, just make him talk. He won't bite your head off."

They hung up after Zach promised to call Alice back with the latest news. Then he and Kate conferred about how to approach Davies. Zach, terrified of making the call, tried to procrastinate. "Maybe we should call him later," he said.

"Why?" said Kate.

"I don't know, it just seems funny to turn around and call him right back after we just hung up."

"This is a good time: we know he's home."

"Do you want to call him?"

"Why?"

"Because I'm scared to death, all right?"

"Okay, I'll call him." Zach felt a powerful mixture of relief and embarrassment as Kate began to dial Davies's number. He and Kate were the only people standing outside on the main street, although cars and trucks passed by regularly. The post office was closing, but business was picking up at the diner down the street, a classic aluminum-clad establishment called the Rest Stop. A couple of pickup trucks and a station wagon were parked outside the diner, and a family of four had just lumbered inside.

Kate said, "Professor Davies? This is Kate, Zach Blumberg's friend?" She sounded nervous. Zach pressed close to her so that he could hear Davies's voice, but she pulled away from him.

She said: "Yes, we were just wondering about Aubrey and Harmondsworth."

There was a long pause. "Professor Davies?" she said. Zach heard him bark, "What about them?"

"We didn't know this before, but we now realize that they were presidents of Yale, and Cryptsmen. Frankly, sir, it seems difficult to believe that you would not recognize their names, particularly when they appear in tandem like that."

She nodded as she listened to a torrent of angry speech. Zach winced and then started jotting down a few words on a cash-register receipt that he had fished out of his pocket. He wrote: "D. must have seen those names already in C.'s thesis." He showed the paper to Kate, who nodded impatiently.

"I'm very, very sorry to imply that you were being dishonest, sir," she said finally. "But now that you've realized that Aubrey and Harmondsworth have a Crypt connection, have you got any ideas about why they would be mentioned in reference to a Stern manuscript?"

Zach pointed again at the receipt, but Kate nodded emphatically to indicate that she had seen it already.

"You have no idea?" she said. "Well, let me put it this way, all right? If you have no idea, then we might as well call it quits and swear in Judge Frye and let Charles lie peacefully in his grave, because we're out of options." She was suppressing tears. "But I think that you're not being honest with us, so this is all your fault. You must have seen those names mentioned in Charles's thesis, yet you didn't say anything to us about them. You're hiding something, something important enough to lie about—although in a totally ineffective way, if I may say so. So why don't you either tell us, or stop wasting our time?"

Kate's face was screwed up in anger. Zach moved closer to the phone so that he could hear Davies better and put his arm around Kate's shoulder to console her, but she felt stiff and unresponsive. After a few seconds of silence, Davies said: "Very well. I'll tell you a few facts, but they will only frustrate you, I'm afraid, as they frustrate me."

"Go ahead," said Kate, with a severe and unbelieving look on her face.

Zach could hear Davies's strong, precise voice quite clearly. He said: "Two things. First, Wendell Frye is the Crypt archivist. We all have club offices or duties, and that's his bailiwick, the Crypt archive. It's extensive, and it's housed in a room on the top floor of the New Haven building. Second, have you ever seen an old-fashioned library in which each bookcase has a plaster bust on top? If you want to identify a book that's on the third shelf under the Chopin bust, you say, 'Chopin three.' Right?"

Kate said, "Right."

"Well, as you might imagine, the Crypt archive is arranged that way, since it was set up in the last century, and the busts are portraits of Cryptsmen who became presidents of Yale. My grandfather Diomedes sits astride the second-to-last bookcase. In the footnotes to his dissertation, Charles identified the Stern manuscripts that he used so that I could examine them at my leisure."

"So you have seen the Stern papers with your own eyes," said Kate. "They're inside the Crypt building."

"What I have chosen to see is a secret, young lady, and so it must remain. We are discussing the Crypt inner sanctum, remember, and I have already divulged enough that if I had any honor, I'd shoot myself."

"Can you get us copies of the relevant material?"

"What did I just say? It's a secret, young lady. That's why they put the papers there. No doubt they were hoping to convert Cryptsmen in each succeeding generation, for we are all natural conspirators and elitists. The Stern archive would be a useful resource for people like Frye to use in making converts. But even those of us who chose not to join their fraudulent enterprise would nevertheless be sworn to eternal secrecy about the contents of the archive."

"Are there any letters from Stern to Frye?"

"Look, for the thousandth time, my lips are sealed."

"What would happen to you if you told us?"

"First of all, I would forfeit my sacred honor. That, to me, is determinative. But on a more practical level, which you might understand better, I would run significant risks. Who pays for my endowed chair? Who runs Yale? Perhaps they even killed Charles after he quoted material from the Crypt secret archives. He broke a sacred oath; I do not want to meet his fate."

"What would happen to us if we got inside the building?"

"There's a powerful lock on the front door and an efficient electronic security device inside. Forget it."

"Give us your key."

"Absolutely not. If I did that, I might as well walk in with you."

"Is that your last word?"

"You heard me: forget it. Forget the whole damn business; it's over."

Kate slammed the receiver into its cradle without saying good-bye. "Did you hear?" she asked Zach.

He nodded. "So, do we call it quits?" she asked.

"Let's get some supper at the Rest Stop and talk it over."

Seated at a booth by the diner's front window, Zach and Kate ate chowder, salad, and cheese steaks while they half-heartedly discussed ways to break into the windowless Crypt building. They talked about climbing onto the roof, breaking down the door in the middle of the night, or overpowering a Cryptsman as he tried to enter the building. When they had rejected a long series of improbable schemes, they lapsed into silence, and Zach examined the State Capitals map printed on his paper place mat. Suddenly he said, "I promised to call Alice to tell her what we learned from Davies."

"Go ahead, then." Kate sounded lethargic, or perhaps just resigned. She remained at the table while Zach found a telephone near the toilets. Alice again answered the phone in her office, and Zach recounted their second conversation with Davies. When he was finished, Alice said, "Look, I might be able to get us into the Crypt building."

"How?"

"Davies is a stalwart, an Old Blue, a true believer. He'd rather die than let us in, I understand that. But I know some other men of his generation, colleagues, who are also Cryptites but may be a little less taken with the whole ideology of the place. Let me see if I can get someone to let us in."

"Us? Are you coming?"

"Here I am in New Haven. Do you think I want to miss the one chance in my life to see the inside of that ridiculous, overendowed, pretentious fraternity house? I'm coming."

"Great, Alice."

"Call me back in two hours, here in my office. I'll see what I can work out."

Not having any better place to go, Zach and Kate waited for the whole two hours in their booth at the diner, paying the rent by buying coffee and several desserts. The restaurant began to empty out after eight o'clock, although truck drivers and state policemen periodically stopped at the bar for coffee. Zach read Charles's thesis, finding it interesting on a purely academic level: he admired many of its insights. Meanwhile, to pass the time, Kate read Zach's dissertation, pausing every ten or fifteen minutes to ask him a question. Just after eight, she said, "I think I'm going to call Hausman, just to make sure he's okay. Do you have his number?"

Zach could not find the number, so Kate went to the telephone to call directory assistance. She returned a few minutes later, saying, "No answer." She shrugged. "I guess he'll be all right."

"Do you want to ask Andrew to stop by his place?"

"Maybe we should if we can't reach him by ten. I'm sure he's okay, though. At this hour, he could easily be out having dinner or something."

At half past eight, Zach called Alice, who said excitedly, "Look, I have a Crypt key and combination. We can go inside tomorrow night."

"What happens if someone catches us?"

"Then we're in serious trouble. The first thing we do is destroy my friend's electronic card-key. Then we just try not to get ourselves killed. He says to go inside after four A.M., since people are very rarely in there then. He gave me some other tips, which I'll tell you about later."

She and Zach made arrangements to meet the following night in New Haven. Then he returned to the table and told Kate what they had arranged. She listened with growing enthusiasm, nodding and even grinning at times.

"One thing bothers me about our plan," Zach said.

"Fear of death?"

"Well, that, too. But what I was thinking about was this. Lots of the Stern papers are going to be in German, right? Judging by Charles's references, there are going to be pages and pages of them—maybe many volumes, since they spill over onto two bookcases."

"Right. So how do we decide really fast what we need to photocopy? Is that your question?"

"Yeah."

"Your friend Professor Webster must know German."

"I'm sure she does, but it's not just the German that will present difficulties. For instance, let's say that all of Stern's correspondence is in the archive. How do we figure out very quickly which letters are written to his grandson about piano lessons, and which are to inner-circle Sternians about getting nihilists onto the Supreme Court? Do you see what I mean? If Alice reads German, she can gradually figure out what's what—but in half an hour? If we knew who was who, then we could use an index to find the good stuff right away. Or at least we could thumb through the pages looking for key names."

"You would recognize names, wouldn't you?"

"Some. I know a few of the Sternians by reputation. But not a lot, and I wouldn't have a clue about who's an insider and who's an outsider."

"You're saying that we need to bring an expert with us."

"Right, like Hausman."

"Do you think he'd come?"

"We could ask him."

Kate nodded and Zach went to the telephone to try calling Hausman again, but with no success. When he returned to the table, shaking his head, Kate said, "I'm a little worried about him now."

"Maybe we should drop by his house. We can at least see

if his car is in the driveway. We're not very far from Ithaca now, are we?"

"No, I don't think so. But what if those guys are in there with him, holding him prisoner or something?"

"That sounds pretty farfetched. But to make sure, we can go in with backup again. Then, if they *are* holding Hausman against his will, we can free him and have them arrested, which might actually help with the Frye case. But I think that's very unlikely."

They discussed the matter further in order to devise a way that would allow them to visit Hausman's place safely. After they had designed a tentative plan, Zach called Andrew to make more logistical arrangements. They agreed that they would keep trying to reach Hausman by telephone, but if he failed to answer by one in the morning, they would look for him at home. They also discussed ways to turn the tables on any would-be ambushers. In the end, they decided that Andrew would back them up from a second car; Mr. Murkowski would not be able to come to Ithaca for a midnight jaunt, but Andrew would bring a couple of graduate-student friends. Fortunately, he still had the automatic pistols that they had removed from the two Sternians earlier that day.

⟨ • Three hours later, Zach and Kate drove down Hausman's street at about ten miles per hour. They were now driving a blue subcompact car that Andrew had borrowed from an undergraduate friend. There was no sign of the Lexus, nor of anyone watching the Hausmans' home, but a light shone on the upper floor. They drove around the block and stopped next to a parked car in which Andrew waited with several friends. Standing on the street, Zach and Andrew held a brief whispered conference to confirm that everyone knew what to do. Then Kate parked the blue subcompact and she and

Zach began walking toward Hausman's street, trying to stay inconspicuous in the deep shadows. Most of the houses in the neighborhood were dark, and the wind rustled the leaves of the tall maples. Andrew and his friends cruised ahead of them in their car.

Hausman's station wagon was not parked in his driveway, but there was still a light burning upstairs. Zach and Kate approached the side door, glad to see that Andrew's car had stopped not far away. Kate held an oversized police whistle in her right hand; Zach tried to conceal a pistol beneath a borrowed baseball jacket. The door was closed so Zach pressed the bell, which buzzed softly in the distance.

After a few minutes of silence, Kate looked at Zach for approval, then opened the screen and gently pushed the main wooden door ajar. Zach, holding the gun in his shaking hand, stepped as quietly as he could into the dark interior of the house. Kate followed him, her hand on his back.

A sudden metallic crashing sound made them leap into the air with fright—but it was just the screen door banging behind them. Zach felt his pounding chest and tried to breathe evenly while Kate fastened the door closed behind them. The side rooms were pitch-dark and forbidding, but the stairs going to the second story were illuminated by a faint light from above. Kate found Zach's hand and held it while they climbed slowly upstairs. The wooden steps made excruciating creaking sounds. Halfway up, Kate grabbed Zach and whispered, "If anyone's here, they've heard us by now."

"I don't think there is anyone," Zach replied with hope but no conviction. "Let's just see if there's anything upstairs that would tell us where he's gone."

Kate put the whistle in her mouth; Zach led the way with the gun still in his hand. They reached the landing and saw that the light was shining from a room down the hall to the right. They tiptoed toward it, Zach in front and Kate following with a bunched-up piece of his shirt in her hand. As they neared the door, they stopped to collect themselves. Kate pointed at the floor, on which appeared to be the indistinct shadow of a man standing around the corner with the light to his back. He remained eerily still, as if he were waiting to surprise them. Zach's heart started pounding again. Kate, her voice cracking slightly, said, "Professor Hausman?"

There was silence and the shadow remained still. It certainly looked like a standing man, although it could have been a trick of the light. Kate put the whistle back in her mouth, and they both peered slowly around the threshold. Zach saw a man's feet near a desk; in a second he realized that they were suspended some distance off the ground. Just as he began to look up toward the man's head, Kate screamed, the whistle flying out of her mouth. She clutched Zach and hid her head in his chest. He forced himself to look up and saw an ashen face staring directly at him, the mouth contorted and the head bent sharply to the side with a rope around its neck. It was Jules Hausman.

CHAPTER 9

1 • For almost three hours they drove rapidly south and east on deserted back roads, fleeing the sight of Hausman, the reach of their enemies, and even the attention of the Ithaca police, who might learn from Hausman's wife that they were somehow linked to his death. They passed ominous, Charles Addams houses with crooked gables and mansard roofs and decrepit gingerbread trim. In the fringes of the Catskills, they saw thick woods with trees swaying wildly in the wind, trout streams, and ancient hills. They didn't speak a word, but sat numbly in the car, mesmerized by the median line. Finally, at four in the morning, they approached a major road and spotted a motel with its sign illuminated. Kate said, "I've got to stop. I can't keep driving."

In their motel room, everything but the painting of the moose above the bed was striped, but nothing matched anything else: not the pile carpet, nor the throw rugs covering the carpet's stains, nor the threadbare bedspread, nor the wallpaper, nor the red globular paper shade that covered the room's one light bulb. They switched off the light and climbed into bed fully clothed, clinging to each other as headlights from the highway cast swiftly moving beams across the room and trucks thundered past.

Zach remained awake for a long time, his nose buried in the back of Kate's head, and he noticed that she too was unable to sleep. His mind returned constantly to the grisly scene in Hausman's study. After Kate had discovered the body and screamed, Andrew and his friends had rushed into the house to rescue them. The scream and the sound of running feet and slamming car doors had probably been loud enough to alert the neighbors. They had tried to leave the house as fast as possible, but first, Zach and Andrew had quickly inspected the study. While they looked, Kate stood silently crying in the hall and Jules Hausman stared blankly toward the door. Papers lay scattered on the floor as if they had been pushed, but there was no suicide note in view. Zach had probably left his fingerprints on several pieces of paper.

Now, lying sleepless in the motel bed, Zach couldn't get the image of Hausman's face out of his mind. But he must have dozed off at last, because suddenly the sun was shining through the curtain and Kate was no longer in bed. He raised himself on one elbow and saw her brushing her teeth in the tiny toilet.

She returned to the bedroom wearing a rueful smile. "Well, *you* got some sleep."

"Did you?"

"I don't think so."

"What time is it?"

"Nine."

They paid for their room and found a diner nearby where they ate breakfast, both slumped over the table with pouches under their eyes.

"Where to?" said Kate.

"We don't have to be in New Haven for what?—eighteen hours," said Zach.

"It'll probably take us no more than four to drive there."
Zach yawned. "Is New York on the way?"

"Pretty much."

"You want to go there and take an afternoon nap to restore our strength?"

"Are you sure it's safe to go to your place?"

"You're right, maybe not. Let's just drive somewhere nice and wait," he said. "A state park or something. Somewhere out of the way."

Their waitress told them about a park that overlooked the Hudson. As they drove, they scanned the radio dial for news broadcasts. There was nothing in the news about Hausman's death—but that would have been a local story at most. In Washington, senators were beginning to make floor speeches for and against the Frye nomination, in anticipation of a vote. The day before, one of the body's most distinguished liberals had delivered a philippic against Frye, accusing him of "judicial murder" because he had sent a convict to the death chamber despite evidence that he might be innocent; Frye had rejected the evidence on procedural grounds. In response, several conservatives took the floor to defend Frye's high intellectual caliber, independence, and commitment to judicial restraint. There was no mention in the news reports about when the Judiciary Committee might move to a vote.

The state park recommended by their waitress turned out to be a narrow strip of land running along the high bluffs that line the Hudson. Although the day had turned overcast and there were occasional sprinkles of rain, the view was magnificent. Zach and Kate sat on a grassy slope overlooking the river. After a few minutes, Kate put her head on Zach's lap and fell asleep; he remained awake, enjoying the idea that he could be her protector for the moment. As she slept, he

turned over in his mind the events of the preceding days, examining them from every possible perspective and constantly
returning to the same conclusions, the same dead ends. By
the time Kate awoke almost an hour later, he had had just
one stray thought.

"What's up?" she said, raising her head from his lap.

"Not much. I'm glad you slept a little."

"Have you just been watching the river?"

"The river and you."

She smiled. "You want to take a turn sleeping?"

"Not really. Listen, I have an idea."

"Yes?"

"I think we should find out whether Charles tried to contact the Judiciary Committee before he died. Maybe he approached the committee to set up a meeting or to give them
some documents. Surely he would have tried to do that. Possibly, a staff member on the bad guys' side then alerted the
Sternians, and they took care of Charles before the meeting
could take place. See, that would explain how they found out
that he was in Washington—through the committee."

"That's a possibility," said Kate after a moment's thought.
"So why doesn't Davies ask the committee staff if they have
a record of Charles on their phone log or in someone's diary
or something? I have the impression that government agen-
cies and politicians always keep records of who they talk to.
I mean, every time there's a scandal in Washington, there's
always a phone log. Sometimes it turns out to be missing or
altered, but someone's always supposed to have kept a
record."

"You want to call Davies and ask him?"

"Your turn. And while you have old Hannibal on the
phone, why don't you ask him when the vote's going to happen?"

There was no public telephone in the park, so they drove into the nearest town and found a phone inside a fast-food restaurant. Zach failed to reach Davies at his hotel, but Kate suggested that he might be visiting the Judiciary Committee. Zach called information and then the committee—all the time worrying about his next phone bill. He asked the receptionist if Professor Davies was present and available.

She was an extremely competent and efficient person, and she had Davies on the line in thirty seconds.

"Professor Davies? Zach."

"Hello, Zach." There was a note of ridicule in his voice whenever he uttered Zach's first name. "Still on the case?"

"In a manner of speaking. When is the vote?"

"Nothing official, but the rumors are bad. My sources tell me that a senator is going to take the floor within hours to demand an explanation for the committee's delay."

"Does that mean it'll all be over in hours?"

"No. That speech will trigger the process of wrapping up the hearings, with closing comments and all that. You probably have until tomorrow afternoon."

"Please try to hold them off as long as you can."

"If you say so, although it's hard to see what difference a few hours can make at this late stage. Face it, Zachary, the game's up."

"Listen, can you help us in one more way?"

"I'd be delighted." He did not sound delighted.

"Ask folks around the committee whether there'd be any record if Charles had called them before he died. Just ask them: is there any record of a Mr. Charles Wilson contacting the committee?"

"That sounds worthwhile. I'll make inquiries. Where can I reach you?"

"Leave a message on my machine in New York; I'll check

it from here." Zach gave Davies his number and then said
good-bye.

2 • They walked into the dining area of the restaurant to
buy lunch. As they scanned the enormous illustrated menu
behind the counter, Zach suddenly shouted: "Oh, my God!"

His voice was loud enough to make several customers turn
around. Kate said, "What? Did you figure something out?"

"Oh, my God!"

"What's the matter?"

"I'm supposed to teach a class today! I completely forgot.
I'm a horrible person; I'm an idiot. I should be fired. What'll
I do?"

"Well, what time is the class?"

"Two."

"You can make it there by then."

"I haven't prepared a thing. I don't even have any books."

"Work on it in the car. Come on."

They were soon on the road again, driving rapidly south.
Zach said repeatedly that he could not teach his class. Was-
n't he trying to hide from the police, block a Supreme Court
nomination, and solve a murder—and he was supposed to
be able to teach a class at the same time? Besides, he had
no books, no time, and no ideas. He asked Kate to stop the
car; he would just not show up. But she adopted a firm tone
and demanded that he concentrate on what he was going to
say. When he responded with more complaints and whining,
she said, "I have an idea. Why don't you tell them about Frye
and the Sternians? It's within the topic of the course, isn't
it? Roughly? It'll definitely wake 'em up."

He resisted for a while, but gradually the idea began to
sound better to him. By the time they had arrived at campus
and parked the car, he was reasonably sure that the class

could go well. He left Kate in the library and entered the grim classroom building with a spring in his step.

It was the second-to-last class, and only four students were present: Dorothy, Fred the Ayn Randian, and two of the women who sat in the back row. The sight of such a small and motley audience disheartened Zach. By now, he had decided to talk to them about the Frye case, but he hadn't worked out a suitable way to present the issues. Once Kate had given him a topic, he had felt so relieved that he had neglected to rehearse his presentation. Now, standing silently before the class, he realized that he couldn't just tell the story of his adventures; that would be too unprofessional—verging on bizarre—and the students probably wouldn't believe him anyway. So, after a few minutes of frantic thought, he finally said, "I want to conduct class a little differently today. Your papers are due next time, and I've asked you not only to state what Nietzsche's grounds for nihilism are, but also to say something about why his ideas are relevant and important. Right? Some of you have been having problems with the second part of the question, I know."

He glanced at Dorothy, who was seated attentively in the front row, but he quickly moved his eyes away in order not to appear to single her out.

"Who here has been following the nomination of Wendell Frye?" Zach asked.

Silence.

"Who knows who Wendell Frye is?"

Fred raised his hand. "Fred?" said Zach.

"He's the guy who wants to get onto the, um, Supreme Court. Isn't he?" Fred seemed very pleased with himself for knowing this.

"That's right," said Zach. "Now, what's his philosophy? Why do some people like him and some people don't?"

"The liberals want to get him 'cause he stands up for individual freedom."

Zach sighed; this was going to be harder than he'd thought. These students didn't know that Frye had anything to say about natural law or original intent, so how could they understand that his positions might be intentionally deceptive? It wouldn't be news to them if natural law or objective truth turned out to be fictions: they had never heard of them in the first place.

"Where did you hear the debate described that way, Fred? Did you read it somewhere?" Zach wanted to play the pedagogue: a good teacher, he thought, would ask Fred about the grounds for his assertion, get him to think critically. But he suspected that everything Fred believed came a priori from the pages of *The Fountainhead*.

Fred shifted uncomfortably in his seat.

"Anyone else?"

Silence, punctuated only by gum-snapping from the back row. Close to panic, Zach decided to take the plunge. "Look, let me tell you a story, okay? You can't say the same thing in your papers, obviously, but maybe it will give you some ideas. At least maybe it'll be interesting, all right? So here's a story for you to think about—a hypothetical story."

It all came out very fast; from the missing dissertation to the death of Jules Hausman, Zach told the whole story more or less as it had happened, omitting only his personal relationship with Kate. As he spoke, he stared at the clock on the back wall, not wanting to make eye contact with his students in case they had begun to suspect him of lunacy. He spoke in a near monotone, like a criminal suspect who has finally agreed to confess everything on videotape. When he was done, he giggled nervously and said, "So that's the story. That's how I'd answer my own question, I guess—about the importance of nihilism, I mean."

He examined his audience. The two women in the back row were slumped in their desks, their huge painted fingernails biting into their cheeks, their mouths hanging open, not out of astonishment but because they were intensely bored. They seemed to be thinking: who *is* this guy? And: will this stuff be on the test? Fred and Dorothy, however, watched him with considerable interest.

He didn't know what to say in conclusion, nor how to begin a discussion. After some moments of silence, Fred said, "Can we *help* you somehow?"

Zach smiled and decided to drop the pretense that his story was fiction. "I appreciate that, Fred. But I don't think there's much you can do."

"Philosophy is cooler than I'd thought." Fred nodded his head appreciatively.

"It's not usually like this," said Zach, trying to be modest.

Staring off into the distance, Dorothy muttered, "Right, it's not usually like that." She seemed to be thinking out loud.

Zach said, "Dorothy? Did you say something?"

"Oh, me? No, it's just that, like—"

"What?" He found her habit of trailing off into silence annoying.

"Okay." She spoke very slowly, composing her words carefully as she went along. "Let me put it this way, all right? You know, I'm trying to do what you said: get ideas from your story about how to write my paper. All right, so I understand that it's important for you to stop this conspiracy; I agree with that. But how does that make nihilism an issue for the rest of us? I mean, this situation is kind of unusual, isn't it?"

She paused for a moment, then continued: "Believing in a whole philosophy of nihilism—that there's no good-in-itself or evil-in-itself—that's *weird,* isn't it? Most people don't worry about things like that; they don't take them seriously. But because of what these plotters believe, they're willing to do bad things, and you need to try to stop them. Good for you. But isn't the problem that they're just kind of screwed up? Maybe because they've read too much philosophy? I'm saying that the problem isn't nihilism; it's worrying too much about nihilism."

Zach was somewhat taken aback. "Well, let me ask you this," he said. "You say that the conspirators are willing to do 'bad' things. But how do you *know* that they're bad, unless there's a difference between good and evil?"

Dorothy considered this question for a while. "You told us a story about a nice old professor with a wife and baby boy who ended up hanging from a rope. That kind of *makes* the point, doesn't it?"

"Do you think so?" Zach was too tired to argue, but relieved that he'd been able to pass the time without disaster. "Well, I'm sorry that we didn't get to Camus. I thought I'd just try to jazz things up a little this time, that's all. But next time—Camus on suicide. Be prepared to discuss the text, and bring your papers."

Dorothy hung around the classroom after he had dismissed the students. Zach said, "Did you bring a draft for me to look at?" He strongly hoped that she had not brought anything.

"No," she said. "I still haven't been able to start the paper. You know, if you don't mind me saying so, I think the assignment is a little unfair. I mean, you want us to say *why* nihilism is relevant and important. Instead, can't we discuss *whether* it is or not? I think the answer is no."

"That's not the assignment, Dorothy," said Zach. "Look, it's a good exercise for you to state an argument for the im-

portance of this stuff—being an English major and all. At
the end of the day, you don't have to believe it: just show me
that you understand it."

"I don't think I do."

"Listen, I'm sure your grade will be fine. Just sit down and
start writing, okay?"

She nodded, but not very convincingly.

3 • Zach found Kate in the basement of the deserted library,
where she was browsing in recent art history periodicals. He
was jubilant after his successful class.

"I knew it would go fine," said Kate.

"Thanks to you."

"True. Listen, I was going to call your answering machine
to see if Davies had left a message, but I didn't know how to
work it."

"Good idea. I'll call."

They found a telephone in a corner of the library, and
Zach called his machine. In addition to six or seven messages for Judah, there were two for Zach. The first was from
Davies. It said: "Zachary Blumberg, this is a message from
Professor H.P.T. Davies. I have learned that the Judiciary
Committee received a package from Charles Wilson on the
tenth; it was delivered by one of the private, express-mail services, and a receptionist signed for it. As you can imagine,
I wanted to examine the contents of this package. Unfortunately, the committee receives hundreds of unsolicited items
each day during a confirmation hearing, including contri-
butions from all manner of paranoids and conspiracy buffs.
Therefore, mail is duly signed for, then sorted into two piles.
Correspondence from well-known people is opened and read
by peons; packages from everyone else are flung into a huge

bin to be looked at when and if someone gets around to—"

Davies's voice was interrupted by the beep of Zach's answering machine, which gave callers a short but unpredictable amount of time to finish their messages. But he must have called again, for the next message resumed in his voice: "Davies again; I shall have to make it quick, I see. Well, the point is, I have spent my afternoon in a most unusual fashion: on my hands and knees going through the committee's mail." He sounded incredulous at the indignity of it. "Some of this stuff is very quaint, I must say. But the upshot of the whole thing is, Charles's package is not there. Sound familiar? Well, that's my news, I'm afraid. Phone me at the Ambassador, if you like."

The second of Zach's messages had been left by Andrew, who said, "Zach, man, this is Andrew; three-fifteen P.M. I'm calling because the cops are looking for you. It's been on the local news. Mrs. Hausman knows that you were doing business with her old man yesterday. She and the kid went away to her folks' place to stay the night; she came back in the morning and found the prof hangin' on a rope. The cops grew suspicious. Added to which, several neighbors saw shady people running in and out of the place—"

The answering machine had interrupted Andrew as well, but he resumed his message after the next beep: "Yeah, so anyway, now they're looking for you. I'd jettison the wheels, if I were you. Call me if you like; hopefully, I won't be in the village lockup when you call."

They decided to leave the car in one of the vast parking lots that ringed campus; they could go to New Haven by public transportation. They retrieved their bags and the two dissertations from the car, then walked to the bus stop where Zach always waited after class. On the way there, Zach said, "It's too bad that Davies couldn't find Charles's package."

Kate said, "It was worth it, though, to make old Hannibal

spend the afternoon on his hands and knees, sorting through envelopes."

After they had waited in the heat for twenty-five minutes, the bus arrived and carried them away from campus, trundling past rest homes and housing developments, shopping malls and stretches of bleak highway. The only people who rode the bus in this part of the world were too young, old, poor, or insane to own a car. Each stop seemed to last forever, as a senior citizen or a mental outpatient clambered on board and fussed with bus vouchers and ID cards. But the bus was air-conditioned and comfortable enough.

They switched from bus to train in an urban center that was really too shallowly rooted and unplanned to be called a town, having sprouted in the 1980's like a nest of crystals in a chemical solution. No continuous sidewalks had yet been laid amid the corporate headquarters, sheathed in mirrors and steel, so they had to make their way gingerly down the margins of busy roads from the bus depot to the Metro-North train station. Zach was used to this, but Kate seemed to find the experience deeply irritating, wincing every time a truck roared past.

They took an empty train to New York, then changed to a full one going north into Connecticut. By now they were both exhausted, hot, and discouraged. They had a brief and testy exchange about who should sit in the one available seat on the train (each one wanted the other to occupy it), but before they could agree, a businessman in a tan suit seized it from them. They had to hang from metal bars until Stamford, then sat squeezed among office workers. Just east of Bridgeport, Zach noticed a headline in a tabloid newspaper that a woman across the aisle was reading: "Frye vote tomorrow; White House is confident." Next to the story was a grinning

photograph of Judge Frye in a bowtie. Zach pointed to it and
Kate nodded, grimacing.

They arrived in New Haven just before eight. The train
station was in a blighted neighborhood near downtown, and
they had to wait forty minutes for one of the city's four cabs
to pick them up. They decided not to go immediately to campus, since that was one of the few places in America where
Sternians might be waiting to surprise them. Zach, whose
knowledge of New Haven after four years of living there
barely surpassed his knowledge of Ulan Bator, did not know
where else to suggest going. He finally thought of the Divinity
School, a miniature Colonial-revival campus that was situ-
ated within walking distance of the heart of Yale, and where
he had once taken a seminar on death-of-God theology. The
taxi duly dropped them by its front gates; they paid the driver and began to wander through modest, neoclassical colon-
nades. The night had turned mild and insects were busy
chirping and buzzing at each other. Traffic could be heard
faintly in the distance, but the school itself was so quiet in
late August that they might almost have been strolling deep
in the countryside. At the back of the campus, they found a
steep hill overlooking the lights of New Haven, where Zach
had often gone before to contemplate the pathos of his life.
This time, he had someone to sit with him, so they waited together until after midnight, saying good-night to the few res-
ident students—mostly cheerful couples with babies in
tow—and watching the house lights flicker off across the city.

After they had heard the midnight bell ring, they started
to walk down the hill toward the center of Yale, using an in-
direct route as a final precaution against being spotted. They
walked down dark, tree-lined streets, past Victorian man-
sions and institutional Yale buildings. Usually, Zach feared
walking these streets at night, because lone graduate stu-

dents were frequently mugged. Tonight, however, he had
other worries to contend with.

As they approached the heart of Yale, the buildings became larger and more homogeneously Gothic. Where loud
voices and music might blare on a hot September night, now
only crickets broke the evening silence; sprinklers made
fountains of the lawns, and a potent smell of cut grass filled
the air. Alice was supposed to be waiting for them in her office inside one of Yale's residential colleges—walled,
vaguely monastic compounds, each containing dormitory
space, a dining hall, faculty offices, and a library. Since the
students were all gone for the summer, the gates of her college were fastened with heavy padlocks. Zach and Kate
peered through the wrought-iron grille at a Gothic inner
courtyard. Seeing no one inside, they searched the sur-
rounding streets for a public telephone, and found one at last
on a nearby thoroughfare that was lined with bars and pizza
joints. Alice answered the phone in her office, and agreed
to let them in the gate of her college.

She met them there five minutes later, dressed in black
slacks, a black turtleneck, and black pumps. "Camouflage,"
she explained, as she unfastened the lock. She shook hands
solemnly with Kate, introducing herself as Alice; Kate
looked starstruck. Then Alice led them through a leafy
Gothic courtyard paved with cobblestones, down a narrow
passage, and across another, smaller courtyard to a me-
dieval-looking door, which was decorated with heavy iron
studs. "Doesn't Yale look *wonderful* without the students!"
she said. "And one can get *work* done here now, without that
infernal noise." However, Zach suspected that Alice's greatest distraction during the semester was not noise, but visits
from her numerous undergraduate friends and admirers.

Her office was a spacious paneled room with leaded

windows and worn leather furniture. A portable television set perched on the desk. Pointing at it, she explained: "I just cannot tear myself away from the hearings, especially now."

She sat Kate and Zach down on a couch, offered them tea and biscuits, and then rummaged among some papers until she had produced a newspaper clipping. Showing it to her guests, she said, "I have been looking through transcripts of the hearings, as reported in the *Times*. Last Tuesday, Fry was asked to list his major intellectual influences. Look who he mentioned."

They skimmed the article until they found the name Otto Stern: Frye had expressed his profound admiration for this great conservative thinker.

As Zach and Kate congratulated Alice for finding this clue, she said, "I have one other item that might be worth looking at." She produced a photocopy of a law-review article by Frye, entitled "Natural Law and Judicial Responsibility." Handing it to Zach, she said, "You probably should read this yourself, to see if I'm right. I had a graduate assistant find it, and then I applied your ingenious method for decoding the Sternians. The beginning of the article says that if we don't believe in natural law, then we'll have no values at all and that will be terrible. Then there's a lot of boring mumbo-jumbo about Aquinas and Jefferson. But right in the middle, Frye quotes a passage from a 1971 article in the *Indiana Law Review*. Wait till you see who wrote that passage."

Zach found a highlighted section in the middle of the article. It was a quoted passage by Robert Bork, attacking moral objectivity. According to Bork, no one could say that any kind of "gratification" was morally superior to any other. Philosophy was supposed to distinguish good forms of pleasure from bad ones, but all moral theories were re-

ally just expressions of personal taste. Every pleasant
sensation—from sexual satisfaction to pride in doing the
right thing—was equally legitimate. Although Bork didn't
say so explicitly, he seemed to imply Nietzsche's dictum:
"Nothing is true and everything is permitted."

"I take it," said Alice, "that that's Frye's real position, too.
He pretends that he's quoting Bork with disapproval, as a
crazy nihilist—but he places this pithy passage bang in the
middle of his article. That practically announces that he's
playing the Sternian game, doesn't it? I mean, it's their classic procedure."

Zach nodded and began to skim the rest of the article.
Meanwhile, Alice asked if she might continue working, since
they ought to wait three more hours before breaking into
Crypt. Zach and Kate nodded and smiled politely, then
watched her as she bent her white head over a pile of papers
on her desk, reading and writing with total concentration by
the light of an old-fashioned desk lamp. Next to her on the
desk stood a cluster of framed photographs showing small
children, a panting Irish setter, and another distinguished-
looking woman of Alice's generation.

Zach couldn't concentrate on the article, although at first
glance he agreed with Alice's interpretation. He put it down
and stared into the distance. After a moment or two, Alice
looked up. "Don't you two have something to occupy your-
selves with? What a terrible hostess I am! Please excuse
me—I must finish a piece for the *PMLA* on approaches to
Donne. If I don't get some writing done tonight, when will I?
You're in the business; you understand how little time there
always seems to be."

They urged her to continue working. Kate browsed
through the bookshelves and picked out one of Alice's own
books to read: *Staircase to God: Images of Transcendence in*

Dante, Wordsworth, and Eliot. Zach put his head down on the arm of the overstuffed couch and tried to nap.

4 • At three-thirty in the morning, Alice gently awakened Zach and Kate by puttering around her office: they were both now sleeping on the couch, one on each arm. When they had opened their eyes and raised their heads, she said, "It's time to get moving."

Kate rubbed her eyes. "You have amazing stamina, Professor Webster."

"Oh, you'll find that you need less sleep as you grow older. When I was your age—back in the Pleistocene—I used to need six whole hours every night or I would be useless the next morning. Now I can do with three."

They conferred briefly about their plan of action. Zach put his and Charles's dissertations in a canvas bag that belonged to Alice, and carried it with him. Alice led the way out of her office, across two college courtyards, and onto the deserted and rather ominous streets of New Haven. They walked a few blocks to the Old Campus, the fortresslike quadrangle that lies at the very center of Yale.

Phelps Gate contained the main office of the campus police, which was open and cheerfully illuminated even at this late hour. Alice waved to the officer on duty and then led them across the lawn of Old Campus toward a small Gothic chapel adorned with rows of spires. "Why are we going this way?" said Zach, knowing that Crypt lay outside the Old Campus walls.

"You'll see," said Alice.

She pushed the chapel door open and led them inside. They stood in the darkness for a few seconds until Alice produced a flashlight and scanned the room with its beam. Overhead, they could vaguely make out ribbed vaulting; slender piers seemed to support the roof. Alice whispered: "When Crypt taps people for membership—you know, recruits them—the brothers don't announce who they are. They just show up in ludicrous hoods, they blindfold the eager inductees, and then they lead them here. In the pitch-dark, the poor fellows don't recognize the place—not that most students come here much anyway."

"Then where do they go?" asked Kate, a quiver of apprehension in her voice.

"Follow me," said Alice, who was obviously enjoying every moment of the adventure. She led the way with her flashlight down the nave of the chapel. She let the beam rest on the altar for a moment, then walked around the back of it. "I'm sure that they pause here for some spooky ritual during the induction ceremony; how could anyone resist? An altar, black hoods—it's deliciously Gothic. But we have work to do."

Kneeling down behind the altar, she let her flashlight play on the stonework. By now, Zach and Kate could dimly make out the interior of the chapel, with its bare white walls and narrow pointed windows. Alice inserted a finger in a crack, winced for an instant, and then withdrew her hand quickly as the stone panel slid forward. "Isn't this fabulous!" she said.

"Why couldn't we just enter Crypt through the front door?" Zach did not like the look of the chasm that had just opened up.

"Someone might see us," Alice explained cheerfully.

She led them down a steep set of stairs into the inky darkness. Once they had descended five or six steps, pressing their hands against the cold stone wall for support, Alice stepped back up the stairs and pulled the stone panel shut behind them. Zach, who had never before suffered from claustrophobia, could now vividly imagine death by suffocation, immurement, thirst, and starvation. He pictured their white bones scattered down the stairs. "Will that open again?" he whispered.

"Of course," said Alice.

At the bottom of the stairs, they found themselves in a long corridor. Overhead, bulky insulated steam pipes ran into the distance. "Look," Alice said, "this is just a standard Yale steam tunnel. You've seen them all over campus. I'm sure there are many entrances that are far more prosaic than the one we just used. Still, I'm only following my friend's instructions."

They walked down the corridor for perhaps fifty yards until they reached a junction. "First right," said Alice, still leading the way with the flashlight. After another twenty or thirty yards, they came upon a drab metal door with the word "Private" stenciled across it in pale blue lettering. Alice pointed the flashlight toward the ceiling and located a steam pipe that turned off from the main corridor and ran into the private area beyond the door. "You see, I *told* the president that Crypt gets its heat from Yale and that we could cut them off unless they admitted women. He denied it outright. But I should have known that he'd lie, since he's a Bell, Bones, and Candle man himself. I'm sure that his society is hooked up to the steam plant, too. Tut, tut."

Next to the door there was a small metal box with a slit down the middle and a tiny red electric light. Alice removed a plastic card from her purse and ran it through the device; the light turned green and a soft buzzing sound emerged from it. Alice removed the card and opened the door. "Quick," she said, stepping inside.

An insistent beeping sound started as they entered the hallway beyond the door. Alice quickly located an electronic keypad glowing in the dark and typed a code onto it. The beeping continued. Alice hastily reentered the code.

Still the beeping continued. She consulted a scrap of paper and began to enter the code for a third time. Finally, Kate said, "Do you have to hit the pound key when you're done?"

"The what key?" said Alice.

Kate pushed the # key and the beeping stopped. "Good for you," said Alice. "I'm still living in the Edwardian period, as you can see."

She pointed the flashlight beam down a concrete corridor that was much like the steam tunnels on the other side of the door, except that now the floor was concealed under a heavy blue carpet, embellished with silver rams' skulls and coffins. A few paces farther on, the hall ended at another door, the handle of which turned easily. Beyond that door, they found themselves in a wide corridor, paved with flagstones and lined with oak paneling and iron sconces.

"I don't know exactly where to go now," Alice whispered, "except that the archive is on the top floor."

Her flashlight beam picked up a flight of stone steps at the end of the corridor. They climbed the steps, passing a broad landing adorned with elk heads, and finally reached a large entrance hall decorated in the Jacobean style with a hammer-beam ceiling, oak paneling, and a series of elaborately framed oil portraits.

On either side of the hall were large rooms into which the flashlight beam projected weakly, picking out nothing but tomblike darkness. A broad flight of steps led upward through the windowless building, and once again they ascended. At both the second and third floors, they stopped briefly to survey their surroundings with the flashlight, but they could see little more than some heavy oak furniture and large, paneled rooms. The staircase that led upward from the third floor was more modest, the paneling having given way to simple plaster walls. On the fourth floor, the stairs stopped and they found themselves in a relatively narrow corridor, simply decorated in the style of a modern office suite. Each side of the corridor was lined with plain, unmarked wooden doors.

The first two doors on the right led to offices; the third admitted them to a large room, on the walls of which they could barely see rows of books in the beam of the flashlight. "This must be the place," said Alice. Zach found a light switch and turned it on; Alice closed the door behind them as they stood blinking in the middle of a library. Once their eyes had adjusted to the light, they could see that the walls were lined with tall bookcases, each surmounted by a plaster bust; in the middle of the room stood a long hardwood table and six high-backed chairs.

"Do you still have the dissertation?" asked Alice.

Zach emptied the canvas bag that he was holding onto the floor, picked up Charles's thesis, and handed it to Alice. "Let's see if any of the letters he cites were addressed to Frye," Alice said.

"Even if they weren't, let's copy them," said Zach.

They identified the busts of Aubrey and Harmondsworth by examining the brass nameplates under each statuette. Under Aubrey's bust was a set of perhaps thirty old-fashioned binders with numbers painted on their imitation-leather spines. Opening one at random, Zach saw that it contained hundreds of letters, some typed and some written with a fountain pen in a cramped handwriting. The first letter that he examined had been written in German, dated March 4, 1948, and signed "Herr Doktor Professor O. Stern."

"I'll look up Charles's references," said Zach. "Why don't you both start browsing through the other letters to see if you pick up anything interesting."

They each began turning the pages of a binder. Zach quickly found one of the letters that Charles had quoted: he couldn't read the German, but he could see that it was addressed to someone he had never heard of.

"Do you know where a copier is?" he asked Alice.

"Yes, my friend said it was across the hall." She was reading intently and did not look up as she spoke.

Zach found his way across the hall to a small office, switched on a photocopier, and waited while it warmed up. When it was ready, he copied the two-page letter and returned to the library. "Find anything?" he asked.

They both shook their heads absentmindedly. One by one, Zach located all of the letters that Charles had cited; none was addressed to Frye, but Zach copied them all anyway. When he returned from one of his trips across the hall, Kate said, "I found a letter to Frye."

"You did?" Zach said excitedly, but she shrugged and passed the volume to him. The letter, written in English, simply said:

1.28.1967

Dear Professor Frye,

Thank you for your invitation to participate in the ABA panel on moral philosophy and the law. I am afraid that I shall be prevented from attending on account of a prior commitment. Best wishes,

O. Stern

"Well, they were hardly best buddies in sixty-seven," Kate said.

"That was a long time ago, though," said Zach, trying to be optimistic.

Alice had been reading letters from the 1940s, but she changed volumes on the ground that no revealing correspondence between Stern and Frye could have taken place before the 1960s. After forty-five minutes of concentrated skimming, they finished examining every volume.

"Nothing between Frye and Stern," said Zach, who was beginning to lose hope.

Alice said, "His last letters were written here in New Haven. It seems inconceivable that he could have spent his retirement here, that his letters could have ended up in Frye's hands, and yet there was no correspondence between them."

"Perhaps they just spoke to each other," said Zach.

Kate added: "Or maybe Frye keeps their letters in *his* personal archive." She had found a cardboard magazine file containing a set of loose papers, which she poured out onto the table. "This seems to be Stern's business and legal stuff," she said.

"How about a will?" asked Alice.

"Yeah," said Zach, "Stern must have left all his letters and notes to Crypt. Or perhaps he left them to Frye. Either way, a will would prove that Frye knew about Stern's nihilism. Otherwise, the old man would never have let him see his private papers."

Kate could not find a will, but she did discover a typewritten inventory of the contents of the box. "The will is *supposed* to be in here," she said.

They sorted through the papers several times, looking for the will or for any other mention of Frye. "It's gone," said Zach.

"Remind you of anything?" said Kate. She walked across the hall to see if the will happened to be filed in the office. She had been gone for four or five minutes when they suddenly heard the unmistakable sound of a door opening downstairs and a short series of electronic beeps.

5 • *Z*ach and Alice froze, listening intently. Zach mouthed silent curses; Alice tiptoed to the door and gently pushed it

closed. They stared at each other in fright.

Silence lasted for what seemed like a very long time, although it might have been less than five minutes. Then someone tapped very lightly on the door.

Alice looked at Zach, and he shrugged. After a few seconds, they heard Kate whisper, "Guys?" Before Alice opened the door, Zach switched off the light. They were immediately plunged into total darkness. Zach heard the door open and close again. Kate whispered very quietly, "Are you guys okay in here?"

"Yeah," whispered Zach.

"Did you see anything out there?" asked Alice.

Kate whispered: "No. But when the light's on in this room, you can see it under the door. Better keep it off."

Zach, sweating profusely and clutching a ream of photocopies in his hand, began to inch forward until he bumped into something on the floor. It turned out to be the canvas bag that he had used to carry the dissertations. He squatted down and stuffed the photocopies into the bag, then remained crouching on the floor.

"Can someone lock that door?" he whispered. He heard some soft scuffling sounds, and then Kate said, "I can feel the doorknob. But I don't feel any lock."

"We'd better just stay in the dark and hope no one comes up," said Zach. He made himself comfortable on the carpeted floor. With nothing to see or do, it was impossible to tell how much time had passed, but it seemed like hours before Kate finally whispered, "Hey, I found something when I was in the office across the hall."

"What?" said Zach.

"A piece of paper listing all the society officers and their phone numbers. It describes Frye as the Crypt archivist."

Zach tried to picture the documents that he had photocopied. "I don't think there's anything on the Stern letters that says 'Crypt,' " he whispered. "Without proof that the letters were filed here, it will mean nothing to say that Frye is the archivist."

Kate said, "What if we *put* something on them?"

"What do you mean?" said Zach.

"I saw a Crypt stamp across the hall. Do you want me to get it?"

"Can you?" said Alice.

"I think so. It was on the desk; I can feel my way there."

"Better be extremely careful," said Alice.

There was more faint shuffling, the door opened very quietly, and then Zach could make out a dim rectangle of less profound darkness.

After five or ten minutes of silence, the door closed again and Kate whispered, "Success—I've got the stamp. There's a light on somewhere downstairs, but I couldn't hear anything. Do you guys want to try to sneak out of the building?"

"Too dangerous," said Alice. "When they leave, we'll hear the alarm being reset and we'll know it's safe."

They waited, the silence punctuated only by their breathing, the darkness broken only by the dial of Alice's watch, which Zach could gradually make out five or ten feet away.

"What time is it?" he whispered.

"Seven," said Alice.

Never did two hours pass more slowly, but by nine o'clock they still had heard nothing from below. Finally, Kate said, "I'm going to do some more reconnaissance."

This time, when she returned, she said, "I think we could get down at least one flight with no problem."

"Why not wait here?" said Alice.

"At this rate, the hearings will be over before we get out," Zach muttered.

Kate added: "And at some point, someone could find us up here. I'd rather make a break for it."

"Okay, but we've got to tidy up first," said Alice. "The papers are lying all over the table, and we've left the flashlight somewhere. We must cover our tracks."

"Can we risk the light?" said Zach.

"I think so," said Kate. "Whoever's here is several floors below us."

After a few seconds, Kate said, "Close your eyes; I'm switching it on."

Even through Zach's eyelids, the light felt painfully bright. When he had adjusted to the glare, he helped Kate and Alice put Stern's correspondence back on the shelf and retrieve the flashlight. Then Alice switched the light back off, and they faced impenetrable darkness once more. Zach sank to his knees and began crawling in the direction of the door, carrying the canvas bag with him. On the way, he bumped into a chair, the wall, and Kate's foot, but at last he found the doorway and followed her out. In the hallway, they could just make out each other's silhouettes. Like three overgrown infants, they crawled down the hall toward the stairs and the tinge of light that emanated from below.

It was difficult to crawl downstairs, but Zach found that he could back down. When they reached the landing below, the light became slightly brighter and it was possible to tiptoe. Kate leaned gingerly over the railing and whispered, "I can't see anything."

Just then, they were startled by a loud roaring noise. At first it was unidentifiable and menacing, but then Alice whispered in Zach's ear: "Vacuum cleaner." She repeated the message to Kate as Zach nodded in relief. They inched their way down the next flight of stairs, with Kate in front. At that point, they could see that only the ground level was illuminated, so they felt safe descending to the second floor. When they reached the landing below that level, Kate peered gingerly around the corner, then beckoned the others to follow her. The ground-floor foyer appeared to be empty, but it was brightly lit and the vacuuming noise was not far off.

While they stood on the landing, peering around the banister at the foyer below them, they suddenly heard a loud electric chime. The vacuum continued to roar until the chime sounded for a second time. At that point, the vacuuming stopped and they heard heavy footsteps downstairs. They backed rapidly up the stairs toward the second floor. They heard a lock turn and a heavy door open, and then a man's voice said, "Hey, Hefty, how're you this morning?"

Another male voice replied, "Good morning, Mr. Stevenson. I was just doing the usual."

"All right. You didn't see anyone in here when you arrived, did you?"

"No, sir, nobody."

"That's funny. The security company called me to say that someone entered the building at four A.M. last night. They just wanted to know if that was all right. As a matter of fact, I thought it was pretty unusual, especially in the middle of the summer. I drove straight here from Hamden as soon as I heard. You sure no one else is here?"

"The place was as dark as a coffin when I showed up at six-thirty."

"Maybe it was just a mistake. Thing is, if someone did check in, they didn't check out. I'm going to look around, make sure we didn't have a burglary or something."

"Okay, Mr. Stevenson. If you need me, shout."

Up on the second floor, Zach, Kate, and Alice hurriedly opened the first door on the left and stepped into pitch darkness, pulling the door shut behind them immediately. The vacuum cleaner started to make its noise again. After a few minutes a light went on in the hall adjacent to them. If someone walked into the room where they stood, they would be completely exposed.

They flattened out against the wall, standing in a row to the left of the door. Immediately, it flew open and strong light flooded the center portion of the room. A man must have been standing in the doorway, surveying the room, for his long shadow fell across the floor. The light also revealed one object in the otherwise bare chamber: a huge, Egyptian-style sarcophagus, carved out of a solid block of basalt. One end was higher than the other and appeared to represent a sphinx's head.

They held their breath and winced for a few seconds; then the door closed.

"Let's get out of here," Kate whispered. She peered through the keyhole. "He's gone upstairs, I think. The alarm's not set. Let's just make a beeline out the front."

She opened the door slowly and peeked her head out, then gave an "okay" sign with her hand. They slipped out of the room, glancing nervously over their shoulders and up the stairs. Once in the hall, they could see that lights had been switched on above them. After running down one flight, they peered around the banister toward the main foyer, which seemed to be empty. The vacuum cleaner was still roaring somewhere below. Kate gestured with her thumb and they bolted down the last flight of stairs, across the foyer, and on toward the main door. Zach grabbed the knob and turned it quickly; then they all piled outside into the intense sunshine of an August day in New Haven. As they pulled the door closed behind them, a middle-aged woman in a tank top looked up in surprise to see two women and a man with a canvas bag rushing out of the Crypt building. When she noticed that they had seen her, she turned away hurriedly.

They ran across the street and into the classroom building opposite, not daring to look back. Once inside, they rushed into an empty lecture hall and closed the door behind them.

"We did it!" said Alice, breathless and beaming.

"Yeah!" said Kate, also grinning.

But then Zach struck his forehead with disgust. "Damn it!" he said.

"What?" said Alice.

Zach peered into the canvas bag, which he was still carrying. "I left my dissertation on the floor. I can just picture it lying there."

6 • They had no choice but to abandon Zach's dissertation. As they walked toward Alice's office by a circuitous route, carefully avoiding the Crypt building, they discussed strategy. They decided to fax Davies the list of Crypt officers and a set of nihilistic letters written by Stern, on which they would place the Crypt stamp. Then a senator could ask Frye for his opinion of Stern. If Frye said that Stern was a great man, the senator could produce the nihilistic letters. If he denied knowing about the letters, then the senator could produce the document that proved that Frye was the Crypt archivist.

They arrived at Alice's office and threw themselves onto her couches, feeling stiff, exhausted, and hungry, but relieved to be safe. After a few minutes, Zach tried to call Davies at the Ambassador Hotel, but he was out. He decided to call his own answering machine, in case Davies had left a message. In fact, there were several messages for Zach, the first of which said: "This is Professor Davies. No word from you so I assume it's all off. Bad luck, old man. I'm going to the hearing room to witness the coronation. See you in New Haven at term time."

"Damn!" said Zach. But before he could explain what he had heard, the second message began: "Hello, Zachary Blumberg, this is Sergeant James Esposito of the Ithaca City

Police. We would like to speak with you in connection with the death of Professor Jules Hausman. In fact, we're asking you to contact us right away. Since you left town so quickly and abandoned your rental car near the Connecticut border, I'm afraid we have been forced to obtain a warrant for your arrest. If you do not contact us, we will have to serve the warrant. If you submit voluntarily to an interview, that'll make everything much easier for all concerned. So please call me right away."

He had left his telephone number and then hung up. Zach described the two messages to Kate and Alice. Then he said, "How can we get through to Davies?"

Kate said: "We could fly to Washington. How long would that take?"

"Too long," said Alice. "The flights from here are very infrequent."

They pondered the problem for a few minutes, growing increasingly pessimistic. Then Alice said, "Hold on a second. I'm friends with our congressman; he's a former student of mine. Maybe I could call his office and get someone to pull Davies out of the hearing."

She started to make the call while Zach switched on her TV, turned it to face the middle of the room, and found the public-affairs channel. The chairman of the committee was making a speech before a packed chamber.

"Judge Frye," he said, "this has been a grueling experience for all of us, I know, but also an immensely educational one, in my opinion. I am just so darn proud of my committee for all the work they've done and for the incredible intelligence they've shown throughout these hearings. That goes for both sides of the aisle—tremendous work. And the staff, of course—great job. Couldn't function without them." He beamed at the row of aides who sat behind the senators on the dais. "All right," he continued, "now I'm going to give

my closing comments, reserving my right to ask more questions later. Then we'll have a final five minutes for each senator, your comments, and a brief caucus before the vote.
Okay with you, Judge?"

Meanwhile, Alice was talking softly on the telephone.
She hung up as the chairman began to read his speech.
"They're sending somebody over to the Senate side," she
said. "Davies will call us here as soon as they find him."

They watched the chairman deliver his remarks, while
Kate applied Crypt stamps to the Stern letters. The chairman offered interminable, vague comments about the importance of the Constitution, the crucial role of the Senate
and the Senate Committee on the Judiciary, the history of
confirmation hearings, the value of bipartisanship, and the
superb qualifications of the nominee. He concluded by saying that, despite opposition within his own party, he was
going to support Judge Frye as the single best-qualified man
for the job.

Just as he was wrapping up, the telephone rang. Alice
picked it up and said: "Hello. . . . Hello, Hannibal, this is
Alice Webster; I've been helping Zachary Blumberg and his
friend. . . . Yes, well, strange bedfellows. Nice to be on the
same side, for a change. . . . Right, we called because we
have some material that we want to fax to you. . . . Yes, send
by fax. . . . It's several things. First, a transcript from last
week's hearings, in which Frye states that he admires Stern.
. . . Right, then some letters from Stern himself that explicitly espouse nihilism. They're in German, I'm afraid. . . . I
know. . . . Well, look, they're the same letters that Charles
quoted. We can send you the relevant pages from his dissertation as well, to serve as a translation."

She made an exasperated face while she listened to
Davies. Then she continued: "Right, right. . . . So if Frye de-
nies knowing about the letters, here's the clincher. They're

stamped with Crypt's logo, and we have a piece of paper stating that Frye is the Crypt archivist. . . . What? . . . Hannibal, you must be joking. . . . Hannibal! . . . My God, whose side *are* you on? . . . All right, that might possibly work. . . . Very well. Go to the Judiciary Committee Office and wait by the fax; call us back as soon as you know anything. . . . Right."

She hung up, looking frustrated and angry.

"What's the matter?" said Zach.

"It would violate his Crypt honor, so-called, if he had any role in revealing the name of a society officer. Also, he won't make public any document that has the Crypt stamp on it."

Kate looked down at the photocopies that she had just finished stamping. "I can white this out," she said.

"Do that," said Alice. "We'll fax him everything and see what he can do. He's going to give the documents to that nice Southern senator, the one who sounds like an old hillbilly but turns out to believe in fairness and justice. He's also got a sharp mind. He has heard our whole story from Davies, and he definitely wants to sink Frye. Did you see him cross-examine the man about his Crypt membership?"

Alice led them out of her office and across the courtyard to the college master's office. The anteroom was a small, cheerful space with two desks, posters and flowers, a fax machine, and a smiling secretary. Union decals were pasted all over the desk.

"Hi, Janice," said Alice. "We're going to fax something, okay?"

"Help yourself, Alice."

They first had to call the Judiciary Committee to get the fax number, then started feeding material to Davies. They wrote the telephone number of the master's office on the cover page so that Davies could call them back. He called right away to say that the documents were arriving, and that he was passing them to the friendly senator by way of a competent staff person.

A small television set rested on a shelf opposite the secretary's desk. "Janice," said Alice, "the Frye confirmation is coming to a close today. Do you mind if we watch?"

"Today's the day? I'd like to watch myself. I hope they skewer the bastard." She used a remote-control device to turn the set on.

A conservative senator was praising Frye fulsomely, and asking such penetrating questions as: "Who do you credit with teaching you to have such a fine judicial temperament: your parents? Or was it the church?"

Frye answered politely, a little smile playing at the corner of his lips. After ten minutes of this, the senator said, "Well, I guess I've gone over my time, Mr. Chairman. Just love talking to the Judge, is all."

The chairman said, "It has been interesting, hasn't it? For you as well, I hope, Judge."

Frye assured him that the hearings had been "most instructive." Then the chairman began to rephrase his earlier remarks about the great educational value of confirmation hearings for the whole American people. After five or ten minutes of this, the camera shifted to the Southern senator who was supposed to be helping them. He began: "Good morning, Judge."

"Good morning, Senator," said Frye, who now looked a bit wary, though still basically smug.

"How are you this morning?" The senator was laying on the drawl.

"I'm fine, Senator."

"That's good. Congratulations on your performance so far. It has been very impressive."

"Thank you, Senator."

"Judge, I just have a couple of questions."

There was a pause. Frye, seeing that a response was expected from him, said, "Go ahead, Senator."

"All right. Now, way back, when was it?—last week sometime, one of us asked you to state your opinion of Otto Stern. Remember that?"

"Yes, Senator, vaguely." It was clear from his face that Frye did not like this line of questioning.

"You said he'd been a formative influence on you, isn't that right?"

"I'm not sure I went that far, Senator."

"Okay, maybe you're right. The words you used, Judge, were 'the most important philosophical influence in my life.' Do you recall those words, Judge?"

"Not precisely, but I'm sure the record is accurate."

"I'm sure it is. We have very fine stenographers here, very fine. All right. Now a funny thing has happened. I've come across some letters written by this fellow Stern that are very interesting. It's been one heck of a long time since I read any philosophy, so maybe you can explain what he means. For instance, listen to this. He says, 'The vast majority of the American public remain blissfully ignorant children, who will swallow whole any pronouncement by an expert with a PhD after his name.' " There was an audible murmur from the audience. " 'This is their great virtue,' " the senator continued over the noise, " 'and it offers us our opening. Having only the most rudimentary education, they are as ignorant of the Death of God and the onslaught of nihilism as the hermit whom Zarathustra encountered in the forest.' I hope I'm pronouncing that name right; I never did study German. Did I pronounce it right, Judge?"

Frye nodded silently, biting his lip. The senator resumed reading: " 'Did Zarathustra tell the old fool that God was dead? Of course not; he was no sadist. He left the man in peaceful oblivion. And so shall we protect our fellow citizens in this innocent young republic; we shall offer them the placebo of a natural-law doctrine, contrived to match the fatuous generalities of their precious Constitution.' "

The room was now filled with excited conversation. The chairman pounded his gavel on the rostrum, demanding order. When at last the audience had settled down, the Southern senator continued: "Judge, since you're such a big fan of Stern's, can you explain to me what he meant by that paragraph I just read?"

Frye was conferring with a dark-suited man to his right.

The senator said, "Would it help if I read a few more letters?"

Frye finally raised his head and said, "Senator, I am profoundly shocked by the document that you just read. It sounds like nothing that Otto Stern could ever have written. It represents all that he hated most. It is appalling, and I feel certain that it is some kind of hoax or forgery that you are the victim of. May I please see the document?"

A sheet of paper was handed down to Frye, who showed it to his companion. After they had conferred for a few more minutes, Frye said, "This is an alleged quotation, contained in someone else's work."

"That's right," said the senator, "but I have the original German text here with me, too. Mr. Chairman, I'd like to ask that both documents be entered into the record."

"Without objection, so ordered," said the chairman.

"May I see the original?" said Frye.

It too was passed to him. "This is a facsimile," he said.

"That's true. Is it your position that it must be a fraud?"

"Yes, Senator, that is my only guess."

"You have never seen it before?"

"Not to my knowledge."

"Do you recognize the handwriting?"

"Not to my knowledge."

A senator who sat near the end of the dais interrupted. "Mr. Chairman, it is ridiculous and totally out of order for new evidence of very questionable merit and relevance to be introduced on the last day of the hearings. I demand that you rule this line of questioning out of order. What does it have to do with the judge's qualifications?"

"The senator may continue his questions," said the chairman.

"This is an outrage," said another senator. "It's turning into a circus."

"Very well," said the chairman. "I was not aware in advance that the senator was going to pursue this line of questioning. The committee will caucus for thirty minutes while the chairman listens to procedural arguments from both sides. Is that satisfactory to you, Judge?"

"Yes. In fact, Mr. Chairman, I would like to request a longer delay. Given just a bit more time, I should be able to prove that these purported documents are forgeries."

"Fine. One hour? All right. The committee will adjourn until twelve-fifteen today." He brought his gavel down with a crash.

7 • "What's Frye up to?" said Zach.

"I don't know, but we'd better try to counter him," said Kate.

"How?"

Alice said, "I know. Let's find that will. I'll call my lawyer right away and ask him where wills are filed."

Janice the secretary said, "What's going on here?"

Alice was using the telephone; Zach ignored Janice's question but asked her, "If you fax something from here, does it say on the fax where it was sent from?"

"Yes. It says right on top, next to the date and time."

"That means that Frye knows we're here," said Zach.

"What's he going to do," said Kate, "send around his goons to beat us up?"

"What is going on here?" Janice repeated. "Are you involved with this?" She pointed at the TV, which showed people filing out of the committee room for the recess while baroque instrumental music played in the background.

Alice hung up. "My lawyer's assistant says that when wills are probated, they get entered into the public records of the probate court. The court in the county where the deceased died usually has jurisdiction. That means that the New Haven probate court may have Stern's will."

"Let's go," said Zach. "Where is it?"

"Do you need a phone book?" asked Janice.

"Yes, please," said Zach.

She handed him a telephone book, and he searched frantically for the probate court's address. "Blue pages," said Janice.

Zach found it in the blue pages; it was downtown. "Kate," he said, "you want to come with me?"

"I'll hold Davies on the line when he calls in," said Alice.

"Can I drive you downtown?" said Janice. "I will if you'll tell me what's going on."

"We'll tell you on the way," said Kate, and they bolted for the door.

Janice's car was parked three blocks away in a university lot. They jogged there and climbed in while Zach breathlessly explained what they were trying to do. Meanwhile, Janice began to drive them through the narrow one-way streets and heavy traffic of New Haven. After making a loop around several Yale colleges, they skirted the New Haven Green, a huge grassy square containing three elegant churches. They passed bus stops where scores of people waited under the grueling sun. They stopped at a light near blighted storefronts with lettering from the 1940s. Two more red lights and another detour through one-way streets delayed them further, but at last they arrived outside a large, grim building that housed the county courts.

Janice waited in the car while Zach and Kate sprinted up the steps and into the dark corridors of the main floor. Breathless, they asked a passing police officer for the probate court's record office. He directed them to the fourth floor. They found a bank of elevators and waited for what seemed like ten minutes for a car that was going up. As they ascended in the crowded elevator, Kate suddenly whispered, "What if Frye's people call the police?"

"What do you mean?" said Zach.

"The Ithaca police. To tell them that we're in Alice's college. They could call the New Haven cops, and we'd be busted."

"You're right," said Zach. "That's what he should do."

At the fourth floor, they jumped out of the elevator and started running down the long, marble-lined hall, glancing hastily at the sign by each door. By now it was twenty-five minutes before noon. They ran all the way down one side of the building, turned right, ran down another side, turned right again, and finally found a door marked "Probate Court: Records." The door was unlocked, and bursting through it they found themselves in a large, dusty room, lit with hanging fluorescent lights, and divided in two by a long wooden partition. On their side of the partition stood a couple of vinyl-backed chairs and a microfilm reader, which was currently being used by a very thin man in an ill-fitting pin-striped suit. On the other side were desks and filing cabinets, as well as four employees: three black women ranging in age from about twenty to sixty, and one fat, elderly white man in suspenders. The women were busily typing or filing; the man sat idly on a stool in the middle of the room.

He said, "Can I help you?"

"We're looking for a will," said Kate.

"Fill out one of those," he said, pointing to a box of forms on the top of the partition, "and the girls will locate the record for you."

Kate scowled at him and took the form. She filled part of it in as she spoke: "Name? Otto Stern. Address? New Haven—we don't know where. Date deceased? Around nineteen eighty. Date probated? Who knows? Social Security number? Beats me."

She handed it back to the man behind the counter.

"The way you filled this out," he said, "only the name's satisfactory."

"How many Otto Sterns can there be?"

"Wills are filed by date deceased. Without a date, it would take the girls forever to find him. So we don't do them without dates. You can find out when he passed away from the county tax office."

"This is an emergency," said Zach. "Can't you help us? We can look through the files ourselves."

The oldest of the women employees got up from her desk and said, "Jim, let me do this. Since you're so busy." She snatched the form away from him and walked back to the files, shaking her head in disgust. Jim said weakly, "Rules are rules."

The woman returned in a few minutes with a microfilm roll. "It's on here," she said, "number 2137B80. You can use the reader when that man is finished with it."

"Thank you very, very much," said Kate.

Zach said, "Can we make a copy?"

"Copies take twenty-four hours," said Jim, obviously glad to bear bad news.

"This is really, truly an emergency," said Kate.

The woman behind the counter said, "There's a reader

that can make copies down the hall in Zoning."

Jim said, "They can't take the roll out of here."

"I'll stay here," said Kate to Zach. "You go make the copy."

Zach grabbed the microfilm roll from her and sprinted out of the office as Jim bellowed in the background. Five doors to the left he found the zoning office, and inside that he discovered a microfilm reader. He had forgotten the number of Stern's file, but he inserted the roll in the reader anyway, and began to page through it. He was good at reading microfilm: he had done it often before in his research. The wills from each year were listed alphabetically, so it didn't take him long to locate Stern's. He copied it hastily, feeding change into the machine. Then he ran back to the probate office, where Kate and Jim were engaged in an angry, jawbone-to-jawbone confrontation. He tossed the roll at Kate, who gave it to Jim, and then they both fled, shouting "Thank you" to the women behind the counter.

They took the stairs down, and then leaped into Janice's car. Zach said, "You were awesome in there."

"What does the will say?" said Kate, still exasperated.

" 'Last Will and Testament of Otto A. Stern'—blah, blah, blah." Zach glanced through the pages rapidly, scanning the faint white-on-black photocopy. "His lawyer wasn't Frye; it was Burton D. Abrams, Esquire, whoever that is. Wait, look at this!" He handed a sheet forward to Kate.

She examined it for a few seconds and then said, "Yes!" She began to read: " 'To my literary executor, Wendell Frye, I bequeath all of my collected correspondence. Any edition that he shall edit of my letters shall omit all items specified in a separate document in his possession.' This is it!"

By now it was ten past noon. They circled back around the green, and then Janice said, "Look, it'll be quicker for you to run there on foot. With these one-ways, I'll have to go practically all the way around the Med School."

Kate thanked her, and they jumped of the car and began sprinting through grassy quadrangles and flagstone-paved passages toward Alice's college. By the time they arrived at the gate, Zach was suppressing violent gasps for breath; Kate looked flushed, but she was much less winded. The first gate that they tried to open was locked, but another one, visible through the grille, was ajar. They jogged around the outside of the college, Zach barely keeping up, and finally arrived at the open gate. Farther down the side of the college, they saw two uniformed Yale police officers getting out of a car. They ducked in through the gate and began running across the courtyard, but at the same time they heard one officer shout, "That's them!"

By the time they had crossed the courtyard, the police were in hot pursuit. They entered a stone passageway and then another courtyard, ignoring shouts of "Stop! Police!" Zach could hardly keep running. Finally, they burst open the door of the master's office and bolted toward the fax machine. Alice leaped from her chair and said, "Just in time. The committee's back." She pointed her finger at the television screen, where the chairman could be seen calling for order. Zach gasped, "Is Davies ready for another fax?"

Alice nodded and Zach started feeding the first sheet of the will into the fax machine, his chest still heaving. He was so nervous and winded that his fingers kept missing the keys. Just as he had finished entering the correct number and pushed "Transmit," the door flew open.

"Freeze!" yelled a police officer, his gun drawn.

On the TV, Frye said, "These purported letters show clear signs of having been tampered with. For example, Mr. Chairman, something has been erased or covered up here."

The police officer again yelled, "Freeze!" Zach's hand was still on the fax machine; he was trying to feed the second page, which had become jammed. His eyes darted back and forth between the officer and the television set.

"Let me see your hands!" said the officer emphatically, pointing the gun at Zach's chest. Zach lifted his hands slowly into the air. He could hear Frye say, "Furthermore, I could give you numerous examples of published works in which Stern said just the opposite. For example—"

"All right, up against the wall," the officer shouted. He ran over to Zach and pushed him violently against a framed poster advertising the British Art Center. Meanwhile, his partner, who had just burst in after him, started snapping handcuffs around Kate's wrists. The fax machine stopped functioning, since the second page of the will was jammed. The telephone rang; Alice picked it up. On the TV, Frye said, "Stern was obviously—beyond any shadow of a doubt— committed to the highest ideals of the Founding Fathers."

Speaking into the phone, Alice said, "We're *trying* to send you the rest. . . . We're having some technical difficulties, largely caused by the fact that Zachary and Kate have just been arrested. . . . That's right. . . . We'll try." She hung up.

The officer who was handcuffing Zach said, "You have the right to remain silent. Anything you do say can be used against you."

Almost simultaneously, Frye said, "Therefore, I demand to know where these facsimiles have come from, who sent them, and who is responsible for such a bizarre fraud."

The Southern senator seemed confused and uncomfortable; he said, "We're just now working on answering that question."

"Mr. Chairman, this is outrageous!" bellowed another senator. "Doesn't he know where this stuff came from? Are we going to hold up a confirmation hearing for a Supreme Court justice just because some garbage showed up this morning on our fax? Any lunatic could've dreamt it up."

Zach and Kate were being bundled out of the room. Alice approached the fax machine and tried to feed the second sheet, but she didn't seem to realize that the committee's fax number had to be reentered before it would work. Zach, handcuffed and with a police officer's strong hand gripping the back of his neck, tried to shout "Retype the number," but he was already outside the office by the time he finished the phrase.

Between the master's office and the door leading outside, there was a small vestibule. Just as Zach and Kate were being propelled across it, the outside door opened and Janice entered.

"Hey, Janice," said the officer who had arrested Zach. "Would you believe I found a murder suspect in your office?"

"Al," said Janice, "you've got my buddies there. There must be some kind of mistake."

The officers stopped. Zach shouted back toward Alice, "You have to retype the Judiciary Committee number."

"What *is* going on here?" said the police officer who was guarding Zach.

"Please let us go back in there for thirty seconds," said Kate. "You'll see the stuff we're faxing show up on TV."

The officer looked doubtful, but Janice said, "Look, Al, I don't know why you're busting these kids; they're trying to do good. Let 'em back in."

"Okay," said the officer, "for thirty seconds. But I'm keeping the cuffs on you." He clearly wanted to know what was going on.

They walked back into the room. Alice was now feeding the whole will into the machine, since she didn't know which page contained the important information. On TV, two senators were engaged in a shouting match over the fairness of introducing new evidence during the last round of a hearing.

At last the whole will disappeared into the machine. On television, the commotion continued, now watched by Alice, Kate, Zach, Janice, and two Yale police officers. Behind the chairman, a door opened and Davies could briefly be seen bursting in with a ream of papers; soon he reappeared and took a seat among the aides on the dais. The chairman started pounding the rostrum for order. When order was finally restored, he said, "The senator has two minutes remaining."

The Southern senator said, "Well, what do you know, Judge? More pieces of paper have arrived." In response to this announcement, there was another angry uproar. The senator continued speaking over the commotion. "It's your testimony that you've never seen these letters before?" he asked.

Frye looked hesitant; the noise subsided as the audience waited for his response. "Yes, Senator," he said.

"Well, I have before me the last will and testament of one Otto A. Stern. And what does it say here? That all of his correspondence is bequeathed to you, sir, but you're supposed to keep some of it secret."

Yet again, the hearing room erupted in pandemonium. When order was restored, the senator said, "To the best of your knowledge, is this will genuine? Remember now, you're under oath, and we can check the original."

Frye conferred with the man to his right, then said, "I prefer to remain silent on the ground that my answer may incriminate me."

More commotion. A senator off camera shouted, "His time's up! His time's up!" Again the gavel pounded the rostrum.

The Southern senator said, "All right, I'd just like to take stock here. We've got an alleged letter from Stern that says some very perplexing and troubling things, to my mind at least. We've got your testimony that you love and respect Professor Stern, and you also claim that he never wrote any evil letters. Then we've got a will, stating that all of Stern's letters ended up in your possession, but some of them were supposed to be kept secret. Finally, you won't tell us if the will's genuine, on the grounds that it might incriminate you." He packed a great deal of innuendo into that last phrase.

"I challenge you to prove that the letters are real," said Frye. "At least, tell us where this stuff is coming from."

"I believe it's coming out of a certain secret society up at Yale," said the senator. Davies, who was still sitting behind him, looked dismayed and tapped his shoulder urgently; the senator had clearly gone beyond what he was supposed to say. But the senator ignored him, asking Frye, "Aren't you a member of the Crypt society, and aren't these letters usually stored inside the society building in New Haven?"

"I prefer to remain silent," said Frye, after a long pause.

"Well, that's your right; that's certainly your right. However, we are fortunate to have sitting right nearby another Crypt member who will be happy to enlighten us. Mr. Chairman, may I swear in an emergency witness?"

There were more shouts of "outrageous" and "out of order"; Davies looked panic-stricken. The senator turned around in his chair and started talking to him, pointing forcefully at the witness table. The chairman joined them and they formed a three-person huddle. After they had argued inaudibly for a few minutes, Davies made his way to the table and sat down next to Frye. They ignored each other studiously. Davies raised his right hand and was sworn in. Then the senator said, "You are Professor Hannibal Davies of Yale University?"

"Yes, Senator."

"And you are a member of the Crypt society?"

"I prefer to remain silent on that point."

"Professor Davies, the Constitution gives you the right not to testify in your own defense; you may remain silent if speaking would incriminate you. But in this case, there is no chance that answering my question might incriminate *you;* we're talking about Judge Frye. If you refuse to testify in order to protect him, then you could go to jail for contempt of Congress. You're under oath. Now, are you a Crypt member?"

"Yes." Davies looked flushed and angry.

"Are you aware of the offices held by other society members?"

"No."

The senator's usual affable manner disappeared. He said icily: "You are under oath, sir. If you have lied here, you can go to jail. Again, do you know who holds which offices inside Crypt?"

"Yes, I do."

"Now we're talking. So, what is Judge Frye's office?"

There was a long pause, during which the committee room was completely silent. Finally, Davies said, "You are asking me to break a solemn oath of secrecy."

"That's right. *I'm* sworn to uphold the Constitution."

Another long pause; Davies was sweating visibly. Frye, next to him at the table, stared straight ahead with his lips pursed. Finally, Davies said, "Very well. I can see that you are going to continue asking me questions that will require me to forswear myself and put my life in peril. But if I bring down the whole house of cards, that may at least protect me from retribution. Therefore, I'll tell you even more than you have asked. First, the letters from which you have quoted are kept in the Crypt archive; I have looked at the originals there myself on several occasions. Second, Frye is the Crypt

archivist. Third, Crypt owns the letters because Stern bequeathed them to Frye, who was his confidant. Otto Stern,
like Frye, was a cryptonihilist, filled with contempt for
democracy and its institutions."

There was more hubbub in the background, but this time
it subsided quickly. Davies continued in a soft but firm
voice: "One more thing, Senator: earlier you were reading a
document that quoted incriminating letters by Otto Stern.
The author of that document was yet another member of
Crypt, a former protégé of Frye's named Charles Wilson. You
were reading from his dissertation, which was stolen from
him several weeks ago. More recently, he contacted this
committee and sent you another document that has since disappeared from the committee's offices. I believe that that
document was Stern's will, but we cannot be sure. We cannot be sure, Senator, because Charles Wilson was recently
found dead in a Virginia motel."

Pandemonium. The room lit up with flashbulbs; senators,
aides, and observers jumped out of their seats. The television camera panned the chamber, revealing a scene of chaos,
and then abruptly returned to focus on the chairman, who
was shouting: "Judge Frye, do not leave this chamber, sir.
You are under oath, sir. You are not excused."

EPILOGUE

1 • On a rainy morning early the following week, Zach, Kate, and Alice sat in Alice's apartment in Greenwich Village, eating bagels and drinking coffee. Zach and Kate had just returned from Ithaca, and Alice wanted to hear all about it.

Zach said: "The Connecticut State Police had to carry out the New York extradition request, so they shipped us up to Ithaca in a police car with a couple of armed guys watching us. But by now it was clear that we weren't very likely murder suspects, so even the guys who were supposed to be guarding us treated us like we were innocent. In fact, they thought it was kind of a joke. When we showed up in Ithaca, the cops there made us tell them the whole story, and then they just asked us to stick around for a couple of days."

Kate said, "Yeah, but after two days, the FBI took over the Hausman case, because now they were investigating a whole interstate conspiracy."

"How did they treat you?" asked Alice.

"They weren't that nice," said Zach, "but they did put us up in a hotel while we were in Ithaca. And we were glad to stay, because we wanted to know what was going on with the investigation."

"And what was going on? The papers have been frustrat-ingly vague."

Kate said: "They subpoenaed all of Frye's records; they started treating Charles's death as a potential murder; they searched Frye's place—the whole deal. The forensics peo-ple found that there was pretty good evidence that Charles had been killed; it wasn't a suicide."

"Right," said Zach, "so then they discovered that Frye possessed a copy of Stern's will with Charles's fingerprints on it. Also, they learned that he had been talking on the hotel phone with a guy whom the FBI was after anyway, some kind of unsavory ex-CIA character. At that point, they offered Frye a plea bargain. There was some back-and-forth be-tween the lawyers, but finally he confessed to conspiracy charges and perjury in return for ratting on several of his buddies. He claims that he didn't know about the murder until after the fact, and they're accepting that."

"What about Hausman?" said Alice.

"Believe it or not," said Kate, "that one really was a sui-cide. At least, the forensics people couldn't find any evi-dence of violence or strange fingerprints or anything."

"Plus," said Zach, "there was a very plausible suicide note in Hausman's handwriting. They didn't find it right away, and they weren't sure at first that it was genuine. But they decided it must be real when they learned that he had sent a similar note to his mother by express mail; and the guy in the post office remembered him sending it. I guess he didn't want his mother to go for too long without an expla-nation."

"What did the note say?"

Kate deferred to Zach to explain. "I don't remember the exact words," he said, "but the gist was that he'd always be-lieved that Otto Stern was the last remaining bulwark against nihilism. When he found out that even Stern was, let's say, beyond good and evil, he didn't see any point to his whole life's work as a philosopher. He was going to kill himself right away, but he wanted to do one more thing—break up the Sternians. So he helped us to recover Charles's thesis, and then ended it all."

Alice let this sink in for a minute, and then asked, "As a philosopher, Zachary, do you find this rational? Isn't there any better response to nihilism?"

"I think the case for extreme cultural relativism is very strong. And that means that there is no objective right or wrong."

"You're not going to do *yourself* in, are you?" said Kate, making a joke of it but sounding genuinely worried.

"No. I take these issues seriously; I think about them all the time; but somehow, they don't seem quite *that* compelling. Old Zach's a wimp, that's the bottom line."

"No, you're just sane," said Alice.

"Is it sanity not to follow your thoughts where they lead you?"

Alice took a sip of coffee and said: "It's sanity not to think that those thoughts matter so very much."

"That sounds rather antiintellectual of you, Alice," said Zach.

"No one has ever called *me* antiintellectual before, Zachary. You know, being against abstract theory is not the same as being antiintellectual. Between your grand statements about the death of truth and so on, and the concrete reality of life down here on earth, there is a vast gulf. I am a literary person; I deal with the concrete realities—love, jealousy, loyalty, rage. I *know* that those are real."

"All right," said Zach, "then tell me this. Why were you so eager to block Judge Frye? Why did you put yourself in serious danger in order to stop him, if you didn't care about the abstract issues?"

"First of all, it was fun. But I also would have been very angry if Wendell Frye had been appointed. He's a liar and hypocrite; we don't need a man like that on the Supreme Court. I don't care much about philosophical issues, but I don't like his dishonesty one bit. Besides, he's a lunatic right-winger even in his public statements. His appointment would have meant a step back for women, the poor, the environment—"

Zach shook his head, but Kate said, "I agree with her."

She and Alice exchanged smiles and then Alice said, "One more question. Did they find your thesis?"

Zach shook his head. "No," he said, "they searched Crypt, but not until two days after we had broken in. By that time, it had vanished. I assume that a Sternian took it and destroyed it once he realized that it might be used as evidence against him. Although another possibility is that the cleaning man might have just tossed it."

"That's terrible," said Alice, and Kate also made a sympathetic face.

"I don't mind much," said Zach. "It was beginning to seem kind of dull to me, actually. Davies has offered me a lectureship and a salary, so I'm going to take the opportunity to start a new project."

"What on?" asked Alice.

"I'm not positive," said Zach, "but I've had an idea that I picked up from something that one of my students said to me last week."

2 • The next day, Zach taught his final class. He began with a discussion of a Camus essay and concluded with a ten-minute speech that he had prepared, in which he summed up the history of existential thought. All told, he was quite pleased with the effect. As class ended, he called for the final

papers, which piled up on his desk as the students passed by, some smiling warmly at him and thanking him, while others slipped out as quickly as they could. Dorothy, however, was still sitting in the back row.

Zach counted the papers and waited for her to approach him, not looking at her directly; but she remained glumly seated. Finally, he looked up and said, "What's the matter? You still couldn't finish your paper?"

She shook her head and suppressed a sob. "Can I have, like, one more week?"

"I'm not allowed to give you an extension."

"I've done a lot of work." She showed him a sheaf of handwritten pages, ripped from a notebook. "My latest draft is thirty pages long," she said.

"Let me look at it." This was going to be a nuisance: he'd have to read all those pages, discuss them at length with Dorothy, and then read another draft a week later. Still, duty called.

"No, it's no good," she said. "I write the stuff down, but it just doesn't make any sense to me."

"All right," said Zach, relieved. "You know, you're very bright, and something you said last week really interested me. Let's talk about it for a minute, and maybe you can get a paper out of it."

Dorothy's face brightened noticeably. Zach said, "You suggested that the story I told last week made a moral argument. Remember that?"

Dorothy nodded, and Zach continued: "Well, if it was my paper, I'd say something like this. An argument is just an effort to persuade another person. Okay? If it works, and the other person's smart and knowledgeable, then it's a good argument. Now, the arguments for nihilism are persuasive, but so are stories about individual good and evil acts. So why should the philosophical arguments, which are actually less

emotionally compelling than the stories, be considered more
authoritative? Do you see what I mean?"

Dorothy nodded again. "Does that mean that you'd let me
write a paper in which I denied that Nietzsche's arguments
were important?" she asked.

Zach realized that he had forbidden this approach the last
time they spoke, but he decided to relent. "Sure," he said.

"And I can have another week?"

"All right."

"Oh, then it's easy," she said cheerfully. "I'll just say that
a story about a murdered father is a persuasive argument
about good and evil. It's as persuasive as some kind of logical argument. I thought of that myself."

"Now, wait a second," said Zach, suddenly annoyed. "It's
not that easy. For one thing, let me tell you how the story
turned out. Hausman—the nice old professor?—he wasn't
killed. It was a suicide. He realized that there was no response to nihilism and took his own life. So the whole story
really was meaningless, and we do need a philosophical response."

"It doesn't seem meaningless to me," said Dorothy. "It
seems to make my point even better. I mean, what a jerk!
He abandoned his wife and kids for that?"

Zach didn't know how to respond. "You just write your
paper, okay? You can conclude what you want, but take
both sides seriously and show me that you understand the
issues. That's all I ask."

≀ • *Z*ach rode back to New York on a train without air-conditioning. The high, vinyl-covered seats were sticky with
sweat and an unpleasant smell emerged from the front of the
car. Ten or twelve elderly suburbanites were traveling together into Manhattan on some kind of outing, and they were

suffering from the heat. Zach watched one old couple across the aisle. They looked hot and weary, but they were clearly enjoying each other's company. The man, to make his wife feel better, pointed out sights through the window, and she dutifully pretended to appreciate them: first a self-storage center painted in gaudy colors, then a glimpse of the Hudson through trees. He wore a baseball cap on his damp, hairless head and wire-rimmed glasses; his bare legs stuck to the plastic seat. Zach noticed his wife's wrinkled old hands and the creases in her arms. He felt pity for the old couple, but not a patronizing pity, because he felt the same way about himself. In his mind, Zach started constructing philosophical pronouncements to express his mood. He experimented with the following proposition: that he and his companions on the train were all uncomfortable, tired, worried creatures, hurtling toward death, trying to squeeze some consolation out of the tenuous bonds of mutual love. Then Dorothy's face passed through his mind, first disconsolate, next relieved after he had given her the extension. Finally, he thought of Kate's warm smile.

For some reason, he remembered how, as a child, he had daydreamed about facing his own impending death. He had imagined postponing his end by just a few seconds through clever delaying tactics, so pleasurable was the mere experience of being alive. He used to concoct whole stories about deliberately falling down on the way to the firing squad, clinging to the disintegrating cliff face during an avalanche, or hiding in the bathtub during a great conflagration. Then he would look at some ordinary inanimate object—like the fake woven seat back that was before him now—and marvel at the joy of mere perception, which was worth savoring and prolonging under any circumstances. He touched the plastic and a droplet of sweat appeared at the tip of his finger.

Alice is right, he thought. What if it's true that there is no such thing as truth and everything is permitted? What does that have to do with whether or not I'm nice to Dorothy? Will it stop that old woman from humoring her husband by pretending to enjoy the sights of Westchester? It isn't that Maistre and Stern and the rest of them are wrong; it's just that their ideas don't seem all that important anymore. In fact, they seem a bit silly, compared to the grown-up business of living. And with that thought, he settled back in his seat and permitted himself to daydream of Kate and happiness.